TIM OWENS

THE SEARCH COMMITTEE

A NOVEL

Tyndale House Publishers, Inc.
Carol Stream, Illinois

Visit Tyndale online at www.tyndale.com.

Visit Tim Owens online at www.timowensauthor.com.

TYNDALE and Tyndale's quill logo are registered trademarks of Tyndale House Publishers, Inc.

The Search Committee: A Novel

Designed by Erik M. Peterson

Edited by Kathryn S. Olson

Published in association with the literary agency of Ethan Ellenberg Literary Agency, 548 Broadway, #5-E, New York, NY 10012.

Scripture quotations are taken from the *Holy Bible*, New Living Translation, copyright © 1996, 2004, 2007 by Tyndale House Foundation. Used by permission of Tyndale House Publishers, Inc., Carol Stream, Illinois 60188. All rights reserved.

This novel is a work of fiction. Names, characters, places, and incidents either are the product of the author's imagination or are used fictitiously. Any resemblance to actual events, locales, organizations, or persons living or dead is entirely coincidental and beyond the intent of either the author or the publisher.

Library of Congress Cataloging-in-Publication Data

Owens, Tim, 1959-
   The search committee : a novel / Tim Owens.
      p. cm.
   ISBN 978-1-4143-6445-2 (sc)
1. Pastoral search committees—Fiction.   2. Presbyterian Church—Fiction.
3. Intergenerational relations—Fiction.   4. Life change events—Fiction.   5. North Carolina—Fiction.   I. Title.
   PS3615.W4844S43 2012
   813'.6—dc22   2011033855

In memory of Nora, the matriarch

ACKNOWLEDGMENTS

When I was much younger and didn't think things through very well, one of my selfish prayers was to ask God for a full life, to experience as much as possible, both good and bad. Of course he obliged, and that is partly how I came up with this story and these characters. It's been in the making for a while.

As for the actual writing part, I had a lot of help in editing, feedback, and encouragement from some special friends before it was picked up by my agent and publisher. Abigail Nelson (my favorite Episcopalian), Russell and Karen Wilson (friends from way back), Rev. Mark Owens (my dad, a retired Southern Baptist minister), Jan Day (former director of Christian education at Summerville Presbyterian Church in Summerville, South Carolina), and a posse of Presbyterian ministers (Rev. Pete Jorgensen, Rev. Dr. Charles Hasty, Rev. Dr. Bryant Harris, Rev. Erin McGee, and Rev. Larry Duncan) all provided encouragement, even after reading some or all of what I'd written.

Only after receiving positive feedback from these friends did my wife, Ruth, who has an MA in English literature, decide it might be a worthwhile read and pick it up. She knows me better than anyone else does and knew what I was trying to say even when I didn't. Thanks, Ruthie. You look great in those pink rubber boots.

Others in my present church who have been a source of inspiration include Rev. Dr. Mike Shelton, Rev. Lamar Carney, Kari Morgan, Smiling Jack (now in heaven), "Admiral" Hromoga, Mr. Charlie, Mr. Bob, Dr. Miller, Miss Mary, Mrs. Louise, the Pritchard cousins, Butch, and many, many others. My daughter, Corinne, who is a much better writer than I am, read it to make sure I didn't embarrass her. And my boys, Mark, Al, and Dave, did their part to keep me humble by reminding me of all the projects I've started and not finished.

My agent, Ethan Ellenberg, took a chance on a first-time author, and I will be forever grateful for that. Karen Watson and Jan Stob at Tyndale have been especially helpful and encouraging, and Kathy Olson, my editor, is basically the cat's meow. She patiently nudged me along, kept me in bounds, and helped me grow spiritually in the process. All of the folks at the Jerry B. Jenkins Christian Writers Guild, which sponsored the Operation First Novel contest, went out of their way to welcome me into their ministry, and I'm grateful to be part of their organization.

Finally I would like to acknowledge the pastors who were kind enough to allow me to use their material for three of the sermons in this book. The sermon in chapter 14 was written by Rev. Erin McGee while she was associate minister at Summerville Presbyterian Church. The idea for the sermon in chapter 27 is from the dissertation of Rev. Dr. Bryant Harris of Mars Hill Presbyterian Church in Acworth, Georgia. The sermon in chapter 40 is based, in part, on a sermon with a similar theme delivered by the Rev. Dr. Charles Hasty while he was interim minister at Summerville Presbyterian Church.

AUTHOR'S NOTE

Search committees are formed by churches in many Protestant denominations when a pastor leaves a church, typically to take a position at another church. The members of the search committee are intended to be representative of their congregation. This is the story of one such search committee.

CHAPTER 1

When a church is without a pastor, or has a vacancy in an associate pastor position, or after the effective date of the dissolution of the pastoral relationship, the congregation shall, with the guidance and permission of the committee on ministry, proceed to elect a pastor or associate pastor in the following manner. The session shall call a congregational meeting to elect a pastor nominating committee, which shall be representative of the whole congregation. This committee's duty shall be to nominate a minister to the congregation for election as pastor or associate pastor.

THE BOOK OF ORDER, PRESBYTERIAN CHURCH (USA): G-14.0530–31

THE CHURCH VAN already had 187,000 miles on it. It was a white Ford Econoline, and Travis figured it was either a '77 or a '78 model because it looked like the van his cousin Jimmy used to drive. The inside, though, was not like Jimmy's at all. Jimmy's metal-flake brown van only had front seats, and the interior, ceiling included, was covered with burnt-orange shag carpeting. Plus, Jimmy had installed a porthole-type window in the shape of a heart on each side, and he had a little wooden cabinet on one side where he kept his cassettes. It was pretty cool.

The church van, on the other hand, had three bench seats plus the two up front, and it smelled like old vinyl. The rubber flooring was sticky, almost like the floor in a movie theater but not quite as bad. Some of the blue seats were cracked and the foam rubber beneath the vinyl had been gouged. Crawling in, no one complained except for Dot, who mumbled something about the smell.

The reason for crawling into the old van for a road trip was that their preacher said he had been called to a church in Atlanta, so they had to go get another one. The word going around was he had finally landed the Big Job. They all understood and accepted his "calling" as a logical progression in an average preacher's career.

He had been with them about seven years and was pretty good at keeping things on an even keel, like the time those charismatics came in and tried to stir things up. The church lost a few members during that period, but he kept them together by preaching for four Sundays in a row on Job. First he preached about how all of Job's farmhands and animals got killed or were run off by the Chaldeans and Sabeans; the next Sunday, Job came down with the boils from head to foot and took to scraping himself with a piece of broken pottery; the third Sunday, Job started whining and his friends turned on him. Before God got him all straightened out on the fourth Sunday, the charismatics got bummed out and left.

Anyway, their preacher was gone now, and they had an interim minister the presbytery had sent over until they could find a new one. Rev. John Haynesworth, the interim minister, was older than their former preacher, with gray hair and silver-rimmed glasses, and taller, without the paunch. He was a nice man and had gone to Davidson. But as a preacher, he often used words and made points most of the congregation didn't comprehend. It was like being in a doctor's office and he was explaining how to interpret an EKG—the guy seemed to know what he was talking about, so you nodded your head in agreement even though you didn't really understand. They hadn't had any new members join since Rev. Haynesworth had taken over the pulpit.

Travis recalled one Sunday when Rev. Haynesworth was preaching about Ecclesiastes, like how the guy who wrote it thought vanity was responsible for everything people did. By the end of the sermon Travis was so confused that he wasn't sure whether vanity was a good thing or not. The guy who wrote Ecclesiastes made some pretty good points, according to the preacher. In any case, the search committee felt some pressure to get somebody good in there and to be quick about it.

Another reason for the rush to get a new preacher was due to two of the young families in the church leaving to help start a new nondenominational church south of town on 301, joining up with some disaffected Methodists and a few Baptist families looking for a more "progressive" church. If *progressive* meant a church that looked a lot like a dollar store, then Travis figured they had reached their goal. The elders in Travis's church had begun to talk amongst themselves about the threat this new church posed to the membership roll.

It wasn't that two families made a big difference—they had 286 members on the roll—but it could be the beginning of something bigger.

On the other hand, the two families that left were always whining about something, so Travis was kind of glad to see them go. He just couldn't understand why they would want to leave one of the prettiest churches in the county. It was an old church with white clapboard siding, a black shingled roof, and a bell tower covered in cedar shakes. The 650-pound bell that had survived a fire in the original church building in 1879 was rung every Sunday morning by an usher at precisely 11:05 a.m., which coincided with the entry of the choir from the back of the choir loft. Inside the sanctuary, the ceiling was made of dark-stained tongue-and-groove boards that met white plastered walls. There was no stained glass, just tall windows with interior dark-stained shutters. Also, the door and window trim had hand-carved designs on the top corners from 1883, when the church was rebuilt. Travis often admired the craftsmanship that had gone into the building and felt a little pride in being part of such an old, established church. Somehow it gave him a sense of legitimacy, a sense of belonging.

Travis Booth was the youngest of the men on the committee. Bill was the oldest, and Travis was young enough to be Bill's son. Travis had grown up in the church, and people said that he and his wife, Jenny, represented the future of their congregation. Jenny interpreted this to mean they needed to start having babies, but Travis wasn't too sure about that.

He tried to be real active at church, and Jenny enjoyed the circles, small Bible-study groups comprised only of women in the church. Jenny was in circle number three. From what Travis could tell, they discussed a lot more than the Bible.

Travis worked as the assistant manager at the Food Lion in town. He thought it was a pretty good job for him, considering where he came from. In addition to working inside and getting a decent paycheck, he got to talk to everybody who came in, because his office was on a platform behind the service desk at the front of the store. His boss didn't mind him talking so much; said it was good for business. Most of his time involved hanging around up front, standing on the platform and looking out over the store, watching the customers and the stockers. Travis never ceased to be amazed at what was thrown away—good stuff. But rules were rules; putting those expiration dates on everything had caused more food to be thrown away than anything else he could think of.

• • •

There were seven altogether on the committee to find a new minister: Travis Booth—representing the young married professional; Bill Duncan—retired from the electric co-op; Frankie Fulford—about seventy, retired from the post office, the leader, more or less; Matt Fischer—early thirties, an out-of-work PhD living at home with his dad; Dot Spivey—a middle-aged gossip machine and housewife; Joyce Lambertson—about sixty, moved down from New York, widowed, and working part-time at the county library;

and Susie Mayfield—a bookkeeper at the electric co-op, late thirties, divorced, and good-looking.

Bill had spent twenty-eight years in one of those jobs that seemed like a good deal to everybody in town. Steady paycheck, good benefits, company truck—there weren't too many of those jobs around. When Travis first met him at some kind of special dinner in the fellowship hall on a Wednesday night, Bill asked Travis what line of work he was in. Travis told him he was the assistant manager at the Food Lion but that he was taking some classes over at Tech to apply toward an engineering degree. Bill replied, "I wish I had made something out of my career like that." Then Travis proceeded to tell him all the details about the credit hours he could use for his degree and how hard the math was. Bill smiled a little and said, "That's good. That's what you have to do nowadays—you have to go after it."

Bill did the driving on the trips and seemed to enjoy it. He liked to point out things as the van drove by them. For example, the van would pass a Golden Corral steak house and Bill would say something like, "Golden Corral . . . I wonder if their hot-food bar is as big as Ryan's." Remarks like these would invariably stir up some conversation.

Following that particular comment, Dot chimed in. "My cousin Roger, over in Rocky Mount—he's a lawyer, you know—he says those hot-food bars get a lot of people sick with food poisoning."

Bill replied, "Is that a fact? I never heard tell of anybody getting sick from the hot-food bar at Ryan's. Which one is he talking about?" He had Dot's number, plus he had probably eaten at every buffet in the state east of I-95.

Dot looked perturbed. "I don't know exactly which one, but it was over in Rocky Mount." She shifted in her seat, obviously satisfied with her answer.

Nobody knew it at the time, but Bill had some serious heart problems. He had told Travis about it on one of the trips when everybody else was asleep. They were driving along in the dark, coming back from a church visit in North Wilkesboro. There was hardly any traffic on 421. Bill said his doctor had put him on a special diet, one of those no-cholesterol, no-fat, no-sugar, no-caffeine, no-nothing types of diets. Plus he couldn't smoke anymore.

A few months back there had been an article in the *Raleigh News & Observer* about how people here in eastern North Carolina had a high rate of heart disease. Something about all the fatback they used in cooking. Travis once had some string beans that had been cooked without fatback; they were so bitter he almost threw up. And fried fatback—talk about something good. Travis wondered how many slices of fried fatback he had eaten in his life; had to be in the thousands.

Anyway, Bill had this heart thing weighing on his mind. He wasn't worried so much about dying himself as he was about leaving behind his wife, Mary Helen. She really loved him, and he really loved her. They'd had one child together, a boy, Billy. He was killed years ago while riding his bicycle down the road to his cousin's house. Billy was eight. Bill and Mary Helen took it real bad.

"Hey, Bill, look at that one," Travis said, pointing to the portable sign in front of a church they were passing. It read, *Treat every day like it's Sonday.* It was a Methodist church sign.

"That's a good one, but I believe the Baptist churches win the prize for having the best signs."

They had seen some good signs along the way, like *If you really love Jesus, you won't be flirting with the devil* and *Give all your problems to God. He'll be up all night anyway.* And the best one so far, in Travis's opinion: *Without the Bread of Life, we're toast.* Everyone had laughed when they saw that one.

Travis had a little blue wire-bound book with him to keep notes on the different preachers they were going to hear. He turned to the back few pages of it and started writing down all the sayings they had seen on church signs. Their church didn't have a sign, but if one was ever put up in the future, he figured it would be good to have some sayings to draw on. You never know. He finished writing down the one they had just passed and closed his notebook.

"Hey, that sign had a different saying on the other side," Bill said as he looked in the rearview mirror. Travis turned around to look, but they were going around a curve and he lost sight of it.

"What did it say?"

Bill chuckled. "It said that atheism is a nonprofit organization, and they spelled *profit* like a *prophet* in the Bible."

Travis opened his notebook and wrote it down.

Dot spoke up. "I heard those people who bought the old dry cleaner's are atheists."

Travis was beginning to think that God had allowed the devil to travel with them in the form of Dot Spivey. She had made it known that she wanted to be on the committee because, in her words, she wanted to "make sure we got a good one." Short and thick in the middle and about fifty years old, she spoke her mind without any regard for whether she might be offending someone and had one of those hairdos that was real short in the back and then stood up on top like a rooster's comb. She wore a lot of makeup and primped all the time, adding more blush or lipstick while looking into a small compact she fished out of her oversize pocketbook. She revered anybody who had money and, conversely, didn't think much of those who didn't. Travis tried to be pleasant, but deep down, he was terrified of her.

• • •

Today they were headed to Charlotte, where among the fifty or so Presbyterian churches there were about eight preachers who were looking to make a move. They hopped over to 74 from 133. It was four-lane now all the way since they finally worked on the stretch through Robeson County where all the Lumbee Indians lived.

By the time they got close, everybody needed to go to the bathroom, so Bill stopped at a BP in Matthews, a small town on the outskirts of Charlotte. He figured they wouldn't be able to go at the church, not knowing their way around and all. After everybody got back in, the women began their primping, especially Dot, who was making a major exercise out of applying her Mary Kay. She was moving her lips so much to spread her lipstick that Travis thought she was going to end up looking like Bozo the Clown. But it turned out alright.

Susie brushed her shoulder-length auburn hair. It didn't take much for her to get fixed up.

Joyce just patted her hair in the back and on the sides. She looked a lot like Rosalynn Carter but dressed more plainly and didn't wear any makeup at all.

Frankie held a compact mirror close to her face and grinned, looking for remains of a Hardee's biscuit between her teeth. Satisfied, she closed the compact and put it back in her purse. Despite her age, Frankie was probably in better shape than anyone else on the committee. Every time she came into the grocery store, Travis noticed she was wearing an exercise suit and tennis shoes. Travis had overheard her tell one of the cashiers that she tried to walk two miles every day.

Looking back at Matt, Travis noticed his hair was all poofed up in the back from where he had been sleeping, but Matt didn't even bother with it.

Travis opened his little notebook. The fella whose application had given him the appearance of being "their kind of man" was forty-seven, married, two kids—one in college, one in elementary school (a surprise?)—and was born in Florida (not a plus). He wanted to pastor a small-town church, like theirs, and he was affordable. He gave no signs of being a liberal and seemed to be strong on family values. On paper he could have passed for a Baptist. The church he was in currently was in the suburbs of Charlotte in a modern-looking building. It was relatively small, similar to their own, so it wouldn't be a big change for this minister.

They drove into the church parking lot right at 10:50 a.m. They had a plan for entering the church without drawing attention. Churches generally didn't throw out the welcome mat for search committees taking a look at their preachers.

Their usual approach was for Frankie and Bill to go in together as an older couple. Dot and Joyce were also to go in together, looking like two friends keeping each other company. However, they made odd companions—Dot with her hairdo, tight dress, and big, dressy pocketbook next to Joyce with her baggy skirt, plain blouse, unfixed hair, and macramé handbag. Then there were Travis, Matt, and Susie. Matt and Susie were supposed to be a couple and Travis was supposed to be Susie's brother. Unfortunately, their plan was compromised this morning when two ushers came out the front door of the church and drew a bead on all of them piling out of the van.

"Shoot," Travis muttered.

The word would be out now; nevertheless, they went in according to plan and sat in different pews. Travis looked through the bulletin to see what hymns they would be singing. Good. Some old ones. None of that snuggle-up-to-Jesus music with guitars and harmonizing. Today they would sing "Holy, Holy, Holy," "A Mighty Fortress," and for closing, "Immortal, Invisible." What a lineup. Travis checked the sermon title to see if it complemented the power hymns. Oddly enough, it didn't. Instead, it was "Blessed Are the Meek." Travis thought the preacher had missed an opportunity there.

Looking around at the congregation, he began to wonder how these people came to live in Charlotte. They were definitely city folk. He couldn't imagine growing up in a big city. Where would the kids play? He just couldn't fathom it. They dressed a little different, more sophisticated. No brown necks with white foreheads among the men, although it was only March, of course. None of the men were in short sleeves. Each had on a coat and tie. Travis and Bill did too, but they were doing something special. Back at home, Bill would have been in short sleeves and so would Travis. Matt . . . maybe not. Actually, there was one guy sitting by himself wearing a T-shirt. He had long hair. Travis figured you got that sort of thing in the city.

Behind the pulpit was a large stained-glass window that Travis soon figured out had symbols related to the Apostles' Creed. It was real nice. The inside of the church was all white except for the burgundy carpet down the main aisle and the burgundy cushions on the white pews. Susie elbowed Travis when she sat down and raised her eyebrows approvingly. The subject of pew cushions had come up a few times in their church but had been voted down by the session due to the cost.

Travis looked over his shoulder and noticed that Dot was red-faced with the giggles. She was blowing it. Oh well. He couldn't see Bill and Frankie. The organist started playing and the choir came in through a side door on the right.

They had on white robes. Then the preacher came in. He was wearing a white robe with a light-green stole. There was a lot of white in this church. The preacher was balding and had let his hair grow a little long in the back. He wore thick-rimmed glasses and had a moustache, all of which meant nothing to Travis. However, glancing over his shoulder, Travis noticed Dot's contorted face and realized this poor guy didn't have a chance. He preached a good sermon, although Travis couldn't remember a lot of what he said—it was about God's grace.

The other logistics issue they always had to deal with was how to communicate with the preacher following the service. They usually tried to go to lunch with him, but it was a challenge to get his attention without giving themselves away to the whole congregation. It had occurred to Travis that it was hard work trying to steal a preacher. There was no easy way to do it.

Travis finally saw Bill and Frankie. They got to the preacher first. Bill said something, and the preacher smiled and motioned him and Frankie to stand over to one side in the narthex. Travis, Susie, and Matt came along and stood beside them without saying anything, and then Dot and Joyce followed suit. After all their covert tactics, they now stood in the receiving line for the entire congregation. It was quite possibly one of the most awkward moments Travis had ever experienced in church. People exiting the church were whispering and gathering in groups at the foot of the steps and then looking back up at them.

Bill looked at Travis and asked, "You ready to make a run

for it?" Travis chuckled nervously, looking down the steps where everybody was standing around. He wished they had parked out back. The women were fidgeting with their skirts and pocketbooks and were pretending not to notice everybody staring at them. Matt had his back to everyone and was looking at some painting on the wall, his hands in his back pockets and his hair still poofed up in the back. Like Matt, the preacher didn't seem fazed at all. He was taking it all in stride.

When the last of the congregation had passed, the preacher just stuck his chin out, looked straight at Travis, and said with raised eyebrows, "Let's go eat."

CHAPTER 2

In the life of a congregation people may gather for prayer in a number of settings. The session is responsible for the authorization of such gatherings. Regularly scheduled prayer meetings which are open to all may take several forms, including the midweek evening service, a morning, midday, or afternoon gathering, and prayer breakfasts and luncheons. Smaller groups may meet regularly as prayer circles, intercessory fellowships, or covenant groups.

THE BOOK OF ORDER, PRESBYTERIAN CHURCH (USA): W-3.5300(C)

TRAVIS LOADED THE FOUR BOXES OF FOOD into the back of his truck. Each box contained the makings of a meal for one family: one whole ham, one package of brown-and-serve rolls, two cans of Del Monte green beans, one can of beets, one box of Stouffer's stuffing mix, one store-bought pecan pie, one bag of red potatoes, one box of Comet rice, and a gravy packet. It was not a bad-looking Easter dinner, considering you got a whole ham, and who cares about canned beans every now and then? Jenny was sitting up front waiting on him. The circles at church had put all this together and enlisted their husbands to help make the deliveries. There were four elderly ladies on Travis and Jenny's list. One lived right in town, but the other three lived out near the county line.

"You know where all these places are?" Travis asked Jenny, who was busy writing something in her day planner.

"What?"

"Do you know where we're going?"

"Well, I thought you knew all the roads around here."

"Yeah, well, I know the one in town, but I don't know these other three. That's way out Blueberry Farm Road but there's not much out there."

"Yep, that's where we're going. Let's go," Jenny said with an upbeat voice, not looking up and still writing in her day planner. "Don't worry. I'll be with you."

"Hmmph," Travis grunted while starting up the truck.

* * *

Travis slowed the truck to read the name of the road on the little green sign. The county had designated money to put a sign on every dirt road so the 911 dispatchers could figure out where the calls were coming from. That way the dispatchers wouldn't have to go on something like, "It's about three-quarters of a mile past the big oak, and then you veer to the left and go about two miles to the swampy area, and when you get past that it's on the right. Go to the end of the dirt road and we're in the trailer behind the blue house."

But a problem had arisen when the local government realized that almost none of the county roads had names. So the maintenance crew embarked on a massive canvassing of the county to speak with the residents on every dirt road, if possible. The residents were asked to decide on a name for their road. This led to a couple of shootings and house burnings as neighbors argued over the name. It also led to some very peculiar road names like Mama's House Boulevard and Dave's Crib Drive and Chigger City Avenue. Most of the names, though, turned out to be the names of the residents themselves, excited about the opportunity to leave a legacy so future generations could admire and reflect on what great people had lived there. These were people of character and significant standing in the community, no doubt, Travis thought with a smirk. This road he and Jenny were looking for was one of those.

"That's it," Jenny said, pointing at the sign. "Ned Simmons Drive."

"Ned Simmons? Now there's a hero for you. A drunk. They named a street after a drunk. He probably doesn't even know it."

"Well, this is for Mrs. Zella Bryant. She lives in that white trailer with the maroon stripe on one end, over there in that low area. See the one with the little porch on the front?"

Travis turned into the mud driveway leading to Mrs. Bryant's house. The whole area seemed to be in a peat bog and was very squishy.

"I hope we can back out of here without getting stuck."

"Will you please snap out of whatever attitude you woke up with this morning?"

"What attitude?"

Travis stopped the truck in front of the trailer. Jenny mumbled something under her breath as she opened the passenger door and hopped out.

"Oh, great, so now you're mad at me."

"Just hush up and help me with this stuff."

Travis sighed heavily and walked around to the back of the truck to get the box of food for Mrs. Bryant. Jenny was already knocking on the door of the screened-in porch.

Travis walked across the small front yard, carrying the box, and could feel his shoes sinking as he stepped on the soft, wet ground.

"Oh, bless you, honey," an old, raspy voice announced as Travis climbed the steps to the front porch. Jenny was holding the door open for him. Entering the house, Travis detected a funny smell.

"Bless you. Bless you. Come on in. You can put it on that table over there against the wall. Bless you, son."

Travis faked a smile and put the box on the table. Glancing around, he noticed small white trash bags containing clothes stacked in different areas. Mothballs—that was the smell. Whew, it was strong in here. How did she live with that smell every day?

Mrs. Bryant was about Jenny's height, a whole head shorter than Travis, and had a tight-fitting elastic blue scarf covering her head. She was wearing a dark-red skirt that had a hemline just below her knees and a long-sleeved beige blouse buttoned all the way up to her neck. She had on beige walking shoes and flesh-colored panty hose that were a little baggy around her ankles. She also had a few gray hairs on her chin, like the beginning of a beard for a fifteen-year-old boy.

"Mrs. Bryant, the Presbyterian women would like to give you this food as part of our mission emphasis program."

"Well, I thank you very much. You all are so kind. Is this your husband?"

"Yes, it is."

"Hi, ma'am. I'm Travis Booth." Travis nodded and Mrs. Bryant walked slowly toward him. She reached out and put a hand on his forearm. Travis looked down at it. It seemed strange to be touching a black person. Her hand was a rich, dark brown and her fingers were thin but tough, like they were used to handling a shovel. Her touch was soft, though, and felt warm. But it didn't feel like any white woman's hand that he could recall. It was a different kind of feel, like someone wearing a tight-fitting leather glove.

"My, my, he is a fine-looking young man. I think you got a good one," Mrs. Bryant said to Jenny while looking at Travis's face.

Travis blushed.

"Yeah, he's a pretty good one most of the time," Jenny said and then chuckled.

"And he's strong, too." Mrs. Bryant tilted her head to see both sides of Travis's body. "And you," she said to Travis, still with her hand on his forearm. "You are blessed to have such a fine and pretty wife. You know that, don't you?"

Travis nodded.

Mrs. Bryant sighed. "Did you know my husband? Milton Bryant? The custodian at the middle school?" She looked intently into Travis's face.

"No, ma'am. I didn't know him."

Then, in another tone of voice that changed the subject, "You know, I used to work for all these people around here." She took her hand off Travis's arm and made a slow, waving motion. "Took care of all of them. Who is your mama and daddy, son?"

"Well, my mama is dead and my daddy doesn't live here anymore. He lives in Tennessee."

"How did your mama die?"

"She had rheumatic fever as a child and it gave her heart disease. She had a stroke when she was thirty, and then a heart attack killed her when she was forty-two," Travis explained matter-of-factly.

"Oh my, I remember when some of that rheumatic was going around. How did your daddy take it?" Mrs. Bryant asked.

Travis paused. "I don't remember. He left right after the funeral." His face began to flush.

"Left right after the funeral? Why, forevermore?" Mrs. Bryant inquired with raised eyebrows.

"He wasn't living with us anymore by then. He had some problems. My aunt raised us after my mom died." Travis looked at the floor.

Mrs. Bryant gave a sad, knowing smile. "I see. Well, there's no reason to feel bad on account of him. Just look at you. You turned out real good." She smiled. Then she turned to Jenny. "Do you have any children?"

"No, not yet. He says we need to get our finances in order first," she replied, tilting her head toward Travis.

"Oh yes." Mrs. Bryant nodded. "It's important to get that straight. You are going to have children, though, aren't you?"

"Yes, we will, and sooner than later." Jenny squinted at Travis.

Mrs. Bryant turned around to face him. "Well, you got to bring them up right because there's a whole lot of trouble for the young folks nowadays."

"That's the truth, alright," Travis responded, feeling at ease again.

"My oh my. I tell you what, there's so much trouble in the world today that it takes me a solid hour and a half to get through my prayer list every morning," Mrs. Bryant said.

"You pray an hour and a half every morning?" Travis asked, trying to imagine Mrs. Bryant sitting at her kitchen table praying.

"Oh yes. It's my favorite time of the day because it's when I am closest to the Lord." Mrs. Bryant touched his arm again. "Mostly, I pray for myself first, to be a blessing to others and like that; then I go through all the sick and shut-ins in our church and here in the community; then lastly I pray my special prayers."

"What kind of special prayers?"

"Well, you know, that's when I pray for Jesus to come back again and resurrect all my family and like that."

"Oh, well, that's nice."

"He talks to me about it," Mrs. Bryant said while looking straight ahead, focusing on something far off and not visible.

"Who talks to you about it?"

"Jesus."

"Really? You can hear his voice?" Travis inquired, wondering what Mrs. Bryant saw or heard that she ascribed to Jesus.

"Yes, clear as a bell."

"You're kidding." He figured it must be the wind whipping across her trailer.

"Oh no, son, I wouldn't kid about something like that. This morning he told me that Milton was doing real good and was really looking forward to seeing me. I told him to tell Milton that I missed him too. Then he told me to stay inside for the next two days on account of bad weather coming."

"He tells you what the weather is going to be?" Travis asked in a slightly sarcastic tone.

"Well, yes, he does. We talk about all kinds of things. Yesterday, we even talked about what kind of a season the Braves will have this year. You know, I listen to every game they play on the radio."

"You talk to Jesus about baseball?"

"Yes," Mrs. Bryant replied, chuckling. "Sometimes we goof around like that. He is my best friend. We talk about everything."

"Travis, we'd better get going," Jenny interrupted. "We've got three more deliveries to make today."

"Oh, honey, I wish you would stay longer. You two are

such a sweet couple. I can tell that your marriage is going to be good and long, like me and Milton had."

"Thank you. That's so nice of you to say. We do need to get going, though." Jenny walked to the front door of the trailer and stepped out onto the little porch. Travis was following her when he felt Mrs. Bryant tugging on his sleeve. He turned around.

"Come here; let me tell you something special," Mrs. Bryant whispered.

Travis looked over his shoulder at Jenny and turned back to Mrs. Bryant as she said, "If you believe just a little, itty-bitty bit, you can say to the mountain, 'Move,' and the mountain has to move."

Travis raised his eyebrows, then turned to walk down the steps.

"Bye, Mrs. Bryant," Jenny said from the yard.

"Bye, sugar. Take care."

• • •

"What was *that* all about?" Travis said while backing the truck out of Mrs. Bryant's mushy driveway.

"What was *what* all about? Talking to Jesus about baseball?" Jenny replied.

"No, not that. That woman's a little off her rocker. What I'm talking about is when you said we were getting ready to have kids."

Jenny's jaw tightened and her face became flushed. "I didn't say it like that. All I said is we would have kids someday. Besides, what's wrong with saying we're going to have kids?"

Travis knew he had said the wrong thing . . . again. Shoot, why had he even opened his mouth? "Nothing. It's just . . . never mind."

"You know something?" Jenny said. "I'm getting tired of having this conversation. If you didn't want to have kids, then I wish I'd known that before I married you. Honestly, Travis, if that's the way you feel, we need to . . ." Jenny stopped and closed her eyes. "I want to have a family, Travis," she said softly.

"Jen, it's not that I don't want them. I've told you I want to have kids."

"Well, then what, for crying out loud, is it?" she said, raising her voice.

"I just don't think it's the right time yet."

"The right time. Yes, we have to make sure it's the right time," Jenny said and looked away.

CHAPTER 3

Through worship people attend to the presence of God in their life.
From a Christian's life in the world comes the need for worship;
in worship one sees the world in light of God's grace; from worship
come vision and power for living in the world.

THE BOOK OF ORDER, PRESBYTERIAN CHURCH (USA): W-5.1002

IT TURNED OUT that the search committee duty was not so bad. Travis liked seeing how other churches operated and what the people in them were like. He also enjoyed seeing the sights along the road. Usually it was just a day trip, so he wasn't away from home for long. But this one coming up was going to be an overnighter.

As he expected, Dot nixed the last guy because, in her words, "He was just too ugly to have to look at every Sunday." Too bad, too, because Travis thought the guy was a pretty good preacher. He wondered what God was going to say to Dot when she showed up at the Pearly Gates.

Today they were headed up to Johnson City, Tennessee, to hear a guy who was looking for a "new challenge." Some people just went around asking for trouble.

• • •

Talk about a long haul. Bill drove almost the whole way while everybody else napped off and on. They left on Saturday morning and had reservations at an EconoLodge just outside Johnson City. It wasn't really in their budget, but it was the only way they could get there and hear the guy without having to leave at 3 a.m. on Sunday morning. And for all they knew, maybe this would be the guy.

On the way up there, Dot started reminiscing about her days growing up on the farm. Her daddy wouldn't let her or her sister help with the farm chores. According to Dot, her daddy didn't want their hands to get ruined. She said this while holding her hands out in front of her with the backs facing up and twisting them a little as if she were inspecting them. She and her sister just helped their mama around the house and sometimes stayed with a black lady down the road when their mama went into town.

Then Dot gave everyone a visual that wouldn't fade from their memories anytime soon. Apparently, she and her sister used to walk around the yard barefoot and in their underwear in the summer ". . . to stay cool, because nobody ever came out to our farm anyway." After sharing that piece of information, she cackled like a hen. Everybody just smiled or laughed politely. The problem Travis had was that rather than a teenaged Dot, he got an image of the current Dot, hairdo and all, walking around with little rolls of fat hanging over a pair of high-waisted panties and a dingy bra strapped on too tight. He started to feel a little nauseated until Bill, seeing a rest area, had the good sense to stop for a break so they could all get a little fresh air.

• • •

Driving through the mountains made everybody a little uneasy. They were way high up, and the old church van was giving all it had. But going up wasn't as bad as going down. It turned out the brakes on the van had probably needed replacing before they even started on this trip. That wasn't such a big deal on flat land so nobody thought to do it. Going down a mountain was a different deal altogether. First they smelled the brakes. Then Bill said something about how they weren't holding so good. The women started squirming in their seats. Even Matt looked a little nervous.

Joyce, it turned out, knew about driving in the mountains. Travis figured she had some practice in New York somewhere. She was a Yankee, more or less; she tried to blend in but it just wasn't working. Travis felt sorry for her. Her husband had talked her into moving south when he took early retirement from Eastman Kodak in Rochester. He said he was lucky to get out when he did. Sure enough, they laid off about fifteen hundred workers the next year. He said the winters were getting too hard. How they settled on this particular town was something of a mystery—something about taxes and being close to Myrtle Beach golf courses. But the guy up and died unexpectedly before he even got to play any golf. So here was Joyce, stuck in this strange place where she didn't know hardly anybody.

She had taken a part-time job at the county library to give her something to do, but it wasn't exactly a place where a lot of meeting and greeting went on. Joyce would try to relate to people by telling stories about the apples in upstate New York or how long the snow stayed on the ground. Everyone would smile and treat her the only way they knew how—like a foreigner. She dressed differently, too. She wore a lot of baggy skirts and tank-top blouses. But Travis liked her. She was genuinely nice, and that meant something.

Anyway, Joyce told Bill to pull over and let her drive. The others glanced at each other nervously, and Travis was about to object when Bill said, "That's a good idea. I bet you're real good at this, coming from up north." Bill had already been impressed by Joyce's working knowledge of the GPS she brought with her for the committee to use in the old church van.

So Joyce got behind the wheel and let out a little nervous laugh. Apparently preparing for the worst, Dot tightened her seat belt. Travis started thinking about how far down the side of the mountain they would roll before they got hung up on some trees. And everybody got real quiet.

Joyce, on the other hand, now looked like she had just been announced as the new homecoming queen. Her whole face brightened and she was almost excited. She put the van in low gear and they started down again. But she hardly used the brakes at all. She just kept shifting back and forth between low and second. Bill was grinning now and looking admiringly at Joyce's skill behind the wheel.

• • •

Bill was the kind of man Travis wanted to be when he got older. No-nonsense, good manners, friendly, he seemed to have his affairs in order. Travis admired him, too, for recovering the way he did after Billy got run over. Travis was nine years old when it happened. Two teenagers were racing their cars against each other and taking up the whole road. One of them hit Billy. The car knocked him clear across the ditch and next to a telephone pole. His cousin Jerry saw the whole thing, because he was waiting for Billy in his front yard. Jerry had been watching him come down the road. He ran inside and called his mom and then rode his bike down to where Billy was. Travis would never forget it. He just happened to be riding by in the car with his daddy. The rescue squad was just pulling up. His daddy told him to stay in the car but he could see Jerry propping up Billy's head. It had been cracked open. Jerry was crying and had blood all over him. And the look on Jerry's face—Travis could still see it.

When his daddy got back to the car, he didn't look like he wanted to talk. All he said was, "I think it killed him. Crazy teenagers ought not to be driving no cars. They don't have enough sense." After that he didn't say anything for the rest of the way home.

Travis remembered the funeral. The church was packed. When they came walking in the church that hot summer afternoon, Bill was whispering to Mary Helen and holding her up as they walked down the aisle. She was crying and wailing so that it was pitiful to watch. Almost everybody in the whole church went to crying, men and women. Travis was too young at the time to know that kind of sadness. The only thing he could think about was Jerry propping up Billy's head and the look on Jerry's face.

At the graveside service Mary Helen was still crying and wailing and asked if the casket could be opened for one last look. Everybody was looking around at each other when Bill stepped up to the casket and, after gently removing the roses, raised the lid. Mary Helen stopped crying, stepped up beside Bill, and leaned over and touched Billy's face with the back of her hand. Then she turned around and walked out from under the tent toward the church. Bill caught up with her and motioned the funeral home guys to get the car ready. Nobody said a word.

• • •

Finally, they got through the worst part of the mountains and could relax enough to enjoy the view. It sure was pretty in these parts. Lots of little farms, not like the hundred-acre spreads they had back home. Travis reckoned these people couldn't be making a whole lot of money off that little bit of land. They probably worked in a mill somewhere and farmed when they could.

Bill touched the window beside him, turned around, smiled, and said, "It's a whole lot cooler up here than it is where we came from." Dot did a little shiver and tensed up her face.

They decided to stop for dinner at a Cracker Barrel. Joyce pulled into the parking lot, parked the van perfectly, turned the ignition off, and handed the keys to Bill, her face beaming. She was in now.

Travis noted that the Cracker Barrel was just like the ones back home. Of course, it would be. He just expected some things to be a little different when they were this far away. They had to wait for about twenty minutes to get a table for seven. The women were enjoying the wait. They were looking at all the knickknacks—like they hadn't seen them a dozen times before at the Cracker Barrel on 95.

Travis decided to try on some sunglasses, because he might be driving later on and he'd left his in his truck. He put on these NASCAR-type sunglasses that didn't have a frame all the way around the lenses. He thought they looked okay on him.

When he turned around there was a kid standing there, looking straight up at him. "Are you Jeff Gordon?"

Travis took off the sunglasses and said, "Nope, but I sure wish I had his money."

The kid just stared at him for a few seconds and then said, "Well, he ain't gonna get much money this year, because he's already 125 points behind Matt Kenseth in the Sprint Cup standings." Not wanting to have a serious talk with what looked to be a seven-year-old smart aleck, Travis just smiled and walked past the kid toward the hostess station, where the others were milling about.

It was packed, so the hostess seated them at a long table where a gray-haired couple sat at one end across from a white-haired woman who was noticeably older, probably one of them's mama. The man and woman were very neatly dressed. They looked like they traveled in one of those big RVs you see on the interstate at the rest areas. Travis smiled at them when he sat down, trying to be polite, but they didn't smile back at all. *Hmmm . . . Yankees? Maybe midwesterners on vacation.*

Travis and the others didn't really pay much attention to the other party after they sat down. Mostly, they were all busy trying to decide on which vegetables to get as sides. Bill said something about the fried squash. Dot whispered something to Susie while looking in the direction of an incredibly overweight young couple sitting at the next table.

Then—"Eat your meat, Mother!" the middle-aged woman semishouted to the older woman at the end of the table.

They all jerked their heads in that direction and just as quickly looked away as if they hadn't heard it. The daughter was wearing a light-blue long-sleeved blouse and a white sweater wrapped around her shoulders with the arms tied together. Her hair was in a permanent and she was wearing makeup, but not much. She was the sternest-looking woman Travis had ever seen. She had the facial features of a male

Greek statue with a permanent scowl—big eyes, flaring nostrils, and thick lips. And the man looked just like her. Maybe they were brother and sister. No, Travis noted they had on wedding bands, so probably not. The mother was wearing an aquamarine velour top. Her hair had been fixed too but was a little mussed in the back. The man was completely focused on eating his meat loaf platter and appeared to be unfazed by this barking of instructions to his mother-in-law.

Then in an almost equally startling tone, the woman said, "Use your knife! You can't cut it with your fork."

The mother fumbled with her knife and tried unsuccessfully to cut her country-fried steak.

"Just give it to me. This is ridiculous," grumbled the middle-aged daughter, stabbing the piece of meat with her fork and lifting it over to her plate. She began cutting it furiously while sighing with disgust. The mother looked straight ahead as the daughter shoveled the cut pieces back onto her plate.

Bill and Frankie were glancing at each other now with furrowed brows. Bill shook his head and looked down at the menu. Only Matt showed no emotion or acknowledgment of what had just happened.

Just then the waitress came to the other end of the table and asked the mother if she wanted more coffee. The mother picked up her cup and, with a noticeably shaky grip, began to hand it to the waitress, until the daughter said in a spiteful tone, "Oh no, you don't. You have already had two cups. You'll be up all night."

The waitress, a chunky-looking local with black hair tied

up in a bun, looked at the mother and said, "You gotta do what she says, don't you?" She was smiling. There was a silent satisfaction on Travis's end of the table.

Right after Travis ordered, the people got up to leave. The middle-aged daughter, maybe feeling a little guilty, said to her mother, "Did you get enough to eat, Mother? Do you want to take something with you in a box?" The mother mumbled something and shuffled toward the exit. The man sucked at his teeth while studying the check.

Finally, when they had all gone to the other side of the Cracker Barrel, where the cashier was located, Dot had to say something. "I wouldn't talk to my mama like that. That woman's got some issues."

Frankie whispered, "Well, she was just plain mean. I'd hate to see what she does to her poor mama when they're home alone."

• • •

Bill paid the cashier with his credit card so they would just have the one receipt to keep up with. They all crawled back into the van and drove for about another fifty miles to Johnson City and found the EconoLodge where they had reservations. The rooms weren't real clean and it turned out that one of the cable channels had some nudity on it that night. Travis figured Dot would have her say about that in the morning. Bill, Matt, and Travis shared one room and the ladies shared another room. The men got a cot for their room so none of them would have to share a bed with another man. Of course, that part was no big deal for the women.

The next morning they got up early so everybody would have time to get dressed. Travis figured the women got up around five thirty to make sure each one had enough time in the bathroom. They loaded up the back of the van with their suitcases and walked over to the Denny's across the parking lot for breakfast. As they were walking, Dot, of course, brought up the topic of hotel-room cleanliness.

"I think it's the sorry help they get nowadays. I mean, so what if it's an EconoLodge? There's no excuse for not having clean sheets on a bed." She was completely miffed by the situation, and Travis noticed that she was strutting across the parking lot like a hen. He wondered if she was going to say anything about the sex show. She never did. It was mixed company, so probably, if they had watched it, the men weren't going to find out.

After breakfast they loaded into the van and headed out to the church they were supposed to visit. It was a start-up church, begun by some people sent from the larger downtown church. It was located at the edge of town near a bunch of new housing developments. The church was smaller than theirs and appeared to be about three to four years old. They tried the splitting-up routine again. This time no ushers spotted them on the way in, so they moved into their positions with a certain level of confidence. There were about a hundred people there that day. Picking up the bulletin, Travis scanned it quickly to see what hymns they would be singing.

Oh no. He didn't recognize a single hymn. He looked them up in the new blue hymnal, and they were all circa 1980. "Well," Travis said to himself, "this is just great." Some snuggle-up-to-Jesus music. He figured they would have a guitar accompanying the choir. Yep, a grubby-looking dude with a moustache, a short beard, and blue jeans came in before the choir and took a seat on a stool. Travis thanked God it was an acoustic guitar and not an electric one. He guessed these people probably weren't rockers like in the Pentecostal churches. They were more Peter, Paul and Mary style, which to Travis was just as bad but not as loud.

Watching them sing along in harmony, Travis had the thought that these people had spent too many summers at camp. Then that got him to thinking about his own summer at the Royal Ambassadors camp for Baptist boys in Asheboro. At the RA camp they slept in these covered wagon deals out in the woods. Travis would never forget his first night there. He was nine years old. His aunt Kay paid for him to go, but his dad was off working somewhere so Aunt Kay's husband had driven him to the camp. His uncle had not been able to knock off work early at his farm, so they were real late getting there. In fact, everyone was already asleep.

The guard went and woke up the camp director to take them to the right group of campers. Apparently, Travis was supposed to be in the Shawnee group. They hiked through the woods down a trail to where there was a group of the covered wagon things. The camp director woke up the counselor for the Shawnee, a college student from Appalachian State named

Mike, who seemed pretty nice. He showed Travis where his cot was. Travis's uncle unrolled his sleeping bag, set it up on the cot, got Travis's pillow out, and laid it at the head of the sleeping bag. He gave Travis a hug. After staring at Travis for about ten seconds, his uncle disappeared into the darkness.

Travis was scared to death. He couldn't get to sleep for all of the night noises in the woods. It was chilly too. After about an hour of just lying on his back and looking at the canvas covering overhead, he heard some voices coming through the woods. It sounded like a group of boys. They were giggling and whispering. Somebody loudly whispered, "Shut up!" Travis didn't know if he should call out to Mike, hide, or what.

All of a sudden they were very close and began running through the covered wagon, spraying shaving cream and squeezing toothpaste on all of the boys lying in their sleeping bags. Travis did the only thing he knew to do. He jumped out of his sleeping bag and started running through the woods. He could see pretty good in the dark, but he was running so fast that he ran right over a couple of small trees that left scratches on his face and arms. He kept running until he could barely hear the yells back at the camp before he stopped to catch his breath.

He spotted a tall sweet gum—although it could have been some other kind of tree; he couldn't tell in the dark. He couldn't reach the first limb so he climbed by scooching up like a bear would. He finally got into some limbs where he could climb pretty easy. When he got up to a point where he felt safe, he stopped to listen. He couldn't hear anything now.

It was quiet like that for about ten minutes. Then he heard some grown-up voices in the distance.

Travis wasn't sure what had happened back there. He figured he would wait until daylight, when he could see what was going on. Then he started worrying about falling asleep and falling out of the tree. He decided he would give it an hour and then crawl down and sleep on the ground.

About fifteen minutes later he heard a man's voice yell, "Travis! Come back to the camp!" He stayed put, because he didn't know these people. He figured it might be some kind of trick. Then he saw seven or eight flashlights in the distance. They were heading off in different directions. One of them was coming his way. Travis watched the light move through the woods, shining this way and then shining that way. Remarkably, the light kept coming directly toward the tree where he was perched. When the light was almost directly beneath him at the foot of the tree, he recognized the grown-up. It was Mike, the counselor he had met with his uncle.

"Hey," Travis said, careful to give his voice a normal tone.

The light immediately flashed up in the tree and the counselor said, "Travis? Where on earth are you?"

"I'm up here."

"Well, get down from that tree. You scared the heck out of us back there."

Travis came down the tree and dropped to the ground from the first limb.

"What are you doing way out here up a tree?"

"I didn't know what was going on and kinda got scared."

"Oh, that. . . . Well, it was just a raid by the Apaches. We'll get them back tomorrow night. Are you alright?"

"Yeah," Travis said casually, not wanting to let on how scared he still was.

Mike took hold of Travis's hand and they walked back to the camp. Everybody else was already back on their cots and asleep. Travis crawled into his sleeping bag. Mike went out to talk to the other grown-ups, and then Travis heard him getting back in bed. Travis fell asleep hoping the other boys wouldn't find out about what he had done.

Later on that week a doctor came to give his testimonial at the camp dinner meeting in the dining hall. He started out talking about hiking with a group of boys in Shining Rock Wilderness. Said they saw fresh bear tracks and had to be careful to keep their food tied up at night. Then he told how one of the boys developed a severe case of appendicitis. They needed to get him to a hospital, but it would have taken about six hours to hike out, plus they would have had to carry the boy.

So the doctor prayed to God and decided to perform an emergency appendectomy. The only surgical supplies he had to use were his barlow knife, a canteen of cold water, and a first-aid kit. But he had faith that God would see him through it. He didn't say how he planned to sew him up.

It was when he started talking about cutting into the boy and having others hold the boy still that Travis started feeling kind of nauseated. Then it hit him all of a sudden. He let loose something like a projectile vomit with macaroni and cheese,

English peas, and hot dog chunks right on the back of the kid sitting in front of him.

He immediately felt better but didn't realize it would start a chain reaction that would disrupt the doctor's testimony and cause a whole mass of boys to bend over double and hurl their guts out. But it did. It was complete and total chaos. Even some of the counselors threw up. Looking across the room, Travis saw metal folding chairs falling over and boys spewing everywhere. Travis had never seen anything like it, before or since. Man, that dining hall smelled to high heaven for the rest of the week.

When his aunt Kay came to pick him up at the end of the week, she asked, "Well, how did it go?"

Mike put his hand on Travis's shoulder and squeezed hard. He said, "It went great. All of the kids had a great time."

Mike was still squeezing Travis's shoulder hard, so he offered, "Yeah, it was great." Mike's grip loosened.

That was Travis's one and only camp experience.

• • •

Whew! The sermon was already over and Travis hadn't heard a word of it. He started to feel guilty about it but then had the thought that it was really the preacher's fault. If he couldn't keep Travis interested, he probably wouldn't do much for anybody else in their church either.

They went out to eat at an Applebee's. It was pretty good. The preacher was real nice, but everybody agreed later that he just wasn't their style. Oh well, they would have to try again.

CHAPTER 4

Q. 1. What is your only comfort, in life and in death?
A. That I belong—body and soul, in life and in death—not to myself
but to my faithful Savior, Jesus Christ, who at the cost of his own
blood has fully paid for all my sins and has completely freed me from
the dominion of the devil; that he protects me so well that without
the will of my Father in heaven not a hair can fall from my head;
indeed, that everything must fit his purpose for my salvation. Therefore,
by his Holy Spirit, he also assures me of eternal life, and makes me
wholeheartedly willing and ready from now on to live for him.

THE BOOK OF CONFESSIONS, PRESBYTERIAN CHURCH (USA):
THE HEIDELBERG CATECHISM, 4.001

FRANKIE RESTED HER HEAD with its tight gray curls against the back of the seat. They were about two hours from home now; maybe she could get a little nap. The tires hitting the concrete sections on I-40 made a steady *click-click* sound and the van rolled over the sections like a boat crossing a large, smooth wave in the ocean. The afternoon sun was shining in on her side of the church van and it warmed that side of her body. She closed her eyes, listening to Bill and Travis in the front. She could barely make out their quiet voices talking about the Braves' chances this year.

Feeling herself fall asleep, she folded her hands in her lap and . . . found herself twenty years younger, in middle age, riding on the back of a motorcycle with her husband, George, in front of her. They were traveling down a dirt road in a desert, followed by a narrow plume of dust. She tightened her grip around George's midsection. His black leather jacket was warm. A bird flew in a rolling, bobbing motion, up and down, alongside them. It was a red-winged blackbird, and Frankie watched it fly beside them with her head pressed against George's back. The red on its wings was flashing like a miniature strobe light as the bird struggled to keep up with the motorcycle. Sometimes it would fall back into the dust cloud behind the bike, but then with a sudden burst of raw determination, it would pierce through the dust and again find its place next to Frankie.

Frankie sat straight up again on the backseat of the motorcycle and looked toward the horizon beyond the bird. There were small white clouds that seemed to be moving fast, and then faster, toward Frankie and George. As the clouds drew closer, George turned his head and noticed them too. The unusual clouds began to move around each other as if they were trying to get into a certain formation, like elephants in the ring at a circus.

Then George and the motorcycle were gone. And the bird, too. Frankie was a little girl again, lying on her back in a meadow, her big brother, Davie, beside her. A slight, warm breeze was blowing. Frankie watched the movement of the tops of the trees above her. The sun felt warm and relaxed her. Dear Davie held her hand as she dug her toes into the gray, moist dirt. The clouds in the sky were white and puffy like the cotton in her daddy's field. Then, somehow, standing over the two of them was her daddy, looking down and blocking the sun. His face was full of red anger. He started to reach down toward Davie.

"No . . . ," Frankie mumbled and awoke in a groggy state.

"What is it, darling?" asked Dot. "Poor thing, you must have been having a real bad dream. You were twitching and shifting like a five-year-old in church. What were you dreaming about?"

"I don't know," Frankie said, now half-awake. Suddenly realizing that everyone in the van was looking at her, she sat erect and yawned wide with her hand covering her mouth. "Well, I thought I was going to get some rest, but I had some kind of bad dream that I can't even remember," she said in a complaining tone of voice, hoping to deflect everyone's attention. It worked. Everybody went back to talking or looking at the newspaper.

Frankie looked out the window and sighed. Laying her head back on the seat, she again fell asleep.

CHAPTER 5

*All time, all space, all matter are created by God and have been
hallowed by Jesus Christ. Christian worship, at particular times,
in special places, with the use of God's material gifts, should lead the
church into the life of the world to participate in God's purpose to
redeem time, to sanctify space, and to transform material reality for
the glory of God.*

THE BOOK OF ORDER, PRESBYTERIAN CHURCH (USA): W-1.3040

IT WAS GOOD FOR MATT to be home with his dad again. They
didn't talk to each other much, but he could tell that his dad
enjoyed his company. Since his mom died two years ago, a lot
had happened. His dad had sold about half of their land and
kept only enough to keep him busy farming. Matt had been
so absorbed in his own problems that he was unaware of his
surroundings most of the time. His girlfriend, Julia, had asked
him why his dad was always so quiet and always working on
something. He hadn't even noticed.

Of course, Matt had been adrift for so long that he had

stopped noticing other people altogether. It was a strange kind of mind numbness, almost like he was floating. It turned out that after all the schooling, the awards, the papers, the everything, there was really nothing in the way of a job that interested him. In fact, hardly anything interested him. There was nobody left to please. That was it. He had spent his entire life pleasing other people and now didn't know what he wanted or who he was. He had a PhD in something that meant nothing to him.

What an idiot he'd been. It was almost like everyone was in on it. Friends and family had encouraged him to keep going after it, get the degrees, work hard and get the rewards down the road. There were no rewards down the road. All those people he had worked so hard to please didn't even think about him anymore. They were just chanting their parts in the mantra. They had their own lives, their own families, and they were all happy. How did they know not to go after it? How did they know it was better to settle down, to have a family and be content? Who told them? Why hadn't they told him about it? He saw it clearly now, but it was too late—he was locked out.

And yet he sometimes longed to have that drive back—the drive that had rocketed him through academia and then into his research career. It was gone, and its absence had a kind of permanence that had settled like a fog around Matt. Was it the pressure to publish every insignificant finding like all of the academics struggling to make tenure, to make some kind of name for themselves? There certainly were enough useless papers published. There were so many that it was impossible to distinguish the breakthrough discoveries from the reporting of irrelevant bench-scale experiments. And there was also the sickening culture of academia, resembling the politics of a third-world country. But that wasn't it. It was more like the sudden realization of the futility of it all. You could spend your entire lifetime in one laboratory investigating the physics of nature just so cell phones could be miniaturized.

He had been let go when the director of the institute, a mentor and a notable African American physicist of Caltech lineage who had often encouraged Matt, came into his semiconductor lab and found him sitting on the floor reading a Walker Percy novel. It was the third time the director had walked into Matt's lab and found him reading something unrelated to his work. The director was already upset that Matt had missed several deadlines related to a jointly funded project with a big telecommunications company. Matt just couldn't get excited about cell phones. The intensity of the research, the drive to carve out a place among peers, the hunger for more knowledge, to keep learning more and more, were gone, all gone. Life had become an upside-down puzzle to him. He could put the pieces together, but there was no meaning to it. All he got at the end was gray cardboard.

And then Julia came along.

He met Julia at the truck stop out by I-95, coming back from Raleigh one weekend. He had been to the library at the university and knew his dad wouldn't have anything to eat at the house. So he pulled over at the truck stop, thinking he would get a good home-cooked meal there. He had never been inside the place before.

He took a seat in a booth covered in black vinyl. Several pieces of black electrical tape had been used to cover up a crack in the seat cushion. The menu was stuck in between the ketchup and the salt and pepper shakers. The table was laminated with silver-flake formica. He hadn't seen that in a while. It hadn't been wiped off after the last customer left, and there was a drop of pancake syrup right in front of Matt. As he was looking at it, a white dishrag with an arm attached made three swoops across the table.

"Sorry about that," the waitress said. Then, taking a step back and putting one hand on her hip, she gazed at Matt for what seemed to be at least fifteen seconds. It was enough to make Matt have a small panic attack, thinking he might have to talk to this woman. He began studying the one-page menu but not seeing or reading anything. This woman was about to engage him in some type of discourse and he really didn't enjoy making chitchat. In fact, he considered engaging in small talk to be a character flaw.

Then she said to him, "You're not a driver, are you." It was more of a statement than a question. Looking up from the menu, Matt was struck by her plain good looks—dark hair, high cheekbones, possibly some American Indian blood way back.

She noticed his reaction and smiled. "You know how I know?" Matt had the uncomfortable realization that he was going to have to say something when she spoke again.

"Your hands. They're not strong enough."

Feeling the blood rush to his ears, Matt nervously said, "No, I'm just a farm boy."

She gave a little laugh and shot back, "No, you're not."

Matt wondered where this girl had come from and why she had decided to humiliate him in front of all these truckers. Sure enough, glancing around, he saw that at least two other tables were looking at him. And he couldn't stop blushing.

"You're a college boy. You look way too smart to farm for a living."

Matt was seriously considering getting up and leaving, but then she continued. "I'm sorry. I give everybody a hard time in here. It's the only fun I get to have. Ain't that right, Roger?"

She looked over at another table, where one of the truckers said, "Yeah, go ahead and break him in, Julia, like you did the rest of us."

Matt was a little relieved to learn that he was not the only victim.

"Am I right?" she said with a grin, pointing her pen at her pad.

"Uh, yeah. I went to college. But I do farm now, so you're only half-right," he said, feeling a little more in control of the situation.

"Okay, well, whatcha want?" She was still smiling at him like she wasn't through with him yet. "Special today is grilled ham-and-cheese with vegetable soup on the side."

"I'll take the special."

"Sweet tea?"

"Yeah."

Julia jotted it down on the pad and then, in a quiet, raspy voice, asked matter-of-factly, "Are you seeing anybody?"

"Excuse me?"

"You know, going with somebody."

Matt did not want to talk to this woman anymore. He was certain the truckers at the other table were chuckling at him now. He looked around to indicate he had no idea why this woman was prying into his life. But they weren't paying attention anymore.

"Uh, yes. I am," he lied, rather solemnly, hoping this would shake her off.

"Oh." She paused. "You live around here?" Now she was speaking in a little more cynical tone.

What on earth did this woman want from him? He just came in here for some lunch and now felt like he was in seventh grade again.

"Yeah, I just moved back home." He looked away, hoping she would leave.

Julia flipped to the second page of her pad and jotted something down, tore off the page, and put it down on the table. Then she walked back toward the kitchen. Matt noticed that she was a little pigeon-toed, but she somehow compensated in a way that made her hips move like a Venezuelan beauty queen's. She was attractive, but in a different kind of way. He picked up the paper, thinking it was his check.

It wasn't. In a girl-style cursive, she had written, *Don't lie to me. 572-4782. Julia.*

Matt couldn't believe it. This was crazy. He immediately wondered if the truckers had seen her put the note on his table and if they knew what she was doing. They probably did, and he was being set up by this woman for total and complete humiliation. He would never come in this place again.

Julia came back out with his tea. She was not smiling now. Instead, her face appeared to be disinterested in the reality around her. She was moving about the room, checking on tables, and her mood had completely changed. She set the glass in front of him politely, then put another note on the table, turned, and walked back to the kitchen. Matt looked down at the note and whispered to himself, "This is unbelievable." Again she had written something in cursive with lots of extra curlicues. This one said, *Saturday, 7 p.m.*

Maybe she was a hooker. He had heard about the women who hung out at rest areas on the interstate and went from truck to truck plying their trade. Maybe she operated out of the truck stop. Yes, she was a hooker. That would explain the brashness.

Julia came back out of the kitchen and circulated among the other tables, filling red plastic glasses with sweet tea. She came by his table and, without asking, filled his glass with more tea. Then she put down another note. This was insane.

Matt picked up the note as she walked away. *I know you're thinking I'm a hooker but I'm not. I would really like to go out with you.*

This could not be happening.

When she brought the food out to his table, Matt didn't

even acknowledge her presence. Maybe, just maybe, she would get the hint and stop the little game. It was so incredibly stupid. She didn't leave a note this time and she didn't say anything. *Good*, Matt thought. Maybe it was over. The truckers who had been chuckling earlier had finished eating and were now making their way back to their rigs. The ham-and-cheese sandwich was flat and greasy but it tasted great. The soup was pretty good too. So the stop here wasn't a complete misadventure.

Julia came from behind the counter at the cash register and laid his check down at the edge of the table—along with another note. *What if this girl starts stalking me?* Matt thought to himself. *She is completely unpredictable.* This note was longer and composed of several complete sentences: *I have made a complete fool of myself. Please forgive me. I am just a very lonely person and you looked like you would make a good friend.* She signed her name at the bottom of the note.

Okay, maybe she had some type of personality disorder. If she were a middle-class girl in a big city, she would be coddled by shrinks and counselors and would make everyone who knew her miserable. Here, though, she was just a little odd. Thinking about it in that way, Matt began to feel sorry for Julia. Then he caught himself and stood up, walked over to the cashier, and paid his bill. He left without looking at her again, and with the notes folded in his pocket.

That's how it had started with Julia.

CHAPTER 6

*For he will conceal me there when troubles come; he will hide me
in his sanctuary. He will place me out of reach on a high rock.*

PSALM 27:5

TRAVIS OPENED THE METAL TRASH CAN behind his house and
pulled out the full bag to put in the back of his truck. He
looked inside the empty can and smiled. It was funny how
certain things brought back memories of his childhood. This
empty trash can, for instance. He remembered hiding inside
one very much like it—though maybe not quite as shiny—
one time while playing with his sister.

"Ready or not, here I come!" Lou Ann had called from
behind the unpainted clapboard house they'd lived in.

Travis had squatted in the trash can, pulling the lid down

over himself. In the complete darkness, his only sensation was the garbage juice oozing between the toes of his bare feet.

"Here I come!" Lou Ann had called again, running around the corner of the house into the dirt front yard.

Travis remembered how he had stayed completely still. He'd heard Lou Ann's footsteps nearby. When it sounded like she was heading back around the house again, he slowly raised the lid and peered out to see if she was within sight. She wasn't. He threw the lid off and jumped out of the can.

Just then Lou Ann yelled, "Aha!" from the back steps. The old house sat on cinder blocks, and apparently she could see Travis's legs by peering beneath the house.

But Travis made it to the front steps, where he yelled, "Safe!" and plopped down.

Lou Ann dashed around to the front of the house and stopped in her tracks.

"Shoot, Travis, that's not fair. Where were you?"

"Ha! I ain't telling you 'cause then you'll know my secret."

"You reckon Mama's up yet?" Lou Ann looked over her shoulder at the front screen door.

"Don't know. Let's go see." Travis stood up. They opened the door to the house and walked inside.

"Law, you better wipe off your feet! You tracking!" Lou Ann whispered.

Travis looked behind him. Sure enough, he was leaving footprints of dirt and garbage juice with each step. He turned and spread the mess around with one foot, trying to make it blend with the linoleum floor.

"Travis Booth! You better get the mop and clean that up or you won't be eating no supper tonight!" his mother hollered as she came into the room carrying the baby with her good arm. The stroke had caused her to drag one leg, and her bad arm hung limp on the side of her body. She had on a dirty sweatshirt and her shoulder-length hair hadn't been brushed. "And when you're done with that, you can start shelling those butter beans Maybelle brought by yesterday—both of you."

Travis walked a wide circle around his mother to get to the kitchen. He grabbed the mop and the bucket and headed out the back door to the spigot by the steps. After filling the bucket halfway he went into the kitchen and started retracing his footsteps with swoops of the damp mop. When he got to the front room he dipped the mop in the bucket and wrung it out by twisting it with his hands. After he finished mopping he carried the mop to the kitchen and threw the dirty water out the back door.

Lou Ann had already set the paper bag full of butter beans between two of the kitchen chairs and had the big plastic bowl on the floor beside the bag. Travis sat down facing Lou Ann, grabbed a handful of butter beans from the bag, and began shelling them.

"These look good," Lou Ann offered to their mama, who was struggling to put the baby in the old high chair the church had brought by.

"Travis, give me a hand here," his mama barked. She couldn't put the belt around the baby and fasten it by herself.

Travis buckled his baby brother, Robby, into his chair and put a dirty bib around his neck. Lou Ann stopped shelling beans and grabbed Robby's bowl and spoon from the dish rack.

"Here, Mama," she said, putting the bowl on the high-chair tray.

Their mama moved over to the refrigerator and retrieved a jar of applesauce.

"Mama, can we go sit on the front steps and shell the beans?" Lou Ann asked.

Their mama pulled a chair next to the high chair and sat down. "Yeah, go on, but you better not spill a one."

Travis grabbed the sack of beans and Lou Ann brought the bowl. They sat on the top step and put the bowl between them. Travis set the sack of butter beans on the next step down.

He looked across the road and up the hill at the Milligans', a tan brick house with a concrete driveway. They had money. The kids, Junior and Charlotte, were about the same ages as Travis and Lou Ann, but the Milligans weren't allowed to play with the Booths. Something about head lice. Travis didn't think that was such a big deal, though, because all you did was get a nice crew cut and wash your head with soap real good. That normally did the trick. Now, Lou Ann had some trouble with it on account of her being a girl and not able to get a crew cut. In any case, Junior and Charlotte's mama didn't want to deal with it. Today Junior and Charlotte were in their carport playing with something—Travis couldn't tell what.

"Hey, what y'all doing?" Travis yelled.

Junior turned around and waved. Then he went back to playing whatever it was they were playing.

"I wish we had a carport," Lou Ann said.

"What for?" Travis asked. "We ain't got no car. Daddy took it with him, and Mama couldn't drive one anyway."

"Well, it would still be nice to have a place to play when it was raining that wasn't so muddy."

• • •

The dump was unattended when Travis drove up to drop off his trash. Usually Roy Elliott manned the dump, nowadays called a "convenience and recycling center," but he was nowhere in sight. Travis enjoyed talking with Roy because he always came away with something he could tell Jenny when he got back to the house.

The last time Travis came to the dump Roy mentioned that a black-and-white mongrel dog had been found and someone had stopped by to see if Roy recognized it. Roy had told the couple that he didn't recognize the dog, but they could leave it with him because everybody ends up at the dump sooner or later, and he was sure the owner of the dog would too.

Such were the nuggets of wisdom delivered by Roy Elliott to whoever would listen.

The other thing about Roy was that he had known about Travis's daddy. Because of that, he had taken a special interest in Travis to encourage him. Roy knew that Travis sure never got any encouragement from his daddy.

Travis's daddy had left them to go work on a dredge boat

down around Charleston. Nobody around home would hire him to work tobacco on account of his drinking. He sent some money home every now and then, but it was barely enough to buy groceries. It wasn't that he didn't make enough money, because the dredge boat jobs were pretty good. They paid alright and the men got to sleep and eat for free on the boat. Somehow, though, his daddy's getting a job didn't do a whole lot for the family. Travis's mama always said his daddy spent all their money on liquor. She said that was why they didn't get to wear new clothes and only had lunch on Tuesdays, Thursdays, and Sundays and why she couldn't afford the medicine she was supposed to be taking.

His daddy did drink a lot. He never hit their mama or them, but he yelled at all of them every time he came home. He was always mad about something.

Once he took Travis and Lou Ann fishing with a gill net on a creek near the Pamlico Sound. He told them to stand on the bank while he rowed the boat out to the middle of the creek and then upstream. His plan was to anchor both ends of the gill net to the bank to form a C, and then he was going to paddle out to the middle of the C and slap the paddle on the water to scare all the fish into the net.

Sounded like a good plan to Travis. However, his daddy hadn't been real clear on what Travis and Lou Ann were supposed to do. They watched him put one end of the net on the bank and then get in the boat and start poling out to the middle of the creek. The end of the gill net on the bank just followed along behind the boat as he poled.

Based on his reaction when he reached the middle of the creek and looked back at Travis and Lou Ann, apparently they were supposed to hold the end of the gill net he had put on the bank. At least that's what they thought he was saying in between all the cussing and yelling.

He slammed his paddle down on the boat real hard and it snapped in half, making him even madder. He threw the end with the handle on it at them, standing on the shore. Fortunately, he had already been drinking and it didn't come anywhere close to hitting them, although the throw caused him to lose his balance and fall out of the boat.

Travis and Lou Ann just stood on the bank with wide eyes, watching it all unfold. Their daddy came stumbling out of the water and told them to go get in the car. They did just that and watched as he put the small rowboat on top of the car and then tied it down with some old rope.

He yelled at them the whole way home. It made Lou Ann cry, but Travis wouldn't even blink. He didn't want to give his daddy the pleasure of making him cry. It was his way of fighting back.

The fishing incident was kind of funny, but there were others that were not. Once his daddy came in from drinking and started yelling at Mama to clean up the house and that a pigpen smelled better and he wanted to know what she was spending all that money on that he had been sending her. Mama had somehow managed to lock herself in her bedroom so he couldn't get to her. Upon figuring this out, Daddy punched a hole in the wall by the door. After that

Travis eased out of bed and locked the door to his and Lou Ann's bedroom.

The next morning their daddy was lying on the floor of the front room, asleep. He had wet his pants. Mama just moved around him and went into the kitchen to fix them something to eat. Travis and Lou Ann also walked around him and followed their mama to the kitchen.

The worst thing about it was they had no other place to go or any way to get there. Their best hope was that he would just get up and leave again, which most of the time he did.

Travis threw the bag of trash into the dumpster and got back in his truck. Driving off, he was disappointed Roy wasn't around to talk with today. Roy always made him feel good.

CHAPTER 7

*The seasons of the Christian year provide a rhythm and content
for personal worship and discipleship. Special seasons, occasions,
and transitions in one's own life also inform personal worship
and discipleship.*

THE BOOK OF ORDER, PRESBYTERIAN CHURCH (USA): W-5.5002

BILL HAD CHECKED WITH HIS INSURANCE MAN to make sure
his life insurance would pay out if this heart disease thing
killed him. The house had been paid for a long time ago.
Truck was paid for. No real obligations except, possibly, Bill's
sister Lydia, who was Jerry's mama, might need taking care
of down the road. She had real bad arthritis and her husband, Clayton, had a stroke six years ago and died from it.
Lydia would only add a little to the grocery bill, though, and
might be good company for Mary Helen. They always did
get along. Mary Helen would be able to live off the insurance

and Social Security and not have to worry about money so much. But her best friend would be gone, and Bill worried that might be too much for her. They were too close.

Nowadays when he looked at her, for some reason he couldn't help but think about when he first asked her out in high school. He had driven over to her house to pick her up for the drive-in and didn't expect to be interviewed by her parents. When he knocked on the door her daddy opened it.

He knew something was up by the way her daddy said, "Come on in." It wasn't a Sunday-afternoon "Come on in." It was more like a football coach opening the door to his office after tryouts and looking kind of solemn at you and saying, "Come on in."

Once inside the house, he didn't see Mary Helen anywhere. Her daddy, with a wave of his hand, motioned him into the living room, where her mother, who also seemed to be in a somber mood, was sitting on the sofa. Bill sat in the overstuffed chair opposite the sofa and smiled at Mary Helen's mama and daddy. They didn't smile back. Something was definitely up.

Mary Helen's daddy sat down heavily and said, "So, Bill, what are your plans?"

Bill's smile disappeared as he tried to figure out if her daddy meant what were his plans tonight or what were his plans for life? He opted for the former and started talking about the show at the drive-in, but her daddy interrupted him and said, "No, what I meant was . . . what are your prospects?"

Actually, Bill had never really thought about his prospects.

He wasn't a big planner and just kind of went along with things. But he knew he had to come up with something, so he said something about working at the hardware store and then maybe taking some vocational classes over at the community college.

Her daddy stared at him for a while. Her mama said nothing and kind of looked around the room like she was as uncomfortable with this as Bill was. Finally, her daddy said, "So, you're not going to college?"

Bill, trying to sound confident, said, "Probably not. I figure I can get a pretty good job around here. I want to stay close to home."

Just about this time Mary Helen came bebopping into the room and plopped down in the other chair. "Are you ready to go?"

Relieved, Bill said, "Sure!" and stood up to go.

Her daddy seemed to sigh but rose anyway and said, more to Mary Helen than to Bill, "Don't be out later than nine thirty." Then he walked out of the room. Her mama just stood, smiled politely, and said, "Y'all have a good time. Be safe."

That was forty-six years ago. Time had flown. Since he retired he had been getting up real early and treating Mary Helen to breakfast in bed every now and then. Usually after breakfast they would do something in the garden or ride into town to pick up some groceries and walk around. Other than that, there wasn't a whole lot to do. He had thought about doing some real farming, but that would be a lot of work and he would need a different kind of tractor. Besides, nobody made any money at farming anymore and none of the young folks wanted to help. So he just piddled with things around the house and in the garden.

Lately, after the last doctor visit, he'd started repairing things around the house that he hadn't gotten around to in a long while. He was trying to make sure everything was fixed up for Mary Helen, but in a way that she wouldn't notice. So he didn't make a big deal out of his little projects and he pretended that they weren't important to him. He finally fixed that noise the attic fan made. It kept clicking on something up there. It was a piece of cardboard from one of the boxes. He thought about how funny it was that people could learn to live with little annoyances that were so easy to fix. Then he started unsticking all the windows. That took some religion to get done. He fixed the storm door off the kitchen at the back of the house so it wouldn't slam shut if you didn't catch it. The tongue-and-groove porch flooring on the front of the house was starting to rot in places. It needed replacing, but that would be a big project and Mary Helen would notice the extra effort for sure. He would need to bring it up at breakfast one morning and make it seem like it had to be done right away or people might get hurt. That would make the big project justifiable and Mary Helen wouldn't think twice about it after that.

She could drive herself around okay but didn't see so well at night. That was alright because they never went anywhere at night anyway. She used to love to plant flowers and still had several beds around the yard. Maybe he would get some cow manure and make her a new bed by the old water oak in the backyard. That might get her going again on flowers, and that would be something to occupy her. And she loved to read, especially stories about far-off places.

Bill thought about how his dog would provide her company and protect the house. He was a Walker hound, though Bill had never hunted with him. The dog definitely had a nose; Bill just didn't enjoy hunting. The dog loved Mary Helen. She fed him most of the time and put bacon pieces in his bowl with his dog food. But the dog wasn't spoiled, and he never tried to come inside or beg for food. He was a good dog—he knew his place.

What if Mary Helen's health started to fail? Who would take care of her? He knew she didn't want to go to a nursing home. That would definitely kill her. She visited old folks at the home on the other side of town and always said the smell was unbearable, a cross between urine and perspiration. She would never be able to leave her house anyway. It was the one material thing she was attached to.

The other thing he worried about was her sad spells. She would just go in her reading room and sleep on the little couch all day sometimes. She would do this for several days in a row. Then she would come out of it and apologize to him for not helping him with something. The spells came more often now.

Maybe he *should* have done something different with his life. Maybe he should have taken her away to another town after Billy was killed. Maybe he should have gone on to college and studied to be an accountant like her daddy wanted her to marry. Then they would have had money to travel and do the things she read about in those books.

He really had just drifted through life, not ever really going after anything. Life was too short. He didn't have time to do anything over. It was done.

CHAPTER 8

The Church is called to a new openness to its own membership,
by affirming itself as a community of diversity, becoming in fact as
well as in faith a community of women and men of all ages, races,
and conditions, and by providing for inclusiveness as a visible sign
of the new humanity.

THE BOOK OF ORDER, PRESBYTERIAN CHURCH (USA): G-3.0401(B)

IT WAS GOING TO BE A HOT ONE.

"Good thing the AC hasn't died on this old Econoline," Bill said, rapping his knuckles on the dash. "Knock on wood."

Today they were headed to New Hanover County to a small church near Wilmington. The guy over there was supposedly real good at adding members by getting a bunch of programs going for young families. Programs with names like "Married for Life" and "The Bible-Based Family" and "Young Adventurers for Christ." They hadn't ever had any programs before at their church, and as far as Travis knew, none of the other churches in their town did either. The Methodists down the street had an AA meeting on Thursday nights, but that was about all. The programs deal was a new thing for the committee to consider.

"Did you get that sign?" Bill asked, looking over at Travis.

"No, what did it say?" Travis responded, opening his little blue notebook.

"It said, *How will you spend eternity? Smoking or nonsmoking?*"

"Baptist?"

"Assembly of God."

Travis wrote it down and closed his notebook. He had about seventeen or eighteen of them now. He looked at Bill and then down the road. They were coming up on another church that had a sign.

Bill read it aloud. "*Big Bang Theory: God spoke, and BANG— it happened.*"

Joyce laughed and shook her head.

"Now that's a good one," Dot chimed in. "They ought to put that on the first page of science books in all the schools."

Matt said from the back of the van, "Well, the Bible doesn't say *how* God created everything, just that he did."

Smart aleck.

"What's the difference?" Dot shot back.

"Well, why couldn't the big bang be the way God created the universe?" Matt offered.

"Simple," said Dot. "Because it don't say nothing in the Bible about no big bang."

"Matt's got a point," Bill said. "As far as I know about it, the Bible doesn't say exactly how God did it."

"He's right; it doesn't say how except for the part about Eve coming from Adam's rib," Frankie said. "And I always wondered about that anyway."

"Are y'all saying you don't believe in the Creation story?" Dot inquired of the group, like some kind of lawyer quizzing somebody on the stand.

"Well, Dot, are you saying that God did it by snapping his fingers?" Bill responded.

"Like the bumper sticker says, *The Bible says it, I believe it, and that settles it*," Dot replied smartly.

Travis avoided making eye contact with anybody for fear they would ask him what he thought about it.

"Uh-oh," Bill said suddenly as he slowed down.

"What's up?" Travis asked.

"Flat tire."

"Oh my, I hope this old van has a spare," said Frankie.

Bill said, "It does, but I'm betting it isn't the best spare in the world. We'll probably have to stop somewhere and try to get the flat repaired or get a new one if we want to be safe on the way home."

"We're going to be late, I reckon," Dot said, issuing her judgment on the situation as always.

Bill eased onto the shoulder and stopped the van.

Shoot. Travis knew he would be the one changing the tire, and it was just hot enough that he would be sweating by the time it was over. There was nothing he hated more than sweating in Sunday clothes. Sometimes when he started he just couldn't stop, and the more he thought about trying to stop sweating, the worse it got. It just started pouring out. Usually when that happened Travis got up and left to get in some cool air. But here he would be stuck in the van. Maybe if they got going quick he could roll down the window and it wouldn't be so bad. It wasn't like he was out of shape. It was more of a nervous thing.

Everybody crawled out of the van and stood around on the side of the road. There wasn't any shade, only a field of soybeans. After everybody was out, Travis opened the back doors and started digging around under the backseat for the jack and lug wrench. He had just found them when he noticed a rolled-up magazine on one side under the seat. He pulled it out and opened it up. *Oh no.* It was the *Sports Illustrated* swimsuit edition. He quickly rolled it up and jammed it back into place.

Travis's mind began to race. *How did that get in here? Did Matt bring it? No, he isn't like that. Maybe some teenagers in the youth group stuck it back there. They went to the roller rink last week.*

He began to step back with the jack and lug wrench but started to worry when he realized that if he didn't show the magazine to everybody now, they might figure he had stuffed it back there. But if he did bring it out, then what would he say? He didn't want to pull it out and say something that implied he was disgusted with that type of magazine. That might be the right thing to do, but Bill, and probably Matt, would know he was lying, and Susie might think he was a little weird too. On the other hand, if he left it alone and somebody else found it, how would he explain not doing anything about it? Dot would be all over him on that one. He prayed for God to deliver him.

Travis made a quick decision to leave it be and to get rid of it later when nobody was around. He went around to the flat tire, where Bill was standing. He had already started to sweat. Predictably, Matt was standing over by the ditch with the women. Travis popped off the hubcap and loosened the nuts with the wrench. Then he got down on all fours to figure out where the jack was supposed to be placed. The sweat was rolling down his face now.

After putting on the spare, he was soaking wet. Here it was right before church, and he was without any other clothes. He felt like just getting out of his suit pants and taking off his tie and dress shirt. At least he would have a chance to cool down.

"Travis, honey, you are completely wet," Frankie noted as the women and Matt started to crawl back into the van.

"Don't sit by me when we get to the church," Dot said and then laughed hysterically.

It can't get any worse than this, Travis thought.

"Well, he can sit by me anytime," Susie offered, smiling at Travis.

Travis wondered if she really meant that. Maybe she had been looking at him, too.

Oh man, what was he thinking? This must be his punishment for his lustful heart. Well, he guessed he deserved it. Riding around on these trips thinking about Susie while

Jenny was at home by herself running the house—it just was not right. Travis wondered if his sins would be read aloud on Judgment Day so that Jenny could hear them. He thought that's what the Bible said. Maybe everybody's would be read at once and his would get lost in the noise. If it was a stand-up thing in front of God and everybody while all his sins were proclaimed, that almost seemed worse than hell to Travis. Now that he thought about it, he did spend a lot more time wondering about Judgment Day than he did about heaven. But who really cared what heaven would be like? It was bound to be nice. He always pictured a bunch of people walking around not having to work and being polite to each other. And the sun was always shining. And everybody was wearing robes.

"I'll stop at the next station and get Travis a Coke to help cool him down," Bill announced. "We're already late, so it won't matter that much."

"Thanks. I appreciate it," Travis replied.

"Oh my, look at this," Joyce said from the back of the van. She was holding up the swimsuit issue, and all the women were looking at it with their mouths open.

"Where'd you get that?" Dot asked, exaggerating a look of shock.

"It was rolled up and tucked down here by the seat."

"I reckon some of the teenage boys left it in the van when they went skating last week," Frankie surmised.

Bill was looking in the rearview mirror, trying to get a glimpse of the cover. Matt and Travis kept silent.

Dot had the magazine now and was going through it page by page while Susie and Frankie looked on.

"Travis, did you bring this along for some serious reading?" Frankie said and laughed.

Travis's face went flush as he stammered, "N-no . . . it wasn't me." He was sweating again. He would never stop it now.

The women were cackling as they pointed out different things about the models. Finally, Dot wrapped up her investigation and said as she handed the magazine back to Joyce, "I wonder what gets in a woman's head to let her picture get taken while she's lying around like that. I wouldn't even consider it."

Thank goodness, Travis thought, trying to not have a vision of Dot as one of the models in the swimsuit issue. But despite his best efforts, there he was, visualizing Dot rolling around in the surf with a seductive look in her eye. He looked at the floorboard, focusing on not getting sick.

Bill was slowing down, and Travis looked up to see a maroon mom-and-pop-type store with white trim, a couple of old gasoline pumps out front, and a two-bay garage.

"Sit tight, bud, and I'll run in and get you a Coke," Bill said.

"Thanks."

Watching Bill walk into the store, Travis noticed that there wasn't a whole lot going on here. Probably one of those places that had dust on the canned goods and you knew they didn't care about expiration dates. They hadn't updated their gas pumps either, because they had the old manual-reset switch on the side. There were two large bay windows on either side of the entrance with black iron bars across them. Travis wondered who in their right mind would think this place was worth robbing.

Bill came back out, stuck his head through the passenger-side window to hand Travis the Coke, and said to everybody, "They said they could fix the flat while we're in church. We'll leave the tire with them and get it on the way back. Matt, give me a hand getting that tire out for those boys."

Matt moved toward the front as Dot opened the side door. Travis looked in the garage bays to see what kind of equipment they had. Not much. What they had were three black guys, each one sitting on a stack of tires about four high. They looked like a flotilla of sorts, just sitting there, staring at the search committee staring at them. Behind them were other stacks of tires and some fan belts hanging on the wall. They didn't have a lift inside either bay, only a little orange portable lift that could be rolled around to where it was needed.

When Travis looked back at the three men, one of them caught his eye. They stared at one another without so much as a smile or nod, no expression at all. Finally, Travis looked away. The man's eyes were full of a tired hatred that couldn't be stared down. Travis glanced back. Still staring. No emotion. No movement.

Finally, Bill and Matt got the tire out of the van and rolled it to the closest bay. At this point, one of the men extracted himself from his perch and walked over to look at the tire. He put his hand on his hip and started scratching his head like he had never seen a tire before. Then, suddenly, some white guy came out the front door of the store and walked over, yelling something at the other two black men still sitting. They reluctantly stood up. Travis looked at the man who had stared him down. Now he was standing with his arms folded across his chest. Still no expression. Travis knew what he was saying, though.

Bill conferred with the white man, nodding and then shaking his hand. He and Matt walked back to the van and crawled in.

"Okay, let's roll," Bill said as he put the van in gear. "I figure we'll be about fifteen minutes late and will probably have to go in after the prayer of confession. At this point, I don't think we need to worry about being incognito. We're going to stick out like a fly in a mayonnaise jar."

"Yeah . . . oh well." Frankie sighed.

They made it to the church and walked in right after the second hymn, just before the sermon started. They sat down together in one of the back pews on the right.

Travis looked up front for the preacher. Something wasn't right. There were two kids sitting in the chairs behind the pulpit and the choir was full of kids. Travis hadn't noticed the ushers when he walked in, but now he saw them sitting in folding chairs just inside the main doors. Kids. About twelve years old.

Travis looked over at Frankie, who was staring at her bulletin with her mouth wide open. She looked down the pew and pointed to a heading at the top of the bulletin. It read, *Youth Sunday!*

CHAPTER 9

"Then at last the LORD said to me, 'You have been wandering around in this hill country long enough; turn to the north.'"
DEUTERONOMY 2:2-3

APPARENTLY, THE LAST PREACHER had written a letter to Bill to schedule another Sunday for the committee's visit when he realized there would be a conflict with the Youth Sunday thing, but Bill didn't get by the church to check his mail. Mary Helen had been having a bad week and he had kept close to home to care for her.

Everyone understood. Bill said he was sorry and he would pay for the gas on the next trip and would apologize to the session. But the others voted him down. Instead, they decided they would all chip in to pay for the gas they'd wasted, and the session didn't need to know a thing about that trip.

This weekend, they were headed south toward the coast to a medium-size church near Camp Lejeune in Jacksonville, North Carolina, one of the hottest places on the planet during July. This particular church had two worship services, one at eight thirty, followed by Sunday school, and then another service at eleven. It was a Lutheran church.

Just this past year, the General Assembly had voted to let Presbyterians and Lutherans swap ministers. None of the committee members had ever been in a Lutheran church and they weren't sure what to expect. About the only thing Travis ever heard about them was that they had to get the plans for any new buildings approved from some higher-ups. Apparently, this was so they wouldn't build anything too, too . . . whatever it was that Lutherans didn't like in the way of buildings.

Today was going to be a tough day. They planned on attending the eight thirty service at the Jacksonville Lutheran church and then they were going to hightail it over to Havelock to catch the eleven o'clock service at a Presbyterian church. That way, they figured they could make up for that last trip. The van had to leave at six thirty in the morning to get to the Jacksonville church on time.

Just as they were getting into Jacksonville, Joyce spoke up. "I am so sorry, but I have to stop somewhere before we get to the church and use the bathroom."

"No problem," Bill replied. "That preacher isn't going anywhere."

Frankie turned around in her seat and asked Joyce, "Is everything alright?"

"Yes, I just need to go to the ladies' room. I think I have a nervous stomach or something."

"You think it was something you ate?" Dot asked.

"Maybe so. I hope I don't make us late."

"It's no big deal. I think I could use the ladies' room too," Frankie said.

Bill pulled into a Shoney's. Nobody was scared about being a little late anymore, because by now they were pretty good at slipping into a church without anybody paying a whole lot of attention to them. Bill went inside the Shoney's with Frankie and Joyce. The rest of the committee stayed put in the van.

"How far is Havelock from Jacksonville?" Susie asked, offering the question to Travis, Matt, and Dot.

"I have no earthly idea," Dot replied.

Travis said, "The GPS here says it's about an hour. Looks like you have to drive around the Croatan National Forest and go up by New Bern before you can get on the road to Havelock."

"I pulled up Google Maps last night and saw some kind of road going right through the national forest that might cut about twenty minutes off our trip if we need to take it," Matt said from the backseat.

Travis leaned forward to examine the GPS screen more

closely. "Yes, there is a dashed line running through it. Looks like it might be a gravel road, though."

"Well, we're going to need every shortcut we can take to get in two sermons this morning in two different towns. I hope I can stay awake through the second one," Dot said, shifting in her seat and pulling on her dress.

"I can't remember; does this first preacher have a family?" Susie asked.

Travis opened up his little notebook. "Yeah, he's married and has one kid who's fifteen years old, a boy." He closed the notebook and glanced at his watch.

"Oh, heavens, I hope he and his wife aren't having to deal with what I'm going through with Shawn. He can't decide if he's fifteen or twenty, and he doesn't know how to be either one. I pray every night that he'll turn out alright," Susie confessed.

"Honey, your boy needs a daddy at home. That's what his problem is," Dot said, dishing out advice like she was dealing cards.

It was such an inconsiderate pronouncement that Travis felt Dot needed a reprimand. Unfortunately, he and Matt were the only ones left to defend Susie, and they weren't any match for Dot.

It wasn't Susie's fault that her husband had run off with another woman and had left Susie with a mortgage payment she couldn't afford and a teenage boy to raise. Her husband, Dale, had run the tire store in town until he got caught fooling around with his office assistant one night behind the store. The chief of police, Sonny Varnum, responding to what he thought was a vandalism incident, put his high beams on them and already had his new video camera rolling for evidence. Somehow, the word got out and a copy of the video showed up on Susie's doorstep one Saturday morning. Dale left town right away. People had to drive forty miles for tires for about two months until somebody else took over his business.

"No . . . daddies leave. That's what his problem is," Susie replied flatly, hardened by a year of whispers behind her back and unsolicited advice from most everybody in town.

Travis didn't think Susie actually wanted to be on the committee, but some of the women had talked her into it. Her son was having some problems if the clothes he wore to church were any indication. They were black. Black T-shirt, black jeans, black boots, and if he was wearing any kind of coat, it was black. And his hair—it was always greasy looking. He had problems.

On the other hand, Susie was real pretty. She was about thirty-seven or thirty-eight and had shoulder-length auburn hair. She was a little full in the hips, but that seemed to come and go. The other thing Travis liked about Susie was that she had the kind of slow, southern farm accent that was genuine—not the kind that most of the women in town had and tried to overdo. On some Sunday mornings Travis would find himself looking at her a little bit longer than he should have. He really needed to work on controlling that lust thing. After casting a glance sideways to see if Jenny had noticed, he would usually try to correct himself by looking in the opposite direction and around at other people coming in down the aisle.

"I'm sorry, honey. Sometimes my tongue runs faster than my manners," Dot said.

"It's okay. You're right; he does need a daddy."

Travis had a vision of him marrying Susie and then adopting Shawn and trying to straighten him out. But that probably wouldn't work, because he was only twelve or thirteen years older than Shawn, and Shawn probably wouldn't take too kindly to that. Then the thought of Jenny waiting alone at home for him popped into the vision. Oh boy, he was truly a sinner.

Frankie opened the sliding side door and stepped up into the van. "They got candy cigarettes behind the counter for sale in there. I haven't seen those around in years."

"Yeah, some company has just started that up again. I saw them in a Cracker Barrel a couple of months ago," Travis said, looking at his watch again. They were probably going to be a little late to the first service.

Joyce crawled in behind Frankie and then Bill came out of the Shoney's, smiling as he walked toward them.

"I wonder what *he's* smiling about," Dot said.

Bill opened the driver's-side door and got in. "Well, the manager in there said the Lutheran church is on the bypass right next to the Atlantis body-piercing and tattoo shop." Bill paused. "He said the Lutherans tried to stop the body-piercing shop from moving in next door, but they didn't have any weight with the city council."

"You know, I don't think I ever heard tell of a politician who was Lutheran. Or at least one who acknowledged it," Frankie said.

"Acknowledged what? Being a politician or a Lutheran?" Bill said, chuckling.

"Well, they better learn some politics fast, because there's no telling what'll go up next to them on the other side in a Marine town," Dot proclaimed.

"You know, there's something almost blasphemous about a body-piercing shop being juxtaposed with a church," Matt said from the back.

Joyce chuckled.

"What, do tell, are you talking about?" Dot asked, looking perplexed and somewhat agitated.

Matt said, "Oh, nothing. Just joking."

Dot rolled her eyes and shook her head disapprovingly.

They found the church and the body-piercing shop. The shop had bars on the windows and was closed. The church had a modern look to it, like most of the Lutheran churches Travis had seen. It was painted gray with white trim and had a gravel parking lot and a red door.

It turned out they were on time after all. They went inside as separate pairings and didn't sit near each other. It was nice and cool in the sanctuary. This church had pew cushions like that other church did. Susie raised her eyebrows approvingly at Travis as she sat down and patted the cushion. This was the second time she had done that. Maybe the session ought to look at that again.

He looked at the bulletin to check out the hymns for the service. Uh-oh. The liturgy wasn't like anything he'd ever seen. All of these recitations and congregational responses, and about half of them had asterisks beside them meaning you had to stand up when saying that part. And the hymns weren't like any he'd ever sung before. He picked up the hymnal and thumbed through it. There was not even a trace of familiar music in there. No "Blessed Assurance," no "Stand Up, Stand Up for Jesus," and no "What a Friend We Have in Jesus."

"Welcome!" a loud voice said. Travis looked up to see the preacher addressing the congregation from floor level down front. He had on a white robe and a rainbow-colored stole. It reminded Travis of a sailboat. And he had a neatly trimmed beard and moustache. A lot of preachers had those nowadays. Travis figured they were trying to look like Jesus' disciples or something. The preacher was about six feet tall and a little overweight, and Travis remembered he was fifty-two from the personal information form the presbytery had sent them.

"Today is the day the Lord has made. Let us rejoice and be glad in it!" the preacher continued. "Do we have any prayer requests?"

"I have two," said a woman across the aisle. "First, my brother's wife's niece's baby just got out of the hospital after a bout with the jaundice and is recovering at home, and the other one is for one of my neighbors down the street, Imogene Robinson. They found a tumor up under her right arm and she has to go in for some exploratory surgery next week."

"We'll certainly remember them in our prayers. Are there

others?" the preacher inquired, looking about the congregation for any hands up in the air. Then he pointed his finger almost directly at Travis and said, "And you, sir?"

Actually, he was pointing at Matt, who had been scratching under his arm and had his elbow slightly raised.

Matt suddenly realized the preacher was talking to him and replied, "Uh . . . yes. I would like to pray for the people of Tibet living under the oppressive rule of the Chinese government."

Good grief! Pretty much everybody in the church turned around to get a look at Matt, who was thumbing through the bulletin now and oblivious to the attention.

Well, their cover was blown, that was for sure. Why couldn't Matt have just said, "Excuse me; I was scratching my arm" or something like that?

Travis looked over at Susie. She was smiling and looking through the bulletin too. He glanced around at the others. They were all trying to keep from laughing. Dot was shaking in her seat and had her hand over her mouth. Joyce, sitting beside Dot, was blushing.

Travis looked back at Matt. Not a clue.

The rest of the service was a blur. A lot of getting up and down, reciting this, responding to that. Travis couldn't tell you the first thing about the sermon or the preacher. He just wanted to move on.

CHAPTER 10

A prudent person foresees danger and takes precautions. The simpleton goes blindly on and suffers the consequences.

PROVERBS 27:12

THE LUTHERAN PREACHER had run a little long with the sermon, and it looked like they were not going to make the eleven o'clock service in Havelock on time.

"Let's take that road through the middle of the Croatan National Forest," Travis said to Bill while pointing at the GPS.

"A shortcut?" asked Bill.

"Yeah, it looks like we can save about twenty minutes going that way," Matt said from the back.

"Better watch out," Dot said, then giggled. "We might end up in Tibet."

"Matt, honey," said Frankie, "we're making fun of ourselves. None of us even knows where Tibet is."

"Well, the guy caught me off guard," Matt replied. "It was the only thing that came to mind. You think everybody in there knew I was from out of town?"

Susie exploded in laughter, then Frankie, then Joyce, and then the rest of them, even Matt, were laughing so hard it hurt.

"Did you see the look on that man's face sitting in front of us?" Dot asked, still chuckling. "I almost wet my pants trying to keep from laughing."

"Oh my." Frankie sighed as everybody calmed down.

It was getting hot now. Travis reached over and turned up the AC. Looking down the road, he could see the heat waves rippling up through the air from the blacktop. When they were getting into the van after the first service, he had noticed that the air was completely still. The loblolly pines seemed to be holding their breath and standing still on purpose. No birds singing, no butterflies, just stillness and heat.

"Is this it?" Bill asked, slowing down as they approached a gravel road. There was a large brown forestry sign that said *Croatan National Forest* and a small green road sign by the ditch that said *Tabby Lake Road*.

"Yep, that's it," Travis said confidently.

"You think we can make good time on a gravel road?" Frankie asked Bill and Travis, pilot and navigator, respectively.

"Well, we got no choice now. It's ten thirty and it's another forty minutes the other way around," Bill replied.

Bill turned onto the hard-packed gravel.

"Make the first legal U-turn," the GPS instructed.

"Uh-oh. That might be an omen," Frankie said.

Bill was soon making about fifty miles per hour with a cloud of dust kicking up behind the van.

"Recalculating route," announced the GPS.

Frankie said, "Well, maybe she's going to take a chance on it like we are."

"Make the first legal U-turn," the GPS repeated.

"Maybe she knows something we don't," Susie said.

Bill said, "I'm just going to turn this thing off if it's alright with y'all. We've already seen where the road comes out on the other side."

Joyce said, "We can turn it on when we get back on a paved road."

Travis leaned back in his seat, savoring the subtle satisfaction that comes with a successful shortcut. After about ten minutes of straight gravel road, there seemed to be a gradual transition to more of a fine sandy road. The dust plume in their wake had grown huge, almost like the old van had space-shuttle rocket boosters on it. It was billowing behind them and settling on the pines along the side of the road. In fact, the pines along both sides of the road were already coated in a white, powdery dust, from other traffic traveling through here, Travis guessed.

Joyce was the first to notice it. "Does anyone else feel like dust is coming in? My teeth feel gritty."

"Mine too," said Susie. "Look on the top of the seat."

Sure enough, there was a fine coating of dust that was

noticeable by swiping a finger across the seat. It was on the dash too. Now Travis's teeth were feeling gritty.

"There must be some kind of gap in the rubber gasket around the doors," Bill said to everyone, looking in the rear-view mirror. "I don't think slowing down will help, and it might make it worse."

"Well, keep going, for goodness' sakes. Let's get through this mess," Dot instructed.

Suddenly, the hard-packed sandy road became a soft sandy road and the van began to fishtail a bit. Bill slowed down somewhat and said, "We might be getting into a little problem here."

"It's gotta go all the way through, because it shows it on Google Maps," Matt said from the back.

"Maybe for a four-wheel drive or a bunch of horses," Bill said. "But it doesn't look too good for an old church van."

"Oh no!" Joyce gasped. "Dot, the dust is really showing on your dress."

Travis looked around at Dot, who was looking down at her solid navy dress and brushing the front of it with her hand. "Well, this is a pretty sight."

The dust was getting pretty thick now, and Travis noticed that Matt's black hair had a frosted look to it. Susie's hair looked a little lighter too.

"Y'all, I can feel the dust on my lips now," said Susie.

"I'm sorry, everybody, but if I slow down we might get stuck," Bill said loudly. He was leaning forward in the driver's seat, watching every undulation in the thick sand of the road.

Susie was clicking her teeth to feel the grit in her mouth. "Oh, Dot, your dress is covered."

Dot looked down and stuck her lips out in disgust.

Everyone was silent for the next mile or so. The dusting continued. Looking around at everybody in the van, Travis noted they had the same painful resignation a dog has when getting a bath.

Bill suddenly announced, "Looks like we're coming out of it. There's some more gravel road coming up." He sat back in his seat again.

"Thank you, Jesus," Frankie said deliberately.

Travis looked up at the road ahead. It was turning back into a gravel road and they were headed into some thicker woods with more shade. But after a relatively short stretch of gravel, the woods became deeper and the road turned into more of a loamy black dirt path. Then they ran into some fairly deep ruts and the road was muddy in the shade of the forest. Again, the van started to fishtail a little and Bill leaned forward.

"What now?" Frankie asked, looking up front out the window.

"Hang on. We've got a little stretch of mud here to get through," Bill replied.

Everybody was silent and just looked out the windows at the dark woods around them. The van jerked and bounced as Bill steered through the ruts. They were probably about ten miles from the paved road they had left behind. No one was commenting about their likely absence from the eleven o'clock service in Havelock. It almost seemed they were pre-destined to miss it.

"Well, look at this," Bill said dryly as he slowed the van. They had made it through the muddy section with hardly any more comments about their fate. Now everybody was craning their necks to look at the road ahead.

In the middle of nowhere, they had come to an inter-section of two black dirt roads, complete with stop signs.

"Matt, did you happen to see any other roads cutting through this forest on Google Maps?" Bill asked, looking a little annoyed.

"No, the only one on the map was Tabby Lake Road. I don't know where this other one comes out," Matt replied, oblivious to the criticism.

"Should we turn the GPS back on?" Joyce asked.

Travis said, "I don't think that will help us. This intersec-tion wasn't on the GPS screen when we looked at it earlier."

Bill waited awhile at the intersection. Up ahead, Tabby Lake Road looked to get muddy again and there was even a little bridge over a small ditch with an axle weight limit sign on it. Somebody in the state highway department had a sense of humor. To the left and right the other road led to parts unknown, but the road seemed a little better. Based on dead reckoning, the Pamlico Sound was to the right somewhere and maybe Highway 17 was to the left somewhere. Bill took a left.

This road was much better as far as dirt roads go. They started making pretty good time again, with no dust. The ladies, sensing that they might make the eleven o'clock service, began to recover by brushing off their dresses and patting their hair. Matt rubbed his head vigorously with both hands and got most of the dust out. Travis dusted off the dash and brushed off the front of his suit coat.

"What is this?" Bill asked himself out loud. Everybody looked out the right side of the van at a small house with a large antenna on the roof and three green, dusty pickups parked on one side.

"It must be a ranger station," Matt said. "Let's stop and ask them how to get out of here." Finally, Matt had said something that made a little sense. Bill pulled into the dirt driveway and turned off the engine.

"I've got to get out of this van and brush myself off," Dot said, meaning for everybody to get out of her way.

"Let's all get out and brush off," Frankie said, and everyone started piling out of the van.

About this time, three park rangers came out the front door of the small house and stared at them a few moments with bewildered looks on their faces. Then they walked slowly toward the van.

"What in the heck are y'all doing out here?" the ranger in front asked, looking at all of them. They stood in kind of a loose formation, and Dot and Susie were still brushing off their dresses. Travis noticed that all three of the men appeared to have several layers of dust on their clothes and had real leathery-looking skin. The wrinkles around the corners of their eyes were highlighted like someone had dusted their faces while they were squinting at the sun.

"Well, Ranger, we're lost. We're not from around here and thought we could take a shortcut from Jacksonville through the Croatan National Forest to get to Havelock quicker than going around on Highway 17," Bill said, representing his platoon of wanderers.

The rangers looked at each other, still with bewildered faces, and then looked back at the motley group. "What gave you that idea?" the ranger in front asked.

"Google Maps," Matt said, stepping up. "It looked like there was a way through here."

Travis said, "It also showed up as a dashed line on the GPS."

"Well, I guess y'all figured out by now that Google and the GPS haven't ever driven down Tabby Lake Road," the ranger replied, chuckling and looking at the men with him.

"Well, yeah, we know now," Bill said. "Could you tell us the quickest way to get back on Highway 17? We're trying to make it to an eleven o'clock church service in Havelock."

Travis tensed up, waiting for the men to break out in laughter, but they didn't. The head ranger said in a slow, polite tone, almost sighing, "Well, all you do is keep going down this road and you'll hit it after about two miles. You ought to be able to make your service on time because you did cut off a good bit of your trip. I don't know if it was worth it, though."

"It wasn't," Dot said, still brushing herself off. Her navy dress looked like it had zebra stripes on it where the wrinkles in her midsection had prevented the dust from settling.

"Are y'all with some kind of gospel singing group or something?"

"No," Bill replied, "we're on a search committee."

The man looked at Bill with smiling eyes. Then all three rangers broke down and started laughing.

At first Travis was embarrassed and Susie seemed a little angry. But then Frankie started laughing and all of them cracked up.

A search committee. Lost. It was too much.

They made it to the church at 11:08 a.m. The service had already started, but the congregation was just getting ready to sing the first hymn so they slipped in without a lot of heads turning. Alright! The hymn was "Come, Thou Fount of Every Blessing." Travis hummed along until they found a seat.

After the anthem and just before the sermon, Travis started to feel real comfortable. It was nice and cool in this church and he was tired after getting up so early. He felt his face muscles begin to relax. The preacher got up and opened with a joke. That stirred him up some, but then the relaxation moved to his shoulders and down his back. Then it moved on down to his hips and thighs. His arms and hands were completely limp. He felt his head start to roll a little. Then came the tell-tale bob—Travis snapped his head back to attention and Susie turned to look at him.

Travis blushed. Okay, now he was awake again. For a little while. Then his jaw began to drop a little. To avert the backward head bob, he purposely sat up straight so that his head would go forward if he drifted off again. Trying hard to focus on the preacher, he squinted. Then his eyes just kind of relaxed into a closed position and he couldn't help himself. His chin slowly dropped to his chest as his breathing became deep and deliberate. This felt so good. He could sit here for days like this. Nothing could interrupt this feeling except . . . *snort!*

Susie, Matt, and the people in front of them turned to look at Travis. Well, now he was awake alright, complete with total humiliation. He glanced over to where Joyce and Dot were sitting and, yes . . . Dot had heard it and was looking at him with raised eyebrows.

Why *did* he volunteer for this?

CHAPTER 11

All praise to God, the Father of our Lord Jesus Christ. God is our merciful Father and the source of all comfort. He comforts us in all our troubles so that we can comfort others. When they are troubled, we will be able to give them the same comfort God has given us.

2 CORINTHIANS 1:3-4

TRAVIS LOOKED OUT ACROSS THE FOOD LION from his platform at the front. A young boy who looked to be around twelve years old, thin as a rail with a crew cut, was pushing a cart through the store. *Been there, done that.* Travis looked around to see if there might be a parent with the boy, but no one called him or joined him as he continued to shop. Travis looked at the contents of his cart: diapers, a loaf of bread, milk, what appeared to be a box of grits, and a bag of dried peas were the items he could make out from his vantage point.

As the boy went by the spices section, Travis watched him glance around quickly and then put a gravy packet in his pocket. A couple of aisles later, in the cooler section, he did the same thing with a package of sandwich meat. At last he came to the cashier with his cart to check out. Travis watched him pull a twenty-dollar bill and some ones out of his back pocket and hand them to the cashier. She gave him some change back, and he grabbed his two plastic bags of groceries and headed for the door.

"Hold it right there, buddy," Travis said in a low voice that wouldn't attract the attention of other shoppers or his cashiers.

The boy jerked his head around to look at Travis. Travis could see in his eyes that he was trying to make a decision about running out of the store or not.

"Come on over here," Travis said, smiling and motioning with his hand.

The boy walked slowly to Travis. The cashier glanced quickly at him walking toward Travis but then turned and continued to check out the next person.

Travis looked at the boy and noted that his clothes were dirty and his hair hadn't been washed in a while. The boy had "tater ridges" on his neck and arms. That's what Travis's mama had called the dirt that got in the creases of Travis's skin on his neck, arms, and legs when he was a boy. Travis squatted down to get eye to eye with the boy, who looked so nervous he would probably jump all the way to the ceiling if Travis said, "Boo!"

"What's your name?" Travis asked.

"W. P.," the boy replied, a plastic bag hanging from each hand at his sides.

"W. P. who?"

The boy took a deep breath. "W. P. Mooney."

"I see," Travis said. "Well, Mr. W. P. Mooney, I'm going to ask you a couple of questions, and if I'm satisfied with your answers, I'll let you go on, okay?"

The boy looked confused and scared but said, "Okay."

"What did you have for breakfast this morning, W. P.?"

"Didn't have no breakfast, sir," the boy replied.

"Okay, well, what did you have for lunch yesterday?" Travis asked.

"Didn't have no lunch yesterday, sir," the boy replied.

"I see," said Travis, looking the boy in the eye.

The boy's eyes grew moist and his face began to turn red. Travis stood up. "Well, it sounds like you need to go on home and get something to eat, then," he said matter-of-factly.

"Okay," the boy replied softly, looking down at the floor. He turned and walked quickly out of the store.

CHAPTER 12

*God's sovereign love is a mystery beyond the reach of man's mind.
Human thought ascribes to God superlatives of power, wisdom,
and goodness. But God reveals his love in Jesus Christ by showing power
in the form of a servant, wisdom in the folly of the cross, and goodness
in receiving sinful men. The power of God's love in Christ to transform
the world discloses that the Redeemer is the Lord and Creator who
made all things to serve the purpose of his love.*

THE BOOK OF CONFESSIONS, PRESBYTERIAN CHURCH (USA):
THE CONFESSION OF 1967, 9.15

DOT TURNED HER CHEVY CORSICA onto the gray, sandy road
between the AME church and the cemetery. The sand was
deep and loose, and the road had large, rolling depressions
that made the Corsica ride more like a boat than a car.

A hunched-over, gray-haired black man was trimming a
row of redbuds growing along the side of the white clapboard
church. That had to be Sonny. Looking on the other side of
the road, Dot noticed that one of the older tombstones had
been pushed over. Probably some of that crowd of poor white
trash did it.

Behind the church and past the cemetery, live oaks shaded one side of the road, forming a half tunnel as the road traveled farther from the highway. Several hundred yards farther, the trees gave way to a clearing with an old white clapboard house with a red-shingled roof and red shutters.

The house was set up on brick columns about three feet high. It had been moved there. Besides a small mimosa tree in the middle of the front yard, there was a tall magnolia on the side of the house and a large pecan tree at the back. Dot remembered helping Ernestine plant the magnolia. She planted it when she was twelve, so that would make the tree almost thirty-five years old. Blue hydrangeas were on either side of the steps leading to the front porch and azaleas were planted along the side of the house. And the gardenia at one of the corners—it always smelled so good when it was in bloom.

There was no distinct driveway, just a worn-down patch of centipede grass beside the dirt road directly in front of the house. Dot pulled the car over and got out. She climbed the redbrick steps to the porch and opened the screen door.

"Mee-Maw, it's me," she announced and then stepped inside.

"I'm back here, sugar," a voice down the hall replied.

Dot walked to the back bedroom, where a white-haired black woman was in bed, lying on top of a white cotton embroidered bedspread. Her brown skin looked leathery and worn. She was wearing a light-blue flower-print cotton dress and had her bare feet propped up on a small red velvet sofa pillow. She was fanning her face with a square church fan that had a picture of Jesus praying on the front, looking upward toward God.

"You're not having another spell, are you?" Dot asked, standing in the doorway.

"No, sugar, it's the heat. It just wears me out and I have to lie down."

Dot moved to the side of the bed, sat down, and gently patted the elderly woman's head. "You shouldn't try to do so much. Nobody's here to see if your kitchen's clean or not."

"Oh, sugar, you know me. I can't keep still in the mornings."

"Was that your husband I passed at the church, trimming the shrubs?"

"Yes. Heavens, Sonny can't keep still, and I told him it was too hot for him to be out in the sun like that."

"Who pushed that tombstone over in the cemetery?"

"Oh, you know, probably some of them teenagers from town. They ride around in them cars on the weekend and stir up trouble."

"Can I get you a glass of ice water or sweet tea while you're resting?"

"No, sugar. I thank you, but I don't think I could raise my head right now to drink it."

Dot stood up. "Let me get it. I'll help you drink it."

"Well, okay, but get you some too. I made some tea this morning. It's in the icebox. And while you're in there, try some of that cantaloupe I cut up for breakfast. Sonny says it's real sweet."

Dot walked back up the hall to the kitchen, where she was

greeted with the smell of salted ham and fried corn bread mixed in with the smell of sweet melon. It was a comfortable aroma and it presented Dot with the memory of her childhood, sitting on the floor with Ernestine, playing jacks and pick-up sticks; running around the outside of the house playing hide-and-seek with her sister; crawling up underneath the house and feeling the cool, dry dirt; doing cartwheels in the sun on the centipede grass while Ernestine watched and clapped.

Dot opened the refrigerator and took out the pitcher of tea. The refrigerator was full of bowls covered with tinfoil. Ernestine always cooked more than anybody could eat, and now with just her and Sonny, it was probably all she could do to keep from fixing a big meal every day for dinner. Dot opened the freezer and took out an ice tray. The freezer had frozen zipper bags of corn and pole beans from Sonny's garden stacked on one side and bags of gray butter beans and stewed tomatoes on the other side. Ernestine spent about half of her time in the summer putting up vegetables for the freezer. She also had a chest freezer on her back porch that was full of frozen vegetables. She usually offered a bag of frozen something to guests as they were leaving her house, turning around and walking back to her freezer as the guests were leaving through the front door, forcing them to politely stay put until she returned with one or two packs of okra or stewed tomatoes or beans, along with a little advice on how much fatback to add when the vegetables were cooked.

Dot poured two glasses and, after putting the pitcher back in the refrigerator, carried the tea down the hall to the back bedroom. Ernestine was asleep with her head back and mouth open, breathing through a shallow snore. Dot sat in an old stuffed rocking chair in the corner of the room and put Ernestine's glass on the floor. Sitting back in the rocker and sipping her tea, she gazed out the window toward the road. Ernestine's snore rose a little and then stopped. Dot looked over at the bed. Ernestine was still breathing through her mouth but had stopped the shallow snoring. Ernestine was eighty-two years old now. She seemed so young when Dot was growing up, but now Dot realized that Ernestine had been in her late forties when she took care of Dot and her sister. What an amazing woman, playing games with two small children all day, cleaning the house, and then cooking dinner for Dot's mama before going home to cook dinner for her own family.

Ernestine awoke with a snort. "I'm sorry. I just drifted off. How long you been sitting there?"

"Just a few minutes. Go on back to sleep and rest some."

"No, I feel better now. . . . Tell me about your committee and your last trip."

"Well, okay. Heaven help me, Mee-Maw, it's a wonder we made it back alive. You know we were trying to make two sermons in one day. Well, we made the first one in Jacksonville on time. It was a Lutheran church. I tell you, those people are different and the preacher wasn't much good either. Anyway, on the way to the second church, that Matt and Travis had the bright idea that we should take a shortcut through the Croatan National Forest."

"The what? I never heard of it."

"Well, I had heard of it, but it ain't nothing but a big old thicket. Anyway, we started through there on a gravel road and it was dusty like you wouldn't believe. It got all in the van and got on my blue dress. You could even feel it in your teeth."

"My oh my. Did you get out alright?"

"Well, we finally ran up on some rangers that showed us how to get out of there, and we barely made it to the church on time, but I had that dust all in my hair and on my dress and it got caked in my makeup around my eyes."

"Mmm-mmm. And that was that Matt's idea?"

"His and Travis's."

"Isn't he the one whose mama just passed a couple years ago?"

"Yes, that's the one. Matt moved back home with his poor daddy but I don't see how he can be much help on a farm. He's got the craziest notions. You should have heard him talking about the Creation story and trying to show how it didn't happen like it says in the Bible."

"And he's in your church? Helping you look for a preacher?"

"I know. It's crazy, isn't it? But that's the way it is now. These younger people think they have it all figured out."

"It's been like that for a long time. What about the Yankee woman? How's she doing?"

"Well, she's right nice to be around. Not like most of them. I told you about her driving in the mountains for us."

"Yeah, I remember that."

"And Bill—you know he's the regular driver—that poor man has it the other way around."

"What do you mean?"

"Well, his wife hasn't been able to lift a finger since their little boy got run over. He waits on her hand and foot."

"Maybe that's real love. I wouldn't think bad of them for that. Losing a young one is something you don't know about till it happens to you."

"Yeah, you're right. I shouldn't judge them like that."

"How about that young woman? She doing any better?"

"Mee-Maw, she's torn up on the inside. You can tell it in her eyes. She hardly talks at all. She's got that boy, you know, and I'm sure he's driving her up the wall, and then the way that sorry husband did her, I know she's hurting."

"I saw her in town one day. She's a good-looking young woman. She needs to get her another man."

"I know she does. But you think there are any around here worth having?"

"Sure there are. This place is just like all the other places. You got good ones and bad ones."

"Well, I don't know of any good ones left."

"Well, you got a good one, didn't you?"

Dot paused. Mee-Maw lifted her head and Dot lowered hers. "Mee-Maw, I think he's getting ready to leave me."

"What are you talking about, child? Leave you? For what?" Mee-Maw propped herself up on her elbows.

"I can tell. He doesn't talk to me and he's always working

late. He hasn't even touched me in two months." Dot sniffed, wiped her eyes, and looked out the window.

"Is that what you came to talk about, sugar?"

Dot sniffed again and nodded. "Mee-Maw, you're the only one I can talk to about it. I'm afraid to tell anybody else. You know they'll say something behind my back and start stuff all over town."

"You think he's got somebody else he's seeing?"

"Yes."

"Who?"

"He's got that new bookkeeper from over in Wallace. Stephanie. She's younger than me, skinny and pretty. I think that's who it is."

"Sugar, you just hold on. He'll get what's coming to him if he's doing that to you."

Dot sniffed again. "What do you mean?"

"I've seen it happen time and time again. It even happened to one of the deacons in our church last year. Some young pretty thing starts paying these old men a little attention and all of a sudden they think they're twenty years old again. But sooner or later, the young pretty thing lays her eyes on somebody else and then the old fool is left all alone— no friends, no family, no nothing. Won't nobody trust them."

"Mee-Maw, I don't care about all that. I'm just mad at myself for not watching my weight . . . and letting myself get like this. He wouldn't be looking around if I had paid more attention to him."

"You wrong about that. First of all, you're a fine-looking

woman. But sometimes a man don't know what he has. He has to lose it first. I tell you, I've seen it happen many a time. You just hold your head high and go on about your business. He'll come crawling back, apologizing and all. Then you got the upper hand; I'll guarantee that."

"But everybody's going to talk. You know none of them like me very much. They'll say I deserved it and all. . . . Maybe I do deserve it."

"Child, will you quit moping about it? Now, you wanted to talk to me, and I'm telling you how it'll happen. Just bide your time and don't pay no attention to what other folks say. Most of the time, they got troubles coming around the corner for them too. I've seen that happen."

"What if he wants a divorce?"

"Tell him no. You're not giving up that easy. Besides, it won't take too long for him to see what he's done. I bet he'll straighten out in one month's time."

"I never thought it would happen to me."

"Now, sugar, you know that the good Lord don't tell you what his plans are for you. Most of the time you got to go through a struggle to get to any good."

Dot moved to the bed and sat down. Then she began to sob and put her head on Mee-Maw's shoulder, hugging her.

"Now, don't get like that," Mee-Maw said, struggling to sit up in the bed. "You going to be fine, sugar. You going to be fine."

CHAPTER 13

*When I think about what I am saying, I shudder. My body trembles.
"Why do the wicked prosper, growing old and powerful?"*

JOB 21:6-7

ANOTHER EARLY START. Travis hoped it wasn't going to be a
wasted trip. The application was signed, *The Rev. Dr. Perry
Chastain, Trinity Presbyterian Church, Conway, South Carolina.*
Heading into South Carolina got Travis edgy. There was a
wildness in those people that you didn't get in North Carolina.

Bill was letting him drive on this one. There really wasn't
a good way to go. They decided to take I-95 to Lumberton,
past South of the Border, then a few more miles to Dillon,
where they could get on 501 to Conway.

Driving toward Lumberton on I-95, they ran into the

barrage of South of the Border billboards, each with a different corny message. Frankie read every single sign they passed. *"Top Banana!"* A mile later she announced, *"Hot Tamales!"* and *"Stuff your trunk with junk!"*

Most of these billboards were relatively new. The classic one that everyone remembered was in South Carolina coming north on I-95 from Florence; it was the motorized one with the sheep jumping over the moon. Now *that* was an old billboard.

"Have any of y'all ever stopped there?" Bill asked after one of Frankie's pronouncements.

"Not me," Frankie replied.

"Me neither," Dot added.

Travis looked in the rearview mirror and saw Susie and Joyce shaking their heads no. Matt was asleep again with his mouth open, so he didn't answer.

"How about you, Travis?" Bill inquired.

"Nope."

"Y'all want to stop for a cup of coffee?" Bill asked, turning around in his seat to look at everybody. "We've got time."

"Sure, why not?" Dot replied.

Soon after they passed Lumberton, the tower with a top in the shape of a huge sombrero came into view and Dot asked, "Why would anybody want to go up in that thing to look at a bunch of tobacco fields?"

"Well, maybe there's something to look at that you don't know about. Why don't we check it out ourselves?" Frankie responded.

"Not me," Susie said from the back of the van. "I'm afraid of heights."

"Me too," Joyce added.

"Alright then, I'll go if you go," Dot said to Frankie, throwing down the gauntlet.

Bill chuckled.

Travis took one hand off the wheel and looked at his watch. They had about thirty minutes to kill as far as he could tell. After they took the exit and drove back under the interstate toward South of the Border, the place took on a completely different view than what you noticed passing by on I-95. From the interstate, it looked like an odd assortment of buildings and flashing lights, with very few people patronizing the place. But once you drove underneath I-95, it was like being right in the middle of Carowinds or Six Flags. They might as well have painted the road purple or yellow or something. The first thing Travis noticed was the big spark-plug statue over by the gas station. Then as he looked back around toward the other side of the road, the whole place kind of surrounded them and they were stretching their necks like guinea hens, trying to see everything from the windows of the van. That is, all of them except Matt; he was still asleep.

Brightly colored concrete statues of Pedro, the fictitious host and subject of most of the billboards on I-95, grinned and welcomed tourists to various stores with different themes. Pedro was modeled after the kind of Mexican dude you learned about in the third grade before they changed all the history books: a short, chunky guy with a handlebar moustache, wearing a sombrero and white pajama-looking clothes. There was Pedro's Concrete Bazaar, Fort Pedro, Pedro's Myrtle Beach Shop, and other retail outlets like El Drugstore and El Antique Shop. In addition to these main tourist draws, there were various pastel-colored buildings intermingled with carnival rides, lights flashing everywhere, a motel, and a whole lot of . . . stuff.

"Looks like they added something on the back there," Bill said.

"Yeah, some kind of Myrtle Beach–looking thing," Frankie added.

"I've never seen this place full. I wonder how they keep it open," said Dot.

"Well, it looks a lot more full from down here than it does from I-95," Frankie replied.

Everybody gazed at the hodgepodge collection of buildings and the tower with the sombrero on top. The tower had to be a landmark for Yankees. Halfway to Miami.

"Where should I stop for coffee?" Travis asked the group.

"How about right in front of that building over there that says *El Coffee Shop*," Dot replied, clucking like a hen.

Travis immediately blushed and Bill, noticing his reaction, said, "Well, there's so much stuff here that it's hard to see the forest for the trees."

"I mean to tell you!" Frankie agreed.

Travis pulled up to El Coffee Shop and parked. Crawling out of the van, Frankie handed Travis a five-dollar bill and said, "Get me and Dot a cup of coffee, Travis, and put a little cream in mine, please."

"I'll take mine black," Dot chimed in.

"We've got a sombrero to climb," Frankie said, stretching and yawning.

Frankie and Dot went off together in the direction of the sombrero tower, Dot lugging her big pocketbook and Frankie continuing to stretch as they walked. Inside the van, Matt awoke from the dead and asked, "Where in the heck are we?"

"Heaven," Susie replied. "Ain't it nice?"

Matt had a bewildered look on his face as he sat up and looked out the windows of the van. "Oh, wow, South of the Border; I can't say that I've ever stopped here before."

"None of us have either," Susie replied. "We're investigating a rumor that Presbyterians who have been accused of smiling are hiding out here."

"Alright then, let's flush them out and burn them alive in Pedro's El Bar-B-Que Pit," Matt shot back. Sometimes he *was* funny. And, man, Susie was a little spunky today. Travis wondered what was up with that.

"Anybody want to check out the Concrete Bazaar with me?" Susie asked Matt and Travis. Before Travis could answer, Matt said, "Sure," and he and Susie went walking off together.

Bill and Joyce had already gone inside the coffee shop. Travis went around the van and made sure all the doors were locked.

Inside, Travis spotted Bill and Joyce at a table by the

window where they could watch Dot and Frankie go up the sombrero tower. "Mind if I join y'all?"

"Sure, bud, have a seat," Bill replied. Joyce looked up and smiled.

Frankie and Dot must have taken the elevator up instead of the stairs, because they were already at the top. Nobody else was up there. Frankie was walking around the perimeter of the observation platform and looking out while Dot was just standing in one place with her hands on her hips, like an admiral, clutching her big pocketbook and looking off in one direction. They were up there for only a few minutes when both of them got back into the elevator to return to the ground. Travis, Bill, and Joyce watched the elevator begin its descent, and then it suddenly stopped about halfway down.

"Uh-oh," Bill said.

They were staring at the elevator now, waiting for it to move. It didn't.

"Is anybody out there running that thing?" Joyce asked.

"I can't see anybody," Bill replied.

Then Bill looked at Travis and said, "You go find somebody in management around here and I'll go out there and see what's going on."

"Alright."

Bill got up and walked outside while Joyce sat at the table with their coffees. Travis walked over to the counter and asked the only waitress in the joint how to get in touch with their maintenance man.

"Oh, he don't work on Sundays."

"Well, we have two ladies stuck in that elevator on the sombrero tower. How do we go about getting them down from there?"

"I don't know. Go over to the gas station and get somebody," she said while looking down and wiping the light-green formica countertop.

Travis walked outside and looked around for some official-looking building, but all he saw were yellow and lime-green buildings with letters on the sides that said *Motel with Carports!* and *Snow Cones!* They used a lot of exclamation points here.

Finally, he saw some kind of official-looking sign that said Office over near the Motel with Carports! A middle-aged lady with jet-black hair in a permanent and wearing a yellow smock top with tight white pants was inside vacuuming the floor. He knocked on the door and entered, but she apparently didn't notice him coming in because of the noise of the vacuum. When she looked up and saw Travis, she dropped the vacuum-cleaner handle and gasped, putting one hand on her heart. The vacuum was still running, so Travis mouthed the word "sorry" as she reached down and turned off the machine.

"My word! You frightened me. I didn't see you come in."

"I'm sorry, ma'am. I didn't mean to scare you. I need to get in touch with somebody in management or your maintenance man or whoever handles the elevator on that sombrero tower. We've got two ladies stuck in there about halfway up."

"Oh my," she said, walking over to the window and looking out at the tower, still holding her hand over her heart.

"Let me call Roger. He'll know what to do." She walked over to the wall phone in the lobby area.

"Thank you, ma'am. Should we just wait over at the tower?"

"Yes. I'll send him right over. How long have they been stuck up there?"

"About five or ten minutes now."

• • •

Travis walked out of the office and toward the tower. Bill was looking up at the elevator and had his hands cupped around his mouth, shouting something up to Dot and Frankie. By the time Travis reached them, a light-blue utility truck with a yellow flashing light drove up to the base of the tower and a man with a fairly large gut got out, pulled up his pants with both hands, and then reached into the truck behind him and grabbed a leather tool belt to strap around his waist.

"What's going on here?" he asked Bill and Travis.

"Two ladies are stuck in your elevator there about halfway up," Bill replied.

"Is that right?"

"Yes, and we're in a big hurry. We've got to get to Conway by eleven o'clock," Bill said to the man.

The man looked at his watch and said, "Hmmph." Then he walked over to the control box at the base of the tower.

"Can you lower it down manually?" Bill asked.

"How much do they weigh?" the man responded.

"The short one will come in around 150 and the tall one about the same," Travis offered.

The man smiled. "I can't lower this thing manually, but don't worry; it's probably just a fuse."

Bill and Travis looked up at the elevator while the man went to work.

"Travis, walk up the stairs to their level and see if you can talk to them," Bill instructed.

"Okay." Travis started the sweat thing again. Oh well.

He made it to their level, but they were inside a metal box with no windows. Travis heard some giggling but couldn't tell if it was Frankie or Dot. There was a little fan vent on the top of the elevator, so he shouted, "Hey, can y'all hear me?"

The giggling stopped. After several seconds of silence, a voice—Dot's—replied, "Noooooo!" This was followed by one of her hysterical laughs. *Why does that woman hate me?*

"Travis, get us down from here. I need to go to the bathroom!" Frankie shouted. Both of them were laughing and giggling nonstop now.

"There's a guy down there working on the controls. He'll get you down in a few minutes. What happened?"

Dot shouted back, "Well, we were just floating down, minding our own business, when this witch flew into the vent to put a sleeping-beauty spell on Frankie. Only she missed and the elevator got it instead!" Another hysterical laugh.

"Stop being mean, Dot," Frankie said. "You won't be laughing if we have to stay in here all day." Then Frankie started laughing again.

Travis knew when to take a hint.

"I'm going down to check how the maintenance man is doing."

"Alright, honey," Frankie replied.

"Tell him to bring us some doughnuts!" Dot shouted, laughing even louder.

Travis walked slowly down the steps to where Bill was. Matt, Susie, and Joyce had come over now and were standing beside Bill. Susie was holding a small, painted plaster figurine of Pedro.

"How are they doing?" Bill asked.

"Oh, they're doing okay. Too bad it's not just Dot stuck in there. We could get her on the way back."

"Ha! That's a good one, Travis," Susie said.

Travis wondered if she thought he was funny.

Suddenly the elevator jerked and began its descent again. The man stood up and brushed off his pants.

"It was just a fuse. I don't know what caused the overload; I'll need to check that out later."

"If you wait just a few seconds, we can introduce you to the problem," Bill said.

Susie and Joyce laughed again. The man just smiled and looked at the elevator coming down.

As soon as it reached the bottom of the tower and the doors opened, Frankie stepped out, looked at the man, and said, "Where's the nearest ladies' room?"

"Over there at the coffee shop is the closest one."

Frankie took off in that direction at a brisk pace.

Dot stepped out and said, "I heard every word y'all said and I'm not going to forget any of it."

Matt and Travis exchanged glances while Dot displayed her best poker face with her lower lip jutted outward.

Suddenly she let loose with one of her cackling laughs. "Had you worried, didn't I, boys?" The three men just looked at each other and shook their heads. As they walked back toward the van, Travis was sweating like a pig and felt a headache coming on.

"Hey, Bill."

"Yeah?"

"I'll be with you in a moment. I'm going over to El Drugstore to get a BC Powder and a Coke for my El Headache."

CHAPTER 14

When she speaks, her words are wise, and she gives instructions with kindness.

PROVERBS 31:26

THEY WERE RUNNING LATE NOW. Travis had the old van pushing eighty miles per hour down the interstate. The Coke/BC combination made his scalp numb, and his headache started to ease off. Finally they got off the interstate and onto 501. Driving down the two-lane, the van parted the Red Sea of tobacco fields. It took them about another hour to get to Conway but they made it right on time. Travis had been driving around four miles per hour over the speed limit the whole way down 501. He figured they'd give him that.

Conway was a pretty little town on the Waccamaw River,

and the old white-brick Presbyterian church sat on a bluff beneath some huge live oaks overlooking the water. It was by far the prettiest church they had visited.

They split up like they normally did and went on inside. Other folks were making their way to the sanctuary from the Sunday school building behind the church. Travis thought a couple of them saw the committee get out of the van, but they didn't look too concerned. He went in with Susie and Matt and they sat down near the middle on the right.

Travis glanced over at Bill and Frankie sitting across the aisle. They were studying the bulletin. He checked the hymn lineup. *Hmmm.* Some old and some new were in the mix, with "Be Thou My Vision" leading off, followed by a Negro spiritual, "Lord, I Want to Be a Christian," and then ending with some new hymn he'd never heard of. This church had both the old red hymnal and the new blue one, probably a compromise of sorts.

The choir started coming in from a side door in the choir loft. Mostly women. Three men. Then Dr. Chastain came out, followed by a woman minister with red hair. Now that was something they hadn't seen yet. Travis glanced over at Dot, but she was not reacting at all.

Dr. Chastain started in on the announcements. He had a loud, deep voice. Travis liked that. And later, he did the children's service too. Travis began to wonder what the woman preacher did, if anything. Dr. Chastain was definitely preaching today because it said so in the bulletin. After the children left the sanctuary with the nursery attendant, he walked back up to the pulpit area and sat down. Now the woman was getting up.

"Welcome. This is the day the Lord has made. Let us rejoice and be glad in it," she said. A typical greeting. "I was walking downtown the other day with my Saint Bernard when I saw one of our younger members, seven-year-old Tommy Ivey, coming down the sidewalk toward me with his mama. When he saw me, he stopped and said, 'Look, mama, there's Dr. Chastain with her saint.'"

Everyone chuckled. Travis frowned. Did the boy call her Dr. Chastain?

The woman was still talking. "I said to Tommy, 'Actually, he is just a dog and not really a saint. They call this type of dog a Saint Bernard because of where they come from.' Tommy replied, 'See, Mama? I told Jimmy Swain that dogs don't go to heaven and he called me a liar.' I quickly departed, allowing Mrs. Ivey to answer that one."

More chuckles. Travis elbowed Susie and nodded toward the woman preacher and then back down at the bulletin, pointing with his finger to the name across from the sermon title. It clearly said *Rev. Dr. Chastain*. There was no way that she was Dr. Chastain. On the application it . . . Now that he thought about it, it never did say whether it was a man or woman preacher, but surely . . . Perry was a boy's name, not a girl's name. . . .

Could this be true? He looked back at Dot. Her eyebrows were raised and she was registering a forced frown with her lower lip jutting outward. Joyce was smiling but seemed surprised. He glanced over at Frankie and Bill. They were both smiling. He looked at Susie. She was smiling too. Matt? He was just Matt, no reaction.

Well, for heaven's sake. Travis couldn't believe they had driven all the way down here to listen to a woman preacher. He knew they existed and all, but there was no way their church would hire one. They would probably be mad when they found out the committee had even gone to visit one. They had wasted more time on these trips. . . .

Dr. Chastain began her sermon. Travis figured he might as well get comfortable and see what she had to say, since they obviously couldn't get up and walk out in the middle of the service.

"I love words," she was saying. "Okay, I know I am a little odd, but I really am fascinated by words. That is probably why I studied Spanish, Latin, Russian, Greek, and Hebrew and enjoyed them so much during my school years.

"But just think about words for a moment. There are funny-sounding words, like *onomatopoeia*, *juxtaposition*, and one of my favorites, *poof*. There are groups of words that can bring a smile to your face, like 'I love you.' And there are words that can bring tears to our eyes, like 'good-bye.' Sure, there are limits to the ability of words to express human emotion and what we see in our world. How can words describe the love you feel for your spouse or the beauty of a glowing sunset as day turns into night? But words, limited as they are, do evoke joy, allow you to imagine places you've never been, and connect us human beings to each other.

"There is a children's saying about words: 'Sticks and stones can break my bones, but words can never hurt me.' We teach our children this saying as a means of inoculating them from bullies—so they will learn to rely on their own depth of self-worth and not listen to the naysayers of the world. But it's really not true. Words *can* hurt. Words can hurt with a depth that mere sticks and stones can't. 'I hate you,' 'I don't love you anymore,' and 'You are not my friend' all have great power to wound."

Travis thought about his daddy's words directed at him— "You're worthless" and "You'll never amount to anything" and "You're even dumber than I thought you were." Yep, she was right; words could hurt.

"Words are powerful in other ways too. Simply say *ain't* to a northerner and watch his face drop. He will have just judged you as an ignorant person, even though your use of the word was simply a colloquialism. Or use a highly complex word—or if you are a minister, throw out as many long, theological terms as you can—and watch the faces around you shudder. They have just judged you as a person so intelligent that they cannot relate to you, much less be your friend.

"Jesus understood words. He knew their power to hurt and to heal, their power to express emotion, intellect, and judgment. And so Jesus crafted his words carefully."

She directed the congregation to look at the Scripture passage printed in the bulletin. It was something from the book of Matthew.

"The first thing Jesus says in this passage is 'Don't be afraid. Take courage. I am here!'"

She paused, then repeated the phrase. "'Don't be afraid. Take courage. I am here!' I believe Jesus intended these as words of comfort, words that create peace.

"But Jesus' words do not end there. Peter, recognizing Jesus, asks Jesus to bid him to come. Jesus simply says, 'Yes, come.' Notice he does not say, 'Peter, hold your horses. I'll be there in a minute.' He does not say, 'Okay, Peter, let's show the world who I am. Come on; I'll make you walk on water.' Nor does he say, 'Peter, what are you thinking?! You cannot walk on water. I am the Son of Man, and you are a mere mortal.'" She paused again and looked around at everyone. Softly, she said, "Jesus simply says, 'Yes, come.'

"And we all know the story. We know what happens next—Peter comes. And he does fine until he realizes what he is doing and fear sneaks up on him. Then Peter begins to sink, screaming, 'Save me, Lord!' Jesus does, in fact, save him, but then says to Peter, 'You have so little faith. Why did you doubt me?'

"'You have so little faith.' Those sound like harsh words. What happened to the forgiving, loving Jesus? The one who brought peace to the frightened souls just moments earlier? 'You have so little faith.'

"Novelist Doris Betts has tried to describe faith and uses a wonderful image. She asserts that faith is not the same as certainty, but it is, rather, 'the decision to keep your eyes open.' Isn't that a great definition? Faith is the decision to keep your eyes open.

"Think about it in terms of Peter and our Scripture passage this morning. Can't you just see Peter walking on the water, smug and smiling, and then suddenly being hit by a fierce wind? His face registers shock, then surprise, and then terror as he starts to sink. Can't you just see him closing his eyes tight and screaming, 'Save me, Lord!'?

"Faith is keeping your eyes open. Keeping your eyes focused on God. Not letting weariness, or doubt, or fear, or even brightness get in the way of keeping focused on God. Faith is keeping your eyes open."

Travis was definitely keeping his eyes open during this sermon. There would be a whole lot of discussion back home when they found out the committee had been to see a female minister. And he wanted to be ready with answers.

"But faith is also delicate. How often have we said of someone, 'He lost his faith,' as if faith is some sort of small object hidden away in a drawer? Or 'She is going through a time of doubt in her faith'? Faith is fragile, and it needs tending. That is one of the reasons we are here this morning— to tend to our faith in worship and study and fellowship.

"So what does Jesus do to nurture Peter's fragile faith? He says, 'You have so little faith. Why did you doubt me?' It sounds like Jesus isn't nurturing at all. It sounds like Jesus is rebuking Peter! 'You have so little faith.' It sounds awfully harsh. Of course, Jesus would be justified in rebuking Peter. Peter had just observed the feeding of the five thousand and now Jesus walking on water. Why should Peter doubt that Jesus would keep him from sinking?

"But maybe Jesus was simply describing who Peter was. Maybe Peter neither took offense nor felt rebuked, but merely recognized his own identity. Jesus could have even said 'You have so little faith' with great kindness and love—" Dr. Chastain's voice softened—"'You have so little faith. Why did you doubt me?' That's a reading of Scripture we usually don't hear, but maybe that is the way it happened. Notice that Peter is, indeed, the only one who asks Jesus if he can come to him. Maybe Peter, who had just a little faith, had more faith than his fellow disciples.

"Maybe that's the point—having a little faith is better than no faith at all. Faith is a strange thing—it is a gift, freely given and perfect, and yet it needs tending. It is something we can't control, and yet our actions do indeed have an effect on it. Faith is hard to define, hard to describe, and sometimes even harder to possess. But when you have it, it is glorious and abiding.

"Take time to nurture your faith. Be bold and keep your eyes open and fixed upon God. And one day God may call you his one of 'little faith.' For even a little faith is better than none.

"In the name of the Father and the Son and the Holy Spirit . . . amen."

Well, that was . . . not so bad. Travis recalled Mrs. Bryant talking about a little, itty-bitty faith. He wondered if it was really possible, with just a little bit of faith, to move a mountain. Seemed like it would take a whole lot more than that.

CHAPTER 15

Q. 131. What are the duties of equals?

A. The duties of equals are: to regard the dignity and worth of each other, in giving honor to go one before another, and to rejoice in each other's gifts and advancement as their own.

THE BOOK OF CONFESSIONS, PRESBYTERIAN CHURCH (USA): THE LARGER CATECHISM, 7.241

AUGUST WAS HOT, MORE SO THAN NORMAL. The heat made it difficult to focus on getting things done quickly and efficiently. The dog days of summer encouraged lollygagging. Complying with the inertia caused by the heat, the committee had not yet reached consensus on any of the candidates. Travis was beginning to think they would never find a minister they could all agree on.

The liaison from the presbytery's commission on ministry was scheduled to meet with the committee on Monday evening at the church, but at the last minute he called

Frankie to say he didn't think they had given some of the ministers he knew proper consideration, so he wasn't going to come. He lived in Greenville and was some kind of professor at East Carolina University. To Travis, it seemed like those presbytery folks were more than a little arrogant, and they always seemed to look out for each other. It was almost like they believed they knew what was best for everybody else, like bishops or something—or even worse, like the government.

Anyway, the guy didn't show, so they had their own meeting. They met in the adult discussion room, where the session met. The sexton apparently forgot they'd scheduled the meeting, because the AC wasn't on. It felt like an oven in there. Dot wasn't the only one who commented on that.

"Let's make this quick. I can't stand to be hot like this," Dot said, crossing her short legs and folding her arms. "All I know is I won't vote for that bald-headed, bug-eyed preacher we saw in Charlotte. I couldn't look at him every Sunday." This was the second time Dot had made this comment, so that guy was definitely out.

"Well, let's do this in an orderly fashion," Frankie said, assuming her leadership role. "Let's go around and each one of us say who we think is the best one so far. Travis, will you do the minutes for us?"

Travis nodded.

"Joyce, why don't you start us off."

Joyce took a deep breath and sat up straight. "Well, I think the Havelock minister was very good—I just feel like he has a very strong faith. He really spoke to me. I think he would really help us grow in our faith as a congregation."

Dot frowned.

"Okay, that's good. Write down as much as you can, Travis. Okay. Bill?"

"Well, I'm inclined to agree with Joyce. I think that man would be good for us, and he's a good preacher, too. My vote's for him."

"Alright. Matt?"

"The woman. I liked the woman minister in Conway the best."

"Good heavens," Dot whined, shaking her head.

"Dot, keep your opinion to yourself," Frankie scolded. "Everybody has a right to their opinion on this committee—even if it doesn't agree with yours."

Man, Frankie got a little hot. Dot blushed a little and Matt, well, he didn't seem insulted at all. He continued. "She was the smartest one so far, and I think a woman minister is just what our church needs." Now he was pushing the envelope.

"Okay. Susie?"

"I honestly don't know yet. I think I liked the woman best too, but I don't think she would be the best thing for our church right now. I'm undecided."

"That's okay. Dot?"

"Well, I'll tell y'all something straight up. I don't think any of the ones we've seen so far would do anything for our church. We need somebody conservative that's got some good family values. I can't vote for anybody that doesn't take the Scriptures as the literal Word of God. That's the way I was raised and that's the way I'll stay."

"Okay, Dot, you've had your say. Travis?"

Travis put his pen down. Looking around the table, he saw that everyone was all tensed up. It really didn't matter to him which one they got. He and Jenny would still keep coming to church. It wasn't like the *preacher* was the church.

"I don't really care. Any of them would probably be alright in my opinion."

Travis paused and then Dot shifted in her seat. Travis noticed and thought, *Oh man, here it comes.*

Sure enough, Dot leaned forward in her seat and fired at Travis. "If you don't care, then what are you doing on the search committee?"

"Watch it, Dot," Frankie warned.

Dot leaned back in her seat again.

"What I mean is . . . Well, I don't think the preacher makes the church. *We* do. I'm not going to stop coming just because the guy I want isn't the one everybody else wants. The woman preacher would be different, that's for sure, but after thinking about it some, I wouldn't be opposed to it."

"So you want the woman?" Frankie inquired.

"Actually, no. I guess if I had to pick one, it would be the guy we saw in Charlotte. He was a good preacher."

"Okay then. One vote for him. I guess it's my turn. Right now, I would have to go with Joyce and Bill. That Havelock preacher seemed pretty down to earth and I liked him as a person. He was a good preacher and he was polite—not loud and talky like that Lutheran guy. Now we have three more preachers lined up to visit. Do we go ahead and visit those, or do we talk about these some more?"

"Well, we haven't found one yet in my opinion, so I say we keep looking," Dot said.

"It wouldn't hurt to keep looking, seeing as how we're not all together on this thing yet," Bill added.

Everybody nodded.

"Alright then, we'll keep going. Let's get out of here. Joyce, how about closing our meeting with prayer?"

"Okay." Joyce bowed her head. "Dear heavenly Father, we ask that you bless our efforts and lead us to the right decision so that your will, not ours, be done. Bless each of us as we go through the remainder of this week and help us to glorify you in all we do. We pray that you will comfort the afflicted and those who care for them. Forgive us of our many sins. We pray in Jesus' name, amen."

"Amen," said Bill.

CHAPTER 16

Share each other's burdens, and in this way obey the law of Christ.

GALATIANS 6:2

THE SCHOOL DISTRICT HAD AGREED TO HIRE MATT to teach high school physics as a temporary employee without benefits, claiming state budget cuts and teacher certification requirements wouldn't let them do otherwise. For his part, Matt was just glad to have a regular paycheck again.

On the first day of school Matt arrived earlier than any of the other teachers. Walking down the same halls he had traveled years before, he took in the smell of waxed floors and wooden desks, remembering how as a student he had been overly self-conscious of his gait. Not athletic or muscular, he couldn't puff out his chest and saunter. Neither did he have any kind of anatomical tic like out-turned feet that he could rely on for a consistent gait. And the arms. As a teenager he always wondered, what do you do with your arms when you walk? How do you get them to swing naturally? It had been uncomfortable to even walk from his desk to the blackboard. He had finally settled on a slightly bowlegged gait with his hands in the pockets of his corduroy jeans. That got him through high school. Later, he discovered his adult gait was identical to his father's, which was more like a shoulders-hunched, tired stomp, determined but with a sense of relief when allowed to stop.

He entered the physics classroom and sat behind the teacher's podium, an elevated desk with a black resin top and a small sink on one side like the chemistry teacher's desk. This was where it had all started for him. During the first week of tenth-grade physics honors class, he was copying the answers to the homework problems he had not done when his teacher, Mrs. Powers, walked up behind him and announced to the entire room, "Class, everyone please put down your pencils and let's wait for Mr. Fischer to finish copying down the answers. He obviously didn't do his homework." From that point forward, Matt became an excellent student. In fact, had he not been cheating that day his life would probably have been much different than it was now. Matt wondered now what that different life might have been.

For a long time after high school Matt was still waiting

for life to happen. At some point, the good grades and long hours studying on weekends were bound to pay off, but Matt couldn't visualize it. Only later did he realize that his inability to visualize how his life would be was a sign that it wouldn't be anything he wanted. He was being groomed to fill a slot somewhere, a slot supposedly coveted by many but only available to a few. That was the driver. It was almost comical that so many smart people would be driven by such a vague, meaningless goal. But that was Matt's track.

• • •

After first-period class was finished, Matt walked down to the teachers' lounge for what the administrators called his "planning period." Coffee-stained tables were available there for teachers to spread out their work, grade papers, and work on lesson plans. Matt preferred to read instead. He was working on Robert Penn Warren's *All the King's Men* for the third time. He sat down at one of the desks and began to read.

"Excuse me; I don't believe we've met," an older woman said, approaching him.

Matt stood up. "Oh, hi, I'm Matt Fischer. I'm teaching physics. On a contract," he said, smiling.

"Oh, well, that's great. I'm Lydia Willetts. I teach mathematics, mostly algebra and geometry." She looked at the desk where Matt had put down his book. "That doesn't look like a physics book," she said, raising her eyebrows.

"Well, no, it's not. I kinda already have an idea of what

I'm going to cover in class for the rest of the day so I'm just relaxing a bit."

The older teacher straightened up and then bent toward Matt and looked over her bifocals. "A bit of advice. I wouldn't let the administrators see you doing that. They'll take away your planning period and make you teach another class." She straightened again.

"Oh, okay," Matt replied, smiling but wanting to end the conversation. "I guess I'll open my calendar and some other books as well."

"Take it from an old-timer," the teacher said, nodding her head as she walked away.

Matt sat down and began to read again.

About five minutes later an older man approached and extended his hand. "Hi, I'm Dan Clarkson. Teach history and coach football. Who are you?"

Matt stood up again and said, "Nice to meet you. I'm Matt Fischer. I was hired on a contract to teach physics for at least this year."

"Oh yeah. That contract business is a pain. You get any benefits?"

"Uh, no. Not part of the deal."

"Well, hang in there and maybe they'll make you permanent soon. We need more men teaching these kids. Need some role models. Know what I mean?"

"Uh, yeah. I guess they do."

"Alright then, I'll let you get back to it," Dan said, patting Matt on the shoulder as he walked away.

Matt sat down and opened his book.

"Is that Matt Fischer?" said a girlish voice approaching him from the other side.

Matt again stood up and faced the woman walking toward him. She was a little heavy with glasses and . . . oh no. It couldn't be. . . .

"Matt Fischer, do you remember me? Susan Suggs? We used to sit beside each other in, geez, most all of our classes!" She opened her arms for a hug.

Matt responded with a forced smile and as stiff a hug as he could muster, trying not to get close to this woman or let her get close to him. Oh no, she was wearing some awful perfume too.

"Yes, I remember you, Susan. Been a long time, huh?" Matt said, again trying to keep her at arm's length.

"You haven't changed one bit," she said with a huge grin.

"Neither have you." Matt forced another smile.

"I can't believe you're back here teaching—what did I hear? Physics? That's just like you. You were always so smart." Still the big grin.

Matt's breathing became shallow. "Um, yeah, decided to come home for a while and help Dad around the farm. You know my mom passed away," he said, seeing if that would erase the grin.

It didn't.

"Well, isn't that sweet of you. I tell you what. This has made my day! Seeing you again and now we get to work together! It's awesome!"

Matt felt the blood leaving his head.

"I can't wait to tell everybody that you're back!" she said with the big grin again. Then, in a whisper, "I'll let you get back to planning now. See you later!"

• • •

One day, three weeks later, after Matt had learned to avoid the teachers' lounge and Susan Suggs, he was sitting at his desk grading tests for his eleventh-grade physics honors class when he felt the presence of someone. He looked up to see Shawn, Susie's son, standing in front of him, holding his book bag by his side. As usual, Shawn was dressed in black jeans and a black T-shirt, and his book bag was black.

Matt said, "Hey, I didn't see you there. What's up?"

"Uh, I need some help with something."

"Let me see, when I was your age taking this class I needed help understanding electric dipole moments. Is that close?"

"Well, you're right; I don't understand electric dipole moments. But that's not what I came to see you about."

Matt put his pen down and sat back in his chair. "Okay, so what's giving you a problem?"

"Actually, it's not about class. I mean, it is, but it's not."

Matt looked at Shawn for several moments and then said, "Pull up a chair."

Shawn put his book bag on the floor and pulled a chair in front of Matt's desk. "So that field trip to the Chapel Hill Planetarium you planned for us . . . uh, you said we would need to bring twenty dollars for admission and for fast food on the way there and back, right?"

"Yep, twenty bucks."

Shawn nodded again. "So, we don't have a whole lot of money, and my mom gets really depressed sometimes, and I don't want to ask her for that because it's not in our budget. So what I'm asking is if I can skip that trip."

Matt wondered if there were others with the same issue. This wasn't exactly the country-club set he was teaching. He leaned forward and said, "Look, man, I'm really sorry. I hadn't even thought about that. Um . . . don't worry about it. I can spot you the twenty dollars until whenever, okay?"

"But I'm not sure when I can pay you back."

"No big deal. And don't tell your mom about this. She doesn't need to worry about it either, okay?"

"Okay. Thanks."

"And don't worry if you can't pay me back for a long time, or even if you can't pay me back at all, okay?"

Shawn nodded again and picked up his book bag and stood up. He turned and left the room.

Matt leaned back in his chair again. Twenty bucks. When was the last time he had to worry about not having twenty bucks? He had enough money in his bank account from being a single working guy that he hadn't had to worry about money even before landing this teaching job. And Susie—so kind, you'd never know she was struggling to put groceries on the table. He needed to pay more attention to other people. Bonehead.

CHAPTER 17

Q. 149. Is any man able perfectly to keep the Commandments of God?
A. No man is able, either of himself, or by any grace received in this
life, perfectly to keep the Commandments of God; but doth daily break
them in thought, word, and deed.

THE BOOK OF CONFESSIONS, PRESBYTERIAN CHURCH (USA):
THE LARGER CATECHISM, 7.259

TRAVIS HAD SOME IDLE TIME while Jenny was at her circle meeting. He sat down at the computer in the den and turned it on. This would be a good time to just relax and surf the web. The only problem with surfing the web was the temptation to go to the E! website and check out that Brooke woman. She was really something else. Her body proportions were almost perfect and she was just plain beautiful. But he knew he shouldn't go to that website because it made him lust and then he felt guilty and heaven knew what Jenny would say if she found out he had been looking at that woman on the Internet. She might leave him over it and everyone in town would think he was some kind of pervert, and then what would he do? No, he wouldn't go to that website this time. Too risky.

Of course, it was only a website and it wasn't like he was actually committing adultery in real life, was it? No, and he remembered reading something a newspaper columnist had written that said it wasn't hurting anybody if you did something alone in the privacy of your home that didn't involve anyone else. That made sense and the guy was probably right.

So why did he feel so guilty every time he went to that website?

It was probably because he lived around a bunch of old-fashioned people who weren't as sophisticated as him and didn't understand how modern society had accepted these things as being perfectly normal. And really it was only a couple of clicks on the mouse. That couldn't hurt anything. Besides, he wasn't really obsessed with that Brooke woman. He could prove it. He could just go to that site and look at her and then return to one of the news websites. Like this.

Travis made his way to the E! website and saw a link to "Brooke on the Beach!" It was just a click. He clicked on the link and a page of photos of Brooke in various bikinis popped up. He methodically went to each of the photos and then went to each of them again . . . and then one more time. Okay, now back to a news website. See, that wasn't bad, was it? It was just the way things were now. She was a beautiful woman and he was only admiring God's creation. No harm done. . . .

Well, he had done it again. He couldn't go online without visiting that website. What a pitiful, worthless sinner. And Jenny was at *church!* He was going straight to hell. God could not take him seriously if he couldn't even refrain from clicking on a website that made him lust. He was too ashamed to even ask for God's forgiveness. He wanted to, but it was too close to the time of the sin. God would think that he thought he could just sin and sin and sin and then ask for forgiveness each time and everything would be alright. He knew it wouldn't be alright. That's not what God meant. No, he would wait until later and take the chance that he wouldn't be struck down before he got around to asking for forgiveness.

"Travis! I'm home!" Jenny yelled as she came in the back door.

Travis quickly turned off the power to the computer, not waiting to shut it down properly, then got up and walked to the kitchen to meet Jenny before she had a chance to go into the den. His face was red and he could feel his ears getting hot.

"Whatcha been doing here by yourself?"

"Oh, nothing. I just laid down on the couch and took a little rest. How was the meeting today?"

"It went pretty good. We're thinking about sponsoring a poor family to help them get off welfare. Are you okay? You look like something's the matter."

"No, I'm fine. That sounds neat. What family?"

"We don't know yet. We're going to get some names from the Department of Social Services and then decide."

"How are y'all going to get them off welfare?"

"Well, we think we can help them find work and then show them how to manage their finances so they stay ahead. Do you have a fever?"

"No, I'm alright. You think they'll want to work?"

"That's why we're getting DSS to help us. We want to help the right ones."

"So, you want me to fix you some dinner?"

"What? You know I've already had dinner. What is wrong with you? I think you need to stay off that computer. It's starting to boil your brain or something."

Now Travis really blushed. Did she know? No, there was no way. He really did need to stay away from the computer, though. It was nothing but pure temptation.

CHAPTER 18

We believe that all things in heaven and on earth, and in all creatures, are preserved and governed by the providence of this wise, eternal and almighty God. For David testifies and says: "The Lord is high above all nations, and his glory above the heavens! Who is like the Lord our God, who is seated on high, who looks far down upon the heavens and the earth?" (Ps. 113:4ff.)

THE BOOK OF CONFESSIONS, PRESBYTERIAN CHURCH (USA):
THE SECOND HELVETIC CONFESSION, 5.029

BILL PULLED INTO HIS DRIVEWAY and drove his truck around to the back of the house. He smiled a little as he looked at the neatly cut lawn. Maybe his simple life was what it was all about, what God wanted for everybody.

Everything in his yard had a sense of order to it. It was the culmination of hard work over the course of many years of doing things the right way. The freshly painted red-and-gray Ford tractor sitting next to the barn seemed to be parked in the perfect spot, and the white brick border around Mary Helen's flower garden both protected and confined the bright-orange tiger lilies and all kinds of different-colored zinnias. Over in the side yard next to the field, three even rows of sunflowers had their heads reared back, looking toward heaven. There weren't any weeds on the edge of the yard either. He kept them all away.

Everything had a proper place, a place reserved for it in a simple backyard.

Bill was just turning off the ignition when he noticed the door to his shed was ajar and his dog was sitting in front of it. That was strange.

Getting out of the truck, he tapped on the horn to get Mary Helen to come to the back porch and then walked across the yard to the shed. As he crossed the yard he whistled for his dog to come, but the dog didn't budge. Now that *was* strange. Then he noticed one of Mary Helen's shoes lying on the ground next to the dog. He began to run.

When he reached the shed, he was breathing hard. He pulled open the door and saw Mary Helen lying facedown on the wooden planks, her arms splayed outward. He knelt down and turned her over. She was unconscious.

"Mary Helen! What happened? What's wrong?"

He patted her cheeks. No response. He put his head next to her mouth to see if she was breathing. She wasn't. He tried to remember how to administer CPR. He had attended a Red Cross class several years ago but he couldn't remember all the details. He tilted Mary Helen's head back and began to press down on her chest in a rocking motion. After about ten of these, he covered her mouth with his lips and blew air into her lungs. Nothing. He tried ten more presses and then blew into her lungs again. Nothing. This was not working. He had to get her to the hospital.

He quickly grabbed her under the arms and tried to lift her to a standing position. But her legs and arms were completely limp. Bill backed out of the shed, dragging Mary Helen and looking over his shoulder at the truck.

His heart was pounding now. He couldn't lift her onto his shoulder, so he had to let her feet drag across the grass. He was completely out of breath and sweating hard when he reached the truck. But he was able to open the passenger door while holding Mary Helen up with one arm. He sat down in the seat, still holding her, and dragged her inside the vehicle by sliding over to the driver's side. Bill ran around the front and closed the passenger door. He returned to the driver's side and started the truck. The dog jumped onto the tailgate, always left down by Bill, and then into the bed of the truck. Bill jerked the truck into reverse, backed out of the driveway onto the highway, and headed toward town.

Mary Helen's head was close enough to rest on Bill's lap as he drove, and he patted her gray hair while steering with the other hand. He glanced down at her face to see if she was breathing or if there was any kind of movement. He reached across the seat and checked her wrist for a pulse. Nothing. He drove faster.

"Lord, don't take her. Don't take her. Please, God, don't take her."

Bill looked at the speedometer and saw he was going

eighty-five miles per hour. It was as fast as the old truck could go. Maybe one of the deputies would see him and give him an escort. He turned on his flashers.

He looked down at Mary Helen again. Her mouth was slightly open but he couldn't feel any air coming from her. What if she was already dead? How could this happen? She wasn't supposed to go first. No, she couldn't be dead. She was just unconscious. What happened to her?

"God, please save my Mary Helen. I love her so much. Don't take her yet. Please, God, don't take her." Bill continued to whisper as tears started forming and blurred his vision. He rubbed his eyes.

The county hospital was on the bypass, and Bill was able to get there without having to stop for any lights. He pulled up to the emergency room door and blew three long blasts on the horn. Bill gently laid Mary Helen's head on the seat and then got out and ran around to the passenger side. He opened the door and was trying to lift her out when two orderlies pressed in next to him.

One of them said, "Sir, let us get her out of there and onto this stretcher." Bill stepped back and watched them place her on the stretcher and then followed them through the glass doors into the emergency room. His dog followed him in. One of the attendants said, "Sir, you can't bring that dog in here."

Bill looked behind him at the dog. The dog had stopped and was sniffing the peculiar aroma of the hospital. Bill pointed to the truck, and the dog quickly ran through the open doors and jumped back into the bed. Bill caught up with the stretcher. Mary Helen was still not moving. They went straight back to an operating room. Bill noticed several nurses hustling toward him and a young doctor barking orders at them.

One of the nurses grabbed Bill by the arm. "Sir, are you her husband? Yes? Could I ask you to remain outside this door? Somebody will help you put on some protective clothing so you can come in with your wife."

Bill stood there, still, in the middle of the organized chaos. He suddenly felt apart from all that was happening around him. Another nurse came toward him, touched his arm, and said, "Please come with me."

He followed her into a small room, where she handed him some hospital clothing to put on. He quickly changed and then went back to the door where the orderlies had taken Mary Helen. The same nurse came up from behind him and said, "Let's go inside now." Bill walked in and found Mary Helen lying on a table with several nurses busily attaching wires to her body. Her blouse had been removed, and Bill noticed her other shoe was missing. An oxygen mask covered her face. She was still not breathing as far as he could tell. The young doctor was still yelling at the nurses.

Bill was stunned. He couldn't move. He couldn't speak. All he could do was stare at Mary Helen's ashen face. He thought, desperately, that if he could just talk to her she would wake up. He continued to focus on her face. The noise around him became muffled.

"Wake up, darling. I've fixed you poached eggs this morning with some buttered toast and strawberry preserves. Get up now, sweetie."

Mary Helen opened her eyes and smiled at him and then reached out to him.

"It's time to go now, darling. Let's get you back home. I've got the truck waiting right by the door."

"Sir, can you tell us what happened or how you found her?" the young doctor asked while looking at some type of monitor.

Bill looked at the doctor and was confused. He looked at Mary Helen. She was still lying on the table, motionless.

"Uh, well . . . I found her lying facedown . . . in my shed when I got home from the drugstore. . . . I don't know what happened," Bill said in a voice he hardly recognized.

"She's not breathing," the doctor said flatly to no one in particular. "I believe she's had a heart attack," he said to Bill while touching Mary Helen's throat, feeling for a pulse and looking at the monitor.

Another nurse quickly rolled in a table with a defibrillator apparatus while still another unsnapped Mary Helen's brassiere in the front. The doctor grabbed the defibrillator and placed the two electrodes on Mary Helen's chest.

"Now!"

A jolt of electricity caused some movement of Mary Helen's midsection but the heart monitor was still registering a flat line. The doctor positioned the electrodes on Mary Helen's chest again.

"Now!"

Again Mary Helen's midsection moved in response. Still no pulse registered on the monitor.

The young doctor stared at the monitor for a moment, holding the electrodes at his sides, one in each hand. Bill was again outside of his body, staring at Mary Helen's face.

The doctor turned around, placed the electrodes firmly on Mary Helen's chest, and tried once more. "Now!"

Again nothing. He slowly returned the defibrillator apparatus to the table and looked up at Bill. "I'm sorry. I couldn't . . . She was already . . . I'm very sorry."

Bill was silent and then quietly said, "I need to talk to her. . . . She can't . . ." He stumbled over to Mary Helen's side. He leaned over the table and put his head next to hers, burying his face in the stretcher. He stayed there, holding on to Mary Helen's motionless body, sobbing.

"Sir, do you have any family members we could help you contact?"

The doctor put his hand on Bill's shoulder. Bill just held on to the stretcher and kept his face next to Mary Helen's.

CHAPTER 19

As the bodies of the faithful are the temples of the Holy Spirit which we truly believe will rise again at the Last Day, Scriptures command that they be honorably and without superstition committed to the earth, and also that honorable mention be made of those saints who have fallen asleep in the Lord, and that all duties of familial piety be shown to those left behind, their widows and orphans. We do not teach that any other care be taken for the dead.

THE BOOK OF CONFESSIONS, PRESBYTERIAN CHURCH (USA):
THE SECOND HELVETIC CONFESSION, 5.235

THE THING ABOUT FUNERALS in their town was that they were usually packed and politicians showed up like it was a Jaycees barbeque. The sheriff was always there with a handful of deputies to give the deceased some form of posthumous respect. Of course, most families were grateful for the gesture and pretended the deceased had actually done something when they were living that deserved such acknowledgment. Besides, what good did it do to question the principles of a dead person? And it wasn't unusual to have several county commissioners take their posts by the entrance as if they were honorary ushers. When the grieving family made their entrance, at least one of the vote-grabbers would make a gesture while everybody was looking, to give the impression they were kin or at least a close acquaintance of the deceased.

But Mary Helen's funeral was different. Maybe it was because she and Bill had kept to themselves mostly. Travis estimated that only about forty or fifty people were present, counting the preacher, the organist, and the rest of the search committee. The search committee all sat together to show a little solidarity in front of the other members of the church, but also to let Bill know he still had a group of friends he could count on. For family, there was Bill's sister sitting up front with Bill . . . and that was it. Another indication of the lack of family was the number of flower arrangements. Three. It was the first time Travis realized how lonely Bill probably was, even when Mary Helen was around.

Their old preacher came back into town to do the service, and there was a small movement afoot to coax him back. He played to it some, but he really didn't want to discuss it. He was dressing a lot nicer now, wearing a dark suit that fit him almost perfectly and, underneath, a shirt with gold cuff links. When he had been their preacher, he always had on a gray or brown suit from Sears and a shirt that had sleeves so long they stuck way out of his coat sleeves. It seemed to Travis like he talked different too. He didn't pronounce *Jesus* the way he used to—*Jah-eee-suss*. Now his pronunciation was more like . . . well, like *Jesus*. But he had come back for the service, and everybody agreed it was nice of him to make the effort.

Travis had tried to catch a glimpse of Bill's face as he walked into the church with his sister and down the aisle past the committee. Bill looked down at the carpet most of the way, but then he looked up at Travis when he got to their pew. And that look. He hadn't ever seen that look on Bill's face before. It wasn't a vacant stare or an intense, furrowed-brow type of look. It was more a look of hopelessness and confusion. It made Travis real uncomfortable and he hadn't known how to respond. So he smiled like a moron.

The whole deal with Mary Helen was that Bill was supposed to go first. That's what Bill had been planning for and that's what the doctors seemed to think too. Now this. Travis didn't think Bill had a plan B.

The highlight of the funeral was when an old country man got up in the pulpit and sang a Squire Parsons tune, "Sweet Beulah Land." Travis recalled he was from that Baptist church out by I-95 just past Arby's, the one that split off from the downtown church. They didn't have that song in their hymnal, so Travis couldn't follow along. It was beautiful, though, and he saw Bill look out the window for a long period during the song. Later, Travis managed to borrow the sheet music from the pianist to copy down the words to the hymn.

The preacher, like all preachers everywhere, tried to smooth things over by pointing out that Mary Helen was with the Lord now and that they should be comforted and joyful in that knowledge. Comfort, yes. Joy, no. All Travis could think about was how Bill was going to manage without her. He had spent the last twenty years taking care of Mary Helen and now, suddenly, that was all over. Plus, he didn't have anybody to talk to at home. That would be the hard part for Travis, not being able to talk to anybody at home. He hated being alone at home, but not quite as bad as he hated staying in a motel room by himself. That was the worst.

At the graveside service, Bill and his sister sat alone under the tent on the metal folding chairs. It was sunny and quiet, except for the sound of the tent flapping in the afternoon breeze. Bill sat there in his dark suit, bent over with his elbows on his knees and his head buried in his hands. His sister, Lydia, sat beside him with her legs crossed and rubbed his back while staring down at the hole in the gray dirt.

The silver-colored casket was open for the beginning of the graveside service. Travis noticed the breeze blowing through Mary Helen's gray hair, giving life to something that was dead. It had always puzzled him to look at dead people. If the mortician got it right and they looked natural, like they were just asleep, he always had the urge to touch their faces to see if by some miracle they might wake up.

Maybe his preoccupation with dead people in caskets had to do with how he reacted to his own mama's death. She had a heart attack when she was forty-two years old and died in her bed on a hot July morning in 1995. Travis was twelve.

He and his sister weren't even there. They were staying with their grandparents, their mama's parents, at their house in Sylva near the mountains. It was an old boarding-house. His grandparents had stopped taking on boarders two decades earlier, but his grandma still kept all the beds made and the rooms set up, just in case. All the boarders' rooms had been upstairs. Travis and his sister slept up there during their summer visits, and that was where they were when they found out about their mama.

He remembered that room vividly. The hard and slick dark-blue linoleum floor was cold on his feet and smelled old and was cracked in several spots. A dark-red throw rug was positioned on the floor at the side of the old iron double bed. The bed was covered with a thin white cotton bedspread and had real springs that squeaked when you got in. They slept under a quilt too because it was cool at night near the mountains, even in July.

He remembered waking up during the night, hearing his sister crying, and sitting up and seeing Aunt Kay standing beside the bed. He heard more voices downstairs. He heard his grandma crying down there and noticed Aunt Kay patting his sister's head.

"What's wrong?"

"Your mama died."

"How?"

"She had a heart attack."

"Oh. Where's Robby?"

"He's with a lady from the church at home."

"Oh."

That was the extent of his reaction upon learning of his mama's death. He didn't cry. He didn't understand how his life had just changed, how everything had just changed. His sister was sobbing into her pillow. For a long time he couldn't forgive himself for not crying. A long time. Then one day—he wasn't exactly sure when—he just stopped thinking about it.

Travis and his sister got up and got dressed and went downstairs. Their grandma looked at them coming down the stairs and really started crying and sobbing. It scared Travis a little. His grandpa had his arms around her shoulders and led her into their bedroom. Aunt Kay came down the stairs behind them with their lime-green suitcase, and Travis remembered thinking how strange it was going to be, traveling at night.

The next thing he remembered was going to the funeral home. It looked like a regular redbrick store right on Main Street, but you couldn't see in the windows from the sidewalk. It had glass doors just like a bank. It was funny, the things he remembered. He went in with Aunt Kay and his sister. His brother was only a toddler so he wasn't there. Aunt Kay took him and Lou Ann into the room where the casket was situated. Lou Ann started crying real loud. He remembered looking around the room, looking at the light coming in through the pale-green curtains.

The room where his mama was lying was actually used as a chapel, and her casket was down by the podium on one end of the room. Travis walked slowly toward it. Aunt Kay was patting Lou Ann's head and whispering something to her. He was just tall enough to look into the casket and see his mama. She looked like she was just taking a nap, lying there in a pink chiffon dress with her hands crossed over her midsection. Her hair was all fixed up. Travis wanted to touch her and wake her up and actually tried to do just that. He reached over the side of the casket, but Aunt Kay was watching him and grabbed his arm. She led him and Lou Ann out of the room.

Later at the church service when they got ready to go down front, he noticed a man in a black suit standing real close to him. He smelled like strong aftershave. It took Travis a few seconds to realize it was his daddy. He had never seen him in a suit before. His daddy didn't speak to him or Lou Ann—he just stood there with his arms folded, looking straight ahead. Travis noticed his daddy's black hair was slicked down with some kind of gel.

Travis looked back toward the sanctuary and could see his mama in the casket down in front of the pulpit. The lid was still open. He noticed a whole lot of people turning around in their pews to look at him. He got a little scared and refused to go down the aisle with his daddy. Lou Ann held back too. His aunt Kay took them back to her house and stayed with them during the funeral service.

About a week later, he and his sister and his baby brother all moved to his aunt Kay's house to live with her son, Jimmy. That's when he got new clothes and started eating three times a day. His daddy never came back.

Seeing his mama lying in that casket did something to him. When he went to any funeral home for visitation nowadays, he couldn't stop looking at the dead person. Looking for some sign of movement or something—he wasn't sure.

The whole deal was strange to him. How could a living body just up and die one day when it had been buying lettuce at the Food Lion the previous day? And when exactly did the soul go on up to heaven? Did it go at the instant of death, or did it hang around for a while?

Maybe that's what he was looking for—the dead person's soul. Some kind of sign from the other side to explain things a little better. After all, no person alive could really tell you what it was like. The closest source of information was lying right there in the casket.

They stopped by Bill's house after the service to drop off some baked ham and sugar snap peas that Jenny had fixed for him. He thanked them and shook Travis's hand, but he didn't say much else to anybody.

Travis wondered for a moment if he would stay on the search committee, but then he realized that was a stupid thought. It was surely the last thing on Bill's mind.

CHAPTER 20

Q. 130. What are the sins of superiors?

A. The sins of superiors are, besides the neglect of the duties required of them, an inordinate seeking of themselves, their own glory, ease, profit or pleasure; commanding things unlawful, or not in the power of inferiors to perform; counseling, encouraging, or favoring them in that which is evil; dissuading, discouraging, or discountenancing them in that which is good; correcting them unduly; careless exposing or leaving them to wrong, temptation, and danger; provoking them to wrath; or in any way dishonoring themselves, or lessening their authority, by an unjust, indiscreet, rigorous, or remiss behavior.

THE BOOK OF CONFESSIONS, PRESBYTERIAN CHURCH (USA):
THE LARGER CATECHISM, 7.240

FRANKIE STOOD UP TO GIVE HER REPORT to the session, most of whom were stern-faced men: a couple of farmers, a few store owners, and two retirees who really didn't spend a whole lot of time socializing. They were in one of the adult Sunday school classrooms, and the cinder-block walls were painted a light beige. The lack of pictures on the walls combined with the smell of floor wax made the room seem as if it were safe from sin. The folding tables were arranged in a horseshoe with the elders sitting around the outside in brown metal folding chairs, the cheap kind. The interim minister sat at the top of the horseshoe and was serving as moderator.

Frankie's mouth was a little dry. "Uh, well . . . we've looked at several prospects who might fit our needs here, but we haven't been able to reach a consensus yet, so we're going to still visit some more churches over the next three months." Frankie chuckled. "I could tell you some stories, though. We've had several big adventures on our trips."

Nobody smiled.

The elders didn't say anything for about ten seconds. Then they started in on her.

Elder 1: "Three months? How much longer do you think it will take for y'all to decide? You know, we're getting into a bad situation here. No offense to the reverend, but some of the younger families have stopped coming. I saw that Harris couple going into the Methodist church last Sunday morning."

Elder 2: "Well, they weren't doing a whole lot anyway."

Elder 1: "I think they were giving pretty good, though, and we need all of that we can get right now, heading into winter and facing those heating bills again."

Elder 3: "We don't want the committee to rush into something that we can't live with later on. I say let them take as much time as they want."

Elder 4: "I would agree, but our numbers are really dropping off now. We need us a motivator in here to get some of those who are on the fence between us and the other churches to come over to our side. We can't get anybody new to join up if we don't have a full-time preacher. Sorry, Reverend, but you understand what I mean, don't you?"

The interim minister slowly nodded.

Elder 5: "I hope the committee is taking its responsibility seriously and not just having fun every weekend. This is not to be taken lightly."

Frankie gritted her teeth while looking at the floor. Gerald Winter and his uppity wife had moved down from Ohio and felt they had a "calling" to educate the poor, stupid locals who had been here all their lives. They had a funny way of going about it, though. They sang in the choir but didn't do any of the grunt work that keeps a church going. Always left right after the Wednesday-night suppers without offering to clean up. Never visited any of the elderly. And if you asked them to do anything at all, they had to check their schedules because their time was "important." But Gerald wanted to make sure that the committee was "serious" about their job.

"Well, Gerald . . . why don't you get up next Sunday with us at five o'clock and come to the church to see how serious we are about our committee's responsibility? And bring your wife. Y'all get up that early, don't you?" Frankie knew his wife wouldn't let him, even if he wanted to. He was whipped. Tried to cover it up by being a jerk.

"Now, Frankie, I didn't mean—"

"Yes, I know what you meant, and I don't appreciate it. In fact, I don't appreciate the attitude that the whole lot of you is displaying right now."

Silence.

"I want all of you to know that we are taking this *very* seriously. And we are aware of the situation with our declining membership. In fact, that's one of the main reasons we want to make sure we have the right man for the job."

Frankie paused when she heard some labored breathing and then a light nasal snore. Looking around the table, she spotted one of the elders nodding off. His head was resting on his chest but he was still holding his pen in a writing position. Now the other elders noticed him too. Frankie rolled her eyes.

Elder 1: "Frankie, look, we're in trouble here. We need y'all to try to hurry it up some."

Elder 3: "No, let them do it right. Otherwise we might end up with somebody we don't want."

The sleeping elder's pen dropped from his grip and fell onto the table. Then, as he took a deep breath, he let out a loud, abrupt snore that awoke him. He quickly glanced around the table and noticed everyone staring at him. His face flushed.

Rev. Haynesworth said, "We may be losing sight of something here. If you really want the process to hurry up, then you need to ask someone other than the search committee."

Elder 1: "Really? Who?"

Rev. Haynesworth smiled and said nothing.

Elder 3: "He means we need to pray about it."

Elder 1 looked down at the table.

Frankie glanced around the room. "One more thing. Gerald, if you or anybody else ever questions the effort our committee is putting forth for this church, for all of you, for our young folks . . . I can promise that *you* will be searching . . . for another search committee."

Silence. Gerald was looking down at his pad, twiddling his pencil.

"Now, if you will excuse me, we will get back to our *fun* this weekend."

Frankie looked around the room but not one of the strong, wise elders would meet her eye. Only Rev. Haynesworth. And he waved with a smile.

CHAPTER 21

I have cried until the tears no longer come; my heart is broken.
My spirit is poured out in agony as I see the desperate plight of my
people. Little children and tiny babies are fainting and dying in
the streets.

LAMENTATIONS 2:11

JENNY KEPT PUSHING THE BABY THING WITH TRAVIS, trying
to convince him that it was time. Travis knew it was time.
He knew *she* was ready. *He* just wasn't ready. Jenny thought
it was because he was afraid he would lose his freedom. That
he didn't want to be tied down. In fact, she was certain of it.
But that really wasn't it. There was another reason. One that
Travis didn't talk about to anyone. He still wasn't over it. It
happened a long time ago at his aunt Kay's house.

"Can you kids watch the baby while I take your mama to
get her hair done?" Aunt Kay had asked Travis, Lou Ann, and

Jimmy. "We'll only be gone an hour." She had brought Travis, his mama, Lou Ann, and Robby over to her house for the day.

"Oh yes!" Lou Ann cried out. To her, their little brother was just like a baby doll—although he was a very messy, stinky baby doll.

Travis's mama turned to him. "Travis, I'm depending on you."

His aunt Kay said, "Travis, honey, the phone number for Bernice's is right there on the kitchen table. You call me if you need anything, okay? And if there's an emergency, call 911."

"Yes, ma'am." Travis looked at the phone on the wall by the refrigerator.

Travis and Jimmy were both eleven, but Travis was always considered the more responsible of the two. Jimmy just let things slip—not intentionally, but mostly because he couldn't keep his mind on one thing for very long.

Aunt Kay helped Travis's mama down the steps and to the car. Her husband was a tobacco farmer and provided for his family to the extent that Aunt Kay didn't have to work, plus she had a car to drive around. She checked up on her sister, Travis's mama, every now and then, but only when Travis's daddy wasn't around. This was one of those times.

It had been Aunt Kay's idea to take Mama to the beauty parlor that Tuesday when they were sure his daddy wouldn't be coming home. Kay had brought a clean blouse for Mama to wear and some slacks of hers and had helped her get cleaned up and changed. Travis, Jimmy, and Lou Ann were to stay together at her house to watch the baby.

Aunt Kay laid Robby on a towel on the rug in the den and covered him with a thin baby blanket. Robby was sound asleep.

"Y'all take turns watching him now," Aunt Kay had said. She had set one of her kitchen chairs beside the towel where Robby was lying for them to sit on when it was their turn.

Travis was the first to watch the baby. Jimmy and Lou Ann had gone outside to the backyard to dig out a fort in the dirt. At home, Robby ate everything that was put in front of him and cried the rest of the time, so Travis was amazed that he was actually asleep.

Travis sat in the chair for a few minutes and then got up to look around. He went down the hall to Aunt Kay's bedroom. She had a big bed with a white cotton bedspread and several extra pillows on top, and the floor was covered with wall-to-wall white carpet. Travis checked his feet to make sure he wasn't tracking. He opened her closet door. She had some nice-looking clothes on hangers and several pairs of shoes placed neatly in a row. Travis thought to himself, *So this is how it is when you have money.*

He heard the baby make a noise and walked back to the den. Whatever it was that stirred him, Robby was fine now, asleep. Travis's stomach felt a little funny, so he went to the bathroom down the hall. That's when it happened.

Travis was sitting on the commode when he heard Robby start to cry. At first he wasn't worried, because that was normal. But then it sounded like the crying was coming from another room, not the den. He finished his business and went back to the den. The towel was still there, but Robby was gone. He had been crawling a little bit at home but not a lot. The crying was loud and continuous now and was coming from the kitchen.

He walked to the kitchen and saw Robby lying on the floor by the refrigerator. A large mousetrap was on his right hand and he was waving it around as he cried louder and louder, gasping for air between each cry. Apparently, he had crawled to the kitchen and put his hand on the contraption, setting it off. Two of Robby's fingers were caught and were turning blue.

Travis grabbed it and tried to pull the bar up from Robby's fingers, but he couldn't budge it. The spring was too strong. He ran to the back door.

"Jimmy, come quick! Robby's got his hand caught in a big mousetrap!" he shouted through the screen door. Jimmy and Lou Ann both jumped up. Travis hurried back to the kitchen, where Robby was lying on the floor, red-faced and crying like Travis had never seen before.

Jimmy and Lou Ann came running. Lou Ann screamed. Jimmy shouted, "Get it off his fingers!"

"I can't! The spring is too strong! I can't get it to open!"

Jimmy grabbed Robby's hand and tried to pull it out but it just wouldn't budge. Robby's fingers were really blue now.

"What do we do?" Lou Ann yelled. "We've gotta do something!"

"I'll call Aunt Kay!" Travis grabbed the phone from the wall and stretched the cord so he could see the phone number on the kitchen table for Bernice's, where his aunt and mama had gone. His hands were jerking and shaking as he pressed the numbers on the keypad. He finally got the number punched in and held the phone tightly against his face, watching Robby crying with the big mousetrap on his hand. Lou Ann was crying uncontrollably now, and Jimmy was prying at the mousetrap where Robby's fingers were still stuck.

"Hello, this is Bernice," a voice said on the other end.

"I gotta speak to Aunt Kay! It's an emergency!" Travis yelled into the phone receiver.

"Okay, son, hold on," Bernice said, irritated at the loud voice.

"Yes?"

"Aunt Kay! This is Travis! Robby got his fingers stuck in a mousetrap and we can't get it off!"

"Oh no! Call 911! No, wait, it will take too long for them to get there. Run down the road to the white house and get Hilda to take him to Dr. Madison's office and we'll meet you there, okay? That'll be quicker."

"Okay!"

Travis hung up the phone. "Y'all wait right here with him. I'm going to get help!"

He ran out the front door toward the neighbors' house just down the road. As he approached the house, a large German shepherd came toward him, barking. Travis crossed to the other side of the road and the dog stopped on the edge of its yard.

"Help! Somebody help!" he yelled at the house.

No answer. Travis looked in the driveway. No car. Nobody

was home. This was the white house Aunt Kay told him to go to. What could he do now? He should've called 911 anyway. He continued down the road as the German shepherd ran along the front of its yard, barking at him. Luckily, the dog wasn't chasing him. Travis saw another house about two football fields away. He ran as fast as he could. He was breathing hard and his heart was pounding. Finally, he reached the house. A car was in the driveway. He ran to the front door and started banging on it.

"Help! Somebody help!"

A woman opened the door. "What is it, son? Calm down."

"It's my baby brother! He's got his hand stuck in a mousetrap and we can't get it off! He's in the kitchen down the road at my aunt Kay's house. She and my mama aren't there! They went to the beauty parlor. They said to meet them at Dr. Madison's!"

"At Kay's house? Come on and get in the car and take me to him," she said.

The woman and Travis drove back to Aunt Kay's house. When they got there they jumped out of the car and ran inside. The baby's crying was shallow and raspy now. Jimmy was holding him and Lou Ann was sobbing in a low voice.

The woman knelt down and pulled the trap apart and off Robby's fingers. She picked him up and carried him, trotting out to her car. "Come on!"

Travis followed her and jumped in the front seat. Jimmy and Lou Ann climbed in the back. The woman handed Robby to Travis.

"Y'all hold on now; we're going to get him to the doctor," she said as she pulled the car out of the driveway.

At the doctor's office, the woman rushed Robby to the back and some nurses began scurrying about. Travis, Jimmy, and Lou Ann sat down in the waiting room just as Aunt Kay came in, half-supporting and half-dragging his mama.

"Where is he?" Mama yelled. Her hair had been fixed up, making her look less crazy but a lot meaner.

"In the back," Travis replied, not meeting her gaze.

Mama and Aunt Kay went through the door the woman had taken Robby through. Travis, Jimmy, and Lou Ann just sat still and stared at the door.

After another two hours the door opened. Travis's mama, Aunt Kay, and the neighbor woman came walking into the waiting room. His mama was holding Robby in one arm with Aunt Kay supporting her bad side. Robby's hand had a big bandage on it. None of the adults looked at Travis, Jimmy, or Lou Ann. They kept walking toward the front door.

Lou Ann asked, "What happened to Robby's hand?"

Travis's mama stopped and turned to Travis. "He lost two fingers."

Lou Ann and Jimmy looked at Travis. He just looked at the floor.

• • •

That was why he wasn't ready yet.

CHAPTER 22

After God had made all other creatures, he created man, male and female, with reasonable and immortal souls, endued with knowledge, righteousness, and true holiness after his own image, having the law of God written in their hearts, and power to fulfill it; and yet under a possibility of transgressing, being left to the liberty of their own will, which was subject unto change.

THE BOOK OF CONFESSIONS, PRESBYTERIAN CHURCH (USA):
THE WESTMINSTER CONFESSION OF FAITH, 6.023

FRANKIE OPENED THE BACK SCREEN DOOR and walked into her kitchen. There was a note taped to the wall phone. She squinted her eyes and walked over to read it. *Call Dot ASAP.*

"George! When did you take this message?"

"What?" her husband yelled from the den.

Frankie took the note off the phone and walked down the hall into the den, where George was watching the History Channel. Looked like another World War II special.

"When did you take this message?"

George picked up the remote control and put the TV on

mute. "Oh . . . about an hour and a half ago. She sounded kinda upset but didn't say anything other than she needed to talk to you."

"So you don't know what it's about?"

"No, I didn't ask. But you know Dot. It could be anything. She's a piece of work."

Frankie walked back to the kitchen. She picked up the church directory off the counter by the phone and looked up Dot's number.

"871-7256. 871-7256. 871-7256," Frankie repeated while picking up the handset and pressing the numbers on the keypad.

"Hello?"

"Dot, it's Frankie. What's wrong?"

Dot sighed. "It's Fred."

"What about him?"

"I saw his car parked behind a woman's house today right here in town."

"So? What was he doing?"

Dot started to sob. "I don't know. He was in there for an hour. I waited on a side street. Saw him drive away. Frankie, it was Susie's house."

"What? You mean he was in there with Susie? He's too old for her. Are you sure it was his car?"

"I wish I wasn't."

"Well, there has to be some explanation. I don't know about Fred, but I know Susie wouldn't do that to you. When is he coming home?"

"He called . . . and—" Dot sighed—"said he was working late . . . had to finish something."

"You stay right there, baby. I'll be right over."

Frankie hung up the phone and stared at the wall. This would get around town like a racehorse. Poor Dot.

"George, I'm going over to Dot's. I'll be back late. You'll have to eat by yourself."

"What?" George came walking into the kitchen.

"Something's up. It's important and it's personal. That's all I can tell you. I'll be back late."

Frankie got into her car, started the engine, and stared straight ahead. What could she do? Maybe Susie could explain. Maybe he was just helping her fix something. George did that sometimes. He liked to fix appliances, and a lot of the neighbors knew he could do it and called on him. Besides, what could Susie see in Fred? He was not in her league. She could get any man, a young, good-looking man if she wanted one. Fred? It just didn't make sense. Frankie backed out of the driveway and headed over to Dot's house.

Dot lived in an older subdivision on the east side of town. From Frankie's house, it took only about five minutes to get there if you took the shortcut down Blueberry Farm Road through the black community.

As Frankie was driving along, she passed a single green dumpster located on a small pull-off area right beside the road. There was an older-looking white man, very thin, in a ball cap, standing there, and he was holding an older-looking white woman wearing bright-green polyester pants and bedroom slippers. He was holding her in his arms as if he were going to carry her somewhere. Their car, a beat-up Dodge, was parked just beyond the dumpster with the trunk open.

Frankie slowed down and made eye contact with the couple. Their sunken blue eyes just stared as she drove slowly past them. *Hmmm.* The woman seemed to be okay with the situation. Looking in her rearview mirror, Frankie saw the man struggling to lift the woman over into the dumpster. *What in the world?* The woman stood up, bent over, then stood up again, handing something to the old man.

Oh my goodness. Sifting through the garbage. What has the world come to? The man would probably blame it on the woman if the sheriff drove by. Like Adam and Eve in the garden. Why did the woman have to do the dirty work? Maybe she enjoyed the scavenging, or maybe he was unable to crawl into the dumpster. Good heavens, it was a crazy scene. Well, it *was* always interesting to see what other people had thrown out. It told you a lot.

Frankie thought about turning around and asking them what they were looking for. Hopefully it wasn't food. The county provided assistance for people like that. Maybe they didn't know. But no, there was no time for that. Dot needed help right now. Maybe she would see them again and would be able to help them then.

Frankie pulled up in Dot's driveway. It was a small, tan brick ranch that Dot had overdecorated with ruffled curtains, and the small living room inside had that country look that was trendy several years ago—actually, more than several years ago. Frankie pulled the car around back, where they usually parked, and walked up to the back screen door.

"Dot?"

"In here."

Frankie opened the door and walked into the kitchen.

Dot was sitting at the table with her elbows propped up and her face resting on her hands. She looked up briefly at Frankie with red, swollen eyes and then buried her face in her hands. "What am I going to do?"

"We're going to meet this thing head-on, together." Frankie patted Dot's head. "I've got an idea."

"What?"

"Let's go over to her house and confront it straight up."

"I can't. I can't believe he did this. And Susie . . . I can't look at her."

"Just come on. I'll do the talking."

"Okay . . . but I'm staying in the car."

Dot stood up and brushed the wrinkles out of the front of her dress. The dress was obviously too tight, but Frankie didn't comment. That was Dot. Frankie watched as she primped her hair with her hands to get it back in its regular shape. Taking a deep breath and exhaling loudly, Dot said, "Let's go."

• • •

Frankie pulled up in Susie's driveway and got out.

"You sure you won't come in?" she asked, leaning down to talk to Dot through the open car door.

"No, I'm staying here."

Frankie walked up to the front door and rang the door-bell. She looked back. Dot had her head buried in her hands again. The door opened.

"Why, hello, Frankie! What are you dropping by for?" Susie said, smiling. She didn't notice Dot sitting in the car. "Come on in. Is something the matter?"

"Well, I'm hoping you can clear something up."

"What is it?"

"Is Shawn here?"

"No. Why? What has he done?"

"He hasn't done anything. I just don't want him to hear this." Frankie paused, looked down, then back up at Susie. "Dot saw Fred's car parked here today. She waited over on that street across the road until he left. She said he was here for an hour."

Frankie watched Susie's face for a clue. Oddly enough, it didn't show any shame or embarrassment at all. Instead, Susie had a puzzled look.

"What was he doing here?" Susie asked in a quiet voice.

"Well, I was kinda hoping you could tell me that."

"Frankie . . . I've been gone all day. Shawn was here, but . . . what would Fred . . . ? Why would Fred be visiting Shawn?"

"So you were gone all day? Fred wasn't here with you?"

"Of course not! Why would I—?"

"Listen, Dot is out in the car. Do you mind if I go get her? She needs to hear all this too. She thought that you and—"

"She thought I was having an affair with Fred?!"

"Well, honey, you have to admit, she had to suspect something, and I'm sure she never suspected that Fred would be coming over here to see Shawn—"

"Me and Fred? Eew, yuck. I'm not *that* desperate. Go get her; we need to talk this thing out."

Frankie walked to the door, opened it, and motioned for Dot to come inside. Dot closed her eyes and opened the car door. She took a big breath again and exhaled loudly while brushing the wrinkles out of the front of her too-tight dress.

Dot and Frankie went inside. Dot was sober-faced now. Susie was sitting on the couch, still looking puzzled. Dot sat in a rocker opposite Susie.

Frankie decided not to sit down. "Uh, Dot . . . it turns out that Susie wasn't here all day."

"Well, what on earth was Fred doing in here?"

"We're not sure. He might have been visiting Shawn, but we can't figure out why. At least we know he wasn't here with Susie."

Dot looked over at Susie. "I'm sorry, honey. I never should have even thought that."

"It's okay. Sometimes you don't know what to think. I know I didn't with Dale."

• • •

Fred opened the back screen door and entered the kitchen. Dot was sitting at the table waiting for him.

"Hi, honey. Sorry I'm late. Looks like I missed supper."

"Where were you?"

"Where was I? At the office, like I told you. What's wrong with you?"

"Oh, nothing . . . just wondering where you were."

Dot stood up and walked to the den. She heard Fred lumber down the hall to the bedroom. When she heard a drawer shut in the bedroom, she picked up the phone and dialed Frankie's house.

"Hello?"

"He's here."

"Okay, bye."

"Bye."

Dot quietly put down the receiver. Then she turned on the TV and sat down on the sofa. Fred came back up the hall. He had taken his shirt and shoes off and had his T-shirt tucked into his pants.

"I guess I'll fix my own plate since you're mad at me."

"Yeah, why don't you do that," Dot replied flatly.

Fred stopped and turned around. "Is something wrong? I know you can't be this mad because I'm a little late coming home. What is it?"

"We can talk about it later."

"Oh, great. I'm really looking forward to that conversation."

Fred stepped into the kitchen and opened the refrigerator. "Did you fix *anything* tonight?"

"Not for you."

She heard him open the pantry and rummage around for something. Probably the peanut butter and a loaf of bread.

About ten minutes later, the doorbell rang. Dot got up and opened the front door. She welcomed Frankie and Susie. "He's in the kitchen. This way."

Fred stood up when they came in. "Evening, ladies. So, Dot, you called your friends to come beat up on me too?"

"Just shut up, Fred, and sit down."

"Okay, alright. Take it easy on the old man," Fred replied with a smile.

"What were you doing at Susie's house today?"

Fred looked surprised. "Well, if I was at Susie's house, why don't you ask Susie what I was doing there?"

Susie frowned. "Ha-ha. Not funny, Fred. I wasn't there. Shawn was. What were you doing there with Shawn?"

Fred smiled. "Oh, we were just hanging out."

"Fred Spivey, you better give us a straight answer or you won't be sleeping here tonight."

"Wait now; just wait a minute. I can see that you girls got your underwear on backward. I guess I'll have to tell you."

"I would highly recommend it," Frankie replied sternly.

"Alright then. You asked for it." Fred stood up again and turned toward Susie. "Your boy stopped by my office several weeks ago and said he needed to talk to an accountant. It was a slow day so I told him to fire away. He wanted to know if I would help him invest some money in stocks. I told him no. He's just a kid and it is illegal for him to do anything with the stock market before he's eighteen.

"He started to get all emotional and tear up, so I asked him what was making him so anxious to invest money in stocks. He told me. After he told me, I decided I would help him. He wanted the money fast. I told him it was not possible or wise to even try to turn a quick buck on the stock market. It fails a lot more often than it works.

"So anyway, he said he didn't care about that. Said it was worth the risk and that he wanted to use me as an alias for him to day-trade online. He's a smart kid. Already knew about it. I told him he could lose all his money doing that. Then I told him a lot of people have lost their retirement savings rolling the dice with online day-trading. He said he didn't care about what other people lost or any of that; he knew he could make money at it. Said he had a thousand dollars that his dad had given him last month."

Susie gasped.

"Yeah, and he said he was willing to risk it all. He did have a good reason, after all. So I agreed to help him set up an online account using my name and Social Security number, and I agreed I would give him some advice on stocks. He didn't need my advice, though. He's been following the market by reading the *Wall Street Journal* in the library every day after school. I wish more kids had his drive. Anyway, I got him started on one of the computers in my office and he was a pretty regular visitor. He was also a pretty good trader, or at least a really lucky trader. Do you know that in the past three weeks, he has turned that one thousand dollars into six thousand? I can't believe it."

Susie gasped again.

"Well, anyway, once he knew what he was doing, he

started trading on his own computer at home. I stopped by there today just to watch him in action. It's really something to see."

Frankie, Susie, and Dot were standing there, speechless, confused, and all three had their mouths open.

Finally, Susie shook her head and snapped out of her trance. "So, what is he planning on doing with the money?"

"Well, he's going to buy you a new car. Says that will make you happy and you won't be so depressed all the time. Says you need something good to happen to you instead of things always turning out bad. He's a good kid. I would be proud if he were my son."

Susie sat down on the floor of the kitchen and started crying.

Frankie asked, "Well, why did his daddy give him the money?"

"He told his dad that he would talk his mother into taking him back if his dad gave him a thousand dollars."

Susie looked up.

Frankie asked, "Was he planning on doing that?"

Fred snorted. "No. He hates the man for what he did. He just took his dad for a thousand dollars. I'm telling you, that kid is going places."

"But can't he still lose it all playing the stock market?"

"Sure he could, but so far he's batting a thousand and he's beating every fund manager alive."

Frankie offered her hand to Susie. "Come on, sweetie. Let's get up and go home."

As Susie got back to her feet with Frankie's help, Dot said, "Fred, I'm sorry. I thought . . ."

"What exactly did you think, Dot?" He shook his head and sat back down to eat his sandwich.

Dot walked Frankie and Susie to the door.

CHAPTER 23

Since God chose you to be the holy people he loves, you must clothe yourselves with tenderhearted mercy, kindness, humility, gentleness, and patience.

COLOSSIANS 3:12

"Ha! Look at that one," Travis blurted out.

The sign read, *Triumph is just a little* umph *added to* try. Bill smiled but didn't comment. He had said hardly a word the whole trip. Travis opened up his notebook to the back pages and wrote it down.

Everybody was being a little quieter than usual, out of respect for Bill. Two weeks had passed since Mary Helen died and no one thought he would stay on the committee. Who could blame him if he didn't? But he'd showed up this morning when they were getting ready to pull out of the parking lot. Travis surrendered the driver's seat and crawled over to his copilot position. Bill parked his car, climbed in, smiled at the group, and said, "How's everybody doing?"

Almost in unison, they all said, "Fine. We're doing good." Nobody asked Bill how he was doing. They just avoided the subject. Why drag it back out again anyway? He knew they cared and they knew he was hurting. No need to have a talk show about it. Travis thought it was a little strange that Bill was rejoining them so soon, but maybe two weeks of grieving was enough for some people.

Today they were headed over to Raleigh to hear a guy who indicated on his personal information form that he was strong on missions work. That had everyone interested because they hadn't ever really done much of that other than give to a fund that supported some missionaries somewhere. Travis thought they were in Madagascar or someplace like that. Maybe Turkey. He didn't know.

Travis wasn't really looking forward to going to this particular church, because Raleigh folks were a little too uppity. City folk. He couldn't figure out why this guy was interested in moving to their town. It just didn't fit. They couldn't pay him like these folks probably did. In Travis's mind, this was shaping up to be another wasted trip. But he guessed the Lord was leading them, so here they went.

Highway 264 to Raleigh was another dull drive through eastern North Carolina, but at least it was a relatively short one. The church was north of town on Six Forks Road in the suburbs.

"Travis, there's another one," Frankie said from the back. This sign read, *The wages of sin is death—quit before payday!*

Joyce laughed out loud. "How do people come up with this stuff?"

"They get them out of the *New Yorker* magazine," Bill responded with a grin.

Everybody looked at Bill.

Then Joyce laughed out loud again. "Now that was a good one, Bill."

Bill smiled. Everybody smiled. He was talking again.

"Hey, Bill, you mind stopping before we get there?" Frankie said. "I gotta go."

"Not a problem, lady."

Travis added, "There's a Shell at the Zebulon exit."

Dot said, "I could go too."

At the Shell station Travis got out of the van and opened the side door for Frankie and Dot. Bill went around the back of the van to pump the gas.

As Frankie and Dot headed to the restroom in the station, Travis put his hands on his hips and looked around the place. Pieces of cotton were rolling along the concrete near the pumps. Out behind the station was a cotton field. Cotton had been making a comeback. Travis guessed it was from all those Levi's shipped to China or wherever. He always thought cotton was an ugly plant, with those white puffs hanging off a scraggly-looking brown bush. To him, it looked like some kind of poor, white-trash Christmas tree.

Now tobacco, there was a pretty plant: big, broad green

leaves on a sturdy green stem with a white top. It looked more like a crop than cotton did. And nowadays cotton farming was messy, too. After it was picked by a machine it looked like half of the crop was left on the ground. Tobacco, on the other hand, was harvested in a more orderly fashion. It was sticky, but to Travis, there was nothing on this earth that smelled better than a packhouse of cured tobacco before it went to the warehouse for auction.

As a kid, he'd always looked forward to the fall, when his uncle's packhouse was emptied and all that was left were the sticks used to hang the tobacco when it was curing. The sticks were about four feet long, just shorter than Travis and Jimmy, and were one inch thick. There would be hundreds of them stacked in a corner. Travis and Jimmy would take them and build elaborate forts inside the packhouse, putting them together like Lincoln Logs. The forts would have different levels and different rooms—Travis and Jimmy got to be pretty good at it. The only thing that limited them was the height of the packhouse ceiling. They would build right up to it and then leave a little room where they could lie down. The sticks were real sturdy too. Travis and Jimmy could crawl all over them and they wouldn't break. Jimmy said they were made out of hickory, but Travis didn't think Jimmy really knew for sure, because Jimmy liked to exaggerate whenever possible.

Oh man, the tobacco warehouses where buyers came to bid on everybody's crop—those were some hopping places. Travis remembered old Mr. Bennett, who ran the warehouse on the north side of town on 301. He let Travis and Jimmy play around down there sometimes, but only after they had picked up all the scrap leaves on the floor for him. Inside the warehouse was this ramp that the trucks backed down to unload the tobacco. And there were wooden dollies for moving the bundles around. Travis and Jimmy would go there when it was slow and climb on one of those dollies, go down the ramp, and roll off onto the concrete before the dolly hit the wall at the bottom.

And there was this gumball machine with Boston Baked Beans candies. Mr. Bennett once showed him and Jimmy how to shake it so that a handful of the beans would come out of the slot without putting the penny in. If they ran out of things to do like that, they would tag along behind the caller and the buyers and try to figure out who had the best crop.

And the smell. The smell of the cured tobacco was smooth, just like the cured leaf felt to the touch. Travis used to feel it just wrap around him. But all of that was gone now. The warehouse where all that action took place was now a discount furniture warehouse with rows of easy chairs wrapped in plastic.

The van pulled into the church parking lot at 10:45 a.m. Travis hopped out and opened the sliding side door so everybody could get out. As he turned back around he heard a motorcycle coming into the parking lot.

It turned out to be a red moped with what appeared to be a skinny elderly lady riding it. She had on a white helmet with no face shield and black goggles and was wearing a long black pleated skirt with a white blouse under a bright-red cardigan sweater. Her helmet had a hand-painted brown cross on one side. She was wearing black leather driving gloves, knee-high hose, and comfortable beige old-lady shoes.

She drove her moped past their van, glanced over at them, and then circled around and came back, stopping just in time to avoid hitting the side of the van. She turned the moped engine off and removed her goggles. Looking at Frankie, she said, "Where are you people from?"

It was a tense moment. If Frankie told her they were visitors, she would know they were probably a search committee. Frankie looked around at Bill and then back at the lady. "We're not from here. We're visiting."

"Search committee, huh?"

"Well . . ."

"It's okay; don't worry. I'm glad you're here. The sooner we can get rid of Satan's puppet in there, the better off we'll be."

No one responded.

"Maybe y'all can do something with him to turn him around. Lord knows I've prayed about it for over a year now, but he's still in there among us." She crawled off her moped and began to remove her helmet.

Dot asked, "Just what is it about him that makes you say that?"

"Ha! You'll see soon enough. You'll see soon enough." The old lady removed her gloves, placed them in her helmet, and without saying another word started toward the front steps of the church, holding her helmet under her arm.

"What was that all about?" Susie asked, looking around at the others.

"I don't have any earthly idea. I think she's stone-cold crazy," Frankie replied.

"That's what I'm afraid of. What if she says something in church about us being here? This could be a real interesting situation we're getting into," Susie said.

"Well, we're here now. Let's go in and make the best of it." Frankie sounded resigned.

They tried to stagger their approach to the front of the church so as not to be so conspicuous. Matt, Susie, and Travis went in last. Travis quickly scanned the congregation to see where the old lady was sitting. There! He nudged Susie and nodded toward the right side near the back. They quickly turned left and went down about halfway and took their seats. They probably should have sat closer to the back in case something happened and they needed to just get up and leave.

Scanning the bulletin, Travis noticed there was a strange hymn lineup. He didn't think he'd ever sung any of these before. And the prayer of confession was a little overdone. Good grief, this pastor wanted them to confess they were worthless. Travis whispered to himself, "Come on; give me a break." This was not headed toward being a good experience, what with the old lady in the back and the strange hymns and the ripping apart of everybody's self-esteem. They must have missed God's will on this one.

A short man, bald-headed with black horn-rimmed glasses and wearing a black robe with an odd-looking clerical collar, came into the sanctuary from a door on the right side of the choir loft after the choir came in from the left. He walked over to the pulpit area and sat down. Travis remembered that this preacher had gone to school in Scotland, so that would explain the collar deal.

Travis turned around to check out Dot's reaction. He was sure she would be contorting her face and whispering about the minister's bald head and his height. Yep, she was. Oh well, another wasted trip. Maybe the sermon would be good.

Alright, the first hymn was starting.

Travis whispered, "What?"

The tune was so irregular . . . so many sharps. . . . Oh man . . . nobody was singing. Why did they put this stuff in the hymnal? He checked the date on the hymn. Just as he thought—nineteen eighty something. This was one of those hymns added when the southern Presbyterian church merged with the northern Presbyterian church. They put some strangely harmonized song like this in the new hymnal and took out "Onward, Christian Soldiers." Brilliant. Travis bet they hadn't even thought about what the kids in Vacation Bible School would have to sing as they carried the US flag and the Christian flag down the aisle for the opening ceremony each day.

So far, Travis noted nothing special about this preacher other than that he smiled a lot—which, to be honest, was a little annoying. Maybe the old lady was right. After the children's sermon down front—something about sharing—the preacher went back to his seat behind the pulpit.

The choir, rather large in number, stood up for the anthem. The director, a gray-haired lady holding some type of wand, raised her hands (and the wand) high over her head. What came next nearly made Travis jump out of his seat.

The men started the song almost shouting the words and with no musical accompaniment. After about two minutes of that, they fell silent while the women did the same thing. It was like a cadre of drill sergeants scolding the little woman with the wand. Man, these people were intense. They finally finished the musical onslaught and took their seats.

The minister glanced back at them to make sure they were all seated, and then he approached the pulpit. "Today our Old Testament reading is from the book of—"

"Satan!" the old lady shouted, standing up with her index finger pointed at the minister.

"Here we go," Susie said, leaning over and whispering in Travis's ear.

The minister didn't respond, though he did nod toward the ushers. This must have been a familiar signal, because four fairly husky men walked swiftly down the aisle from the rear of the church and converged on the old lady's pew.

But she was ready for them. She began swinging her helmet around her head and looked like she was going to nail one of them any second. "The cross is my defender!"

"Well, that explains the cross on the helmet," Travis muttered to Susie.

"Miss Lettie, please now, come on and go with us," one of the ushers pleaded.

Suddenly, one of the other men grabbed the helmet as it orbited near him and, almost simultaneously, another one grabbed her arm and began pulling her toward the aisle, where the other two could help. The old lady was resisting mightily but to no avail.

About this time Travis began to wonder how the congregation was responding to this scene. He scanned the pews in front of him and over to his left and then to his right. He was shocked to see that no one was even turning around in their seats to watch the commotion. He looked up at the minister. He was just standing there quietly, moving his notes around.

The four men had the old lady now with two of them holding her arms, flanking her, one in front of her, and the other one behind her. They finally reached the narthex and took her outside.

Turning around, Travis looked up at the minister, who was now smiling at the congregation. "For those of you visiting with us today, we welcome you to our place of worship. I offer our sincerest apology for what you have just witnessed.

"Miss Lettie is a dear old soul, but her mind is nearly gone and she has become quite deranged. We all love her very much and do everything we can to help her, but sometimes she causes a stir and we have to escort her out of the sanctuary so that we will be able to worship. Someone is with her in the fellowship hall and will attend to her during the worship service and make sure that she gets home safely.

"Again, please accept our apology for the interruption, but Miss Lettie is part of our church family, and we feel that she should have the opportunity to worship just as we do. Please remember her in your prayers."

Man alive! Talk about a tough situation. Travis wasn't sure his church could put up with that every Sunday. *Hmmph.* Everybody here seemed okay with it, though.

"Today our Old Testament reading is from the book of Genesis, chapter 16, verses 1 through 4. Listen to the Word of God.

"Now Sarai, Abram's wife, had not been able to bear children for him. But she had an Egyptian servant named Hagar. So Sarai said to Abram, 'The Lord has prevented me from having children. Go and sleep with my servant. Perhaps I can have children through her.' . . ."

As the minister continued with the Scripture reading, Travis began to daydream about the possibility of Jenny allowing him to be with another woman. The whole marriage thing was such a big deal to women. It was too bad the multiple-wives deal in the Old Testament wasn't allowed anymore. If it were and if he could get Jenny to agree to it, he could possibly take Susie for his second wife, spending equal time with each one.

Why were women so jealous? It wasn't like he would love either one less. Travis spent a while envisioning himself being a responsible husband for two women. It seemed like it could work, alternating days at each house, cutting the grass, fixing things when they broke, maybe a little romance every now and then. Then an alarm went off in his head—he would have to answer to and take care of *two* women. The one he had right now hardly allowed him a spare moment. Oh boy, it definitely would not work.

Why was he even thinking about this? And in church of all places. It was shameful, possibly blasphemous, and definitely adulterous. He was worse than an unrepentant sinner. What if Jenny knew that he had these thoughts? It would hurt her for sure, but she would also be mad, plenty mad.

He hunched his shoulders forward and felt a hot flash run through his body. He glanced at Susie beside him.

Time to think about something else. He thought about the grocery store and the manager's mentioning it might be time for a raise. If he did get a raise, then maybe he could talk Jenny into letting him get one of those big gas grills on sale at Walmart. Of course, she might want to spend it on painting the kitchen—again. Or maybe buying some garden equipment like a new tiller. Or new clothes. He'd heard a new Goodwill store opened over in Goldsboro and it was just like shopping in a department store. Real nice. He wondered where Susie bought her clothes. They always seemed to fit her so well.

Okay, he needed to think about something else. Maybe they could use the extra money to catch up on their pledge. But that little bit of raise alone wouldn't do it. They needed to cut something out of their budget and catch up again. What could they cut? The once-a-week Ryan's buffet would save about twenty dollars a week. And the cable package could be changed back to the basic package. Between those two things they could catch up by Christmas.

Shoot, he had done it again. The sermon was over and he couldn't tell you one thing about it. Travis looked around to gauge the others' reactions. Bill was nodding off. *Good.* Travis figured they wouldn't hire a guy from Raleigh anyway.

CHAPTER 24

Those who have the gift of celibacy from heaven, so that from the heart or with their whole soul are pure and continent and are not aflame with passion, let them serve the Lord in that calling, as long as they feel endued with that divine gift; and let them not lift up themselves above others, but let them serve the Lord continuously in simplicity and humility (1 Cor. 7:7ff.). For such are more apt to attend to divine things than those who are distracted with the private affairs of a family. But if, again, the gift be taken away, and they feel a continual burning, let them call to mind the words of the apostle: "It is better to marry than to be aflame" (1 Cor. 7:9).

THE BOOK OF CONFESSIONS, PRESBYTERIAN CHURCH (USA):
THE SECOND HELVETIC CONFESSION, 5.245

AFTER MATT ASKED HER OUT ON THAT FIRST DATE, Julia had been stopping by the house on a pretty regular basis. She hit it off right away with his dad, who seemed not to mind her spending so much time there. There was still something about her that Matt couldn't figure out—it was almost like two different people living in the same body. At the house, she was the pretty, relaxed, quiet Julia, but around the truck stop she was the brash, flirtatious, gum-smacking Julia. Maybe it was just a role-playing thing at the truck stop. In any case, it was hard to tell which one was the real Julia.

Matt was in love with the quiet one. Their favorite thing to do together was to sit in the rockers on the front porch after supper and look across the fields at the red-orange sky, just rocking without saying a word. On this particular evening, Matt's dad came out on the front porch and announced that he had to run into town to the Food Lion.

The red taillights on his dad's truck grew smaller as the truck headed toward town. They continued to sit in silence for several minutes. Julia squeezed Matt's hand and stopped rocking.

"What is it?" Matt asked.

"Let's go inside. I'm cold."

"Okay."

After Matt pulled the front door shut, he walked over to the door leading to the kitchen and turned off the overhead light. The only light in the room now was coming in from the kitchen. Then he joined Julia on the couch.

Suddenly, the back door to the kitchen opened.

"Matt? Anybody here?" Matt's dad asked loudly, coming in and standing in the middle of the kitchen.

Matt, getting up quickly, lost his balance and fell onto the floor. Hearing the noise, his dad came running into the front room, flipping on the overhead light as he entered. Julia stood up and was brushing down the front of her blouse. Matt, struggling to stand up, felt the blood rush to his face.

"What is going on?" Matt's dad asked, now standing in the middle of the front room.

"Uh, sorry, Dad. We just didn't expect you back so soon."

Matt couldn't look his dad in the eye. He brushed the front of his pants and glanced over at Julia, noticing that her cheeks were flushed and that she looked confused in addition to being embarrassed.

"I see. Well, I forgot my wallet."

Matt's dad walked out of the room and into his bedroom. Matt heard him shuffling around some change on his dresser. Then he came back into the front room.

"I'll be going now. I'll probably be gone for about forty-five minutes . . . if that's okay."

Matt smiled nervously. He felt the guilt of a fourteen-year-old.

"I need to get going anyway," Julia piped up, looking down at the floor.

Matt's dad walked back through the kitchen and out the door.

Matt sighed. "Yeah . . . right."

• • •

The next morning Matt got up after hearing his dad making coffee in the kitchen. He put on his bathrobe and went in to sit down for breakfast.

"Morning."

"Morning."

"Sorry about last night."

Matt's dad was pouring a cup of coffee and said without turning around, "No problem." A minute later, he added, "So, are you two an item now?"

"I don't know."

Matt's dad took a swig of coffee and turned around. "Nothing wrong with it. She's a nice girl." He took another swig of coffee. "Look, I need your help in a little while getting that disc harrow hooked up."

"Okay, give me a few minutes and I'll be out there."

"Alright," Matt's dad said as he walked out of the kitchen.

Matt headed back to his bedroom and sat down on the side of his bed. The closet door was open and he could see the box in the back of the closet that contained some of his old papers and notes from graduate school. Meaningless. He slid the box out into the room where he could open it. Inside, he saw several black binders of notes from different courses and some floppy disks of data from various bench-scale experiments he had performed. He really needed to throw this stuff out. He reached into the box and moved some of the binders around to see if there was anything worth keeping. Picking up a folder labeled *P. CHEM*, he suddenly remembered the professor who had taught that particular class. White-haired Professor Leeks, grumpy but with a cunning sense of humor.

He opened the folder, and a midquarter exam fell onto the floor. There was a large red A on the front by Matt's name. He didn't remember this exam. The first question was "Summarize, in a paragraph of no more than ten sentences, the Einstein-Podolsky-Rosen (EPR) paradox as discussed in class." Matt flipped the pages to see what he had written for the answer. There it was.

The Einstein-Podolsky-Rosen (EPR) paradox argues
that quantum mechanical theory is incomplete
because it can be shown that two physical quantities
corresponding to noncommuting operators can
be determined with certainty under conditions
that are equivalent to simultaneous measurement.
The argument is based on a system involving two
quantum objects coming together, interacting for a
short time, and then no longer interacting. . . .

Matt had written in the margin, "End of official answer.
Unofficial comments beyond the ten-sentence limit are given
on the back of this page." Matt turned the page over.

On second thought, and considering my
nonrelevantistic (pun intended) position in the
quantum mechanical field (or are we assuming
no field?), I've decided to record my additional
comments in a parallel universe where points cannot
be subtracted for going beyond the ten-sentence
limit. Of course, I could be in trouble if you believe
in the nonlocal ontological connection. . . .

Matt stared at the paper and smiled. Even in discussing the
cornerstone of modern physics, the southerner's curse of nar-
cissistic oratory bubbled to the surface. But he had actually
written that answer and those words and now . . . all he had
was a vague memory of Professor Leeks standing in front of

the class, leaning against the chalkboard, discussing something about Schrödinger's equation. That's all that was left. It saddened him to think all of that was gone, and with little or no chance of return. That part of his life had vanished, standing still while the masses of PhDs continued on, in constant pursuit of the next physics milestone, hoping to get their names etched in the history books. He briefly entertained the thought of returning to that world. Could he make it? Maybe, but the real question was, would he want to? He couldn't be sure about it.

CHAPTER 25

Keep on asking, and you will receive what you ask for. Keep on seeking,
and you will find. Keep on knocking, and the door will be opened
to you. For everyone who asks, receives. Everyone who seeks, finds.
And to everyone who knocks, the door will be opened.

MATTHEW 7:7-8

REV. JOHN HAYNESWORTH looked at his watch. Three o'clock.
Still nothing on paper. This interim-pastor assignment was
getting harder every week. And stewardship season was on the
horizon. Not exactly the type of subject that inspired people.

John sighed and looked around the room. The church
had rented one of five efficiencies at the local motel, the Blue
Vista Motor Lodge, for him until they found a new minister.
The efficiency that had been provided for him was a little
too efficient. One room, a sink, a stove and refrigerator, both
olive green, in the back corner on top of a small square patch

of bright-green linoleum. In the opposite corner, a shower and a toilet. A folding bamboo screen partially hid the toilet from view, but you could see it from the kitchen area. A fold-down bed, a thirteen-inch television set on a small table—no cable. A wingback chair covered in gold cloth with little American eagles forming a striped pattern, a borrowed desk, and brown indoor-outdoor carpet. An amateurish painting on the wall of a sea captain, head and shoulders, in yellow rain gear, smoking a pipe. A window-mounted air conditioner that sounded like a turboprop when you turned it on. One light. Actually, a single lightbulb with a pull chain, mounted to the ceiling. He should have opted for the housing allowance. Oh well. At least it was quiet most of the time.

He still wasn't sure what he was doing here. God's will? These people had no way of knowing his past, not that it was important. Shallotte, North Carolina—where was that? Only child, lifelong bachelor, no family remaining now; it was easy to not have any roots anywhere. Bachelorhood was not a conscious choice as much as it was just never having the opportunity to develop a relationship with a woman.

Well, not really. There was Ann Lingerfelt in the eleventh grade. She hadn't necessarily been pretty, but she wasn't ugly either. He could never figure out why she'd asked him to the prom. She'd lived with her mom, who had cystic fibrosis, in a trailer on Highway 130 about three miles west of town. She was a little too forward, but not in a bad way. She'd even brought him flowers once. Thank God no one had seen that—high school humiliation lasted for life.

Ann's dad was a drunk, and one day he had disappeared with no explanation. A year later, her mom received a letter from Jacksonville, Florida, saying that he had started a new life with someone else. Ann had stayed with her mother after graduation and took care of her for as long as John had stayed in touch. She'd never married, as far as he knew, and never left Shallotte.

She would have made a good wife, graceful and polite, the sort a congregation prescribes for their minister. But bachelorhood had somehow arrived at his doorstep early on and, meeting no resistance, eventually came to be the distinguishing characteristic that everyone remembered about him. Ann Lingerfelt . . . he hadn't thought about her in a long time.

The telephone began to ring and it startled him. In this one-room apartment, it sounded like a fire alarm. He picked up the old-fashioned receiver. "Hello?"

"Reverend?"

"Yes."

"This is Matt Fischer."

"Hello, Matt. What can I do for you?"

"Well, I would like to talk with you in private about something. A personal matter."

"I see. Well, I have some time available tomorrow afternoon. I'll be at the church office. Can it wait until then?"

"Yes, that will be alright. I'll see you then."

"Okay, I'll be looking for you."

"Okay. Good-bye."

"Bye." John hung up the phone. Matt Fischer. Some type of scientist, he recalled, living at home with his dad. Wasn't he on the search committee? Yes, he was. John couldn't recall having spoken with him before.

Ann Lingerfelt. What had become of her? She had wanted to be a flight attendant—a stewardess, as they were called back then. He remembered her talking about it. She had never flown but thought flying around the country and visiting different cities would be *so* exciting. And she thought the uniforms were so pretty and colorful. Like many high school dreams, it didn't seem so far-fetched at the time.

John's dream had been to become a doctor. After all, in high school he was smart, had a scholarship to attend Davidson, and wanted to help people. It seemed like a good plan. Organic chemistry at Davidson changed all of that.

And Shallotte. Shallotte had been a vibrant small town when he was growing up. The whole town would show up for the Christmas parade and football games. The football team had been state champions when he was a junior in high school. Every boy was expected to play. John had tried out but hadn't made it. Too small.

And his classmates . . . all white. There were no African Americans in his class or even in the entire high school. No, actually, there was one. James Davis rode on the same school bus as John, but John got off before he did, so he never really knew where James had lived. Shallotte . . . He hadn't been back in at least thirty years, and the last time was for his mother's funeral, which was poorly attended. Several people had spoken to him at the graveside service but he had not recognized anyone. His father had died much earlier. He had no other family there.

John recalled how much he had wanted to leave that small-town culture behind when he was in high school. Ann Lingerfelt had wanted to leave too. He had. She hadn't.

• • •

The next day John kept the door to his office open as he worked on his sermon. The church secretary didn't work on Wednesdays, so he wanted to be able to hear people coming in. Nonetheless, he was startled when he heard a voice from the doorway.

"Excuse me, Rev. Haynesworth?"

John looked up. *Must be Matt.* "You scared me. I didn't hear you come in." He stood up and extended his hand. "And call me John."

"Okay." Matt stepped over to shake his hand. After an awkward silence, he said, "Uh, I need to talk with you about something personal."

"Okay, I'll keep it in confidence. Have a seat. I'm the only one here."

Matt closed the door and sat in one of the two metal folding chairs in front of John's desk.

John moved his sermon notes aside and sat back in his chair. "Matt, before we get started, tell me a little about yourself. I'm trying to get to know folks here a little better. Part of the job." He smiled.

"Okay, let's see, where to start? Well, I suppose I'll give you the quick tour. I live with my dad right now. I have a PhD in material science and was working at the National Institute of Standards and Technology in Washington, DC, until I got fired. So I came home."

"Why did you get fired?"

"Well . . . I just lost all interest in my work. I was doing R&D on semiconductor fabrication. Now I know my doldrums were really my depression in overdrive. I had a dark cloud hovering over me constantly. Couldn't think straight. I had been told to get some help but I didn't listen. So I got fired."

"You have a problem with depression?"

"Diagnosed as chronic depression, but it seems to be more prevalent on weekends than during the week, and it's not every weekend."

John said, "Lots of people deal with depression. Are you taking any medication?"

"Yes, about 400 milligrams of Wellbutrin every day. It's not working as good as it once did, but I haven't been back to my therapist to get it changed."

"Maybe you should do that," John said.

"Yes, I know. And I will. But that's not what I wanted to talk about."

"Oh, I'm sorry. What is it, then?"

"It's just something I can't figure out."

"What's that?"

"Well—and this may sound juvenile, even laughable, I guess—I just can't figure out what I'm supposed to do with my life. I'm thirty-two years old. I was on an academic path for so long. It was hard to do, but it was easy to know what to do. Now . . . now I don't even know if I'm supposed to be on a path."

John looked at Matt for a few seconds. "So you need a burning bush?"

Matt grinned. "Yes, that would help."

"So do I," John said. "I suppose we all do. Matt, I don't have an answer for you. The good thing, though, is that you're asking the question. You know what? I *do* have an answer for you and it's this." He shook his head. "Hey, I'm teaching myself a lesson now. You need to be open to whatever God's will is for you. When or how it's revealed to you is not something you can control, though." He chuckled. "I need to write this down for a sermon idea. Thanks for stopping by!"

"Do you really believe God reveals his will to us, or do we just try to do the right thing and it seems like that is God's will?"

"Wow, these are hard questions. I need to get my seminary notes out," John said. "Just kidding. I think that a lot of people probably do the latter, and all things considered, it's not a bad thing. It just might not be what God had in mind for them. It's hard to know."

"So do you think what you're doing is God's will for your life?"

"Wait a minute; you're the one asking for help, not me." John laughed. Then he considered the question. "I hope it is. It's not a bad miss if it isn't."

Matt said, "So I need to be on the lookout for God's revelation of his will for my life. What about all those people who are killed in accidents and for no apparent reason? What if I'm one of them?"

"Don't know. There are many things that just can't be explained. But you're a scientist. Do you have a hard time believing all the things that most folks believe without questioning?"

"Yes and no. I see God everywhere. What's hard to believe is that Jesus is the Son of God. It doesn't seem like the God who created the universe would be that tangible. It's not logical."

"Hang on while I write that down. Another sermon idea!" John grabbed a pen and made a note. "Yes, that would be where Jesus comes in. That's the message of the Crucifixion. The tangible part."

Matt leaned back in his chair and crossed his arms. "We're being honest here, right?"

John nodded.

"Okay, so can I ask you an honest question?"

John nodded again but felt some tension in his chest.

"Why didn't you ever marry?" Matt said. "If that's too personal, just say so."

"No, that's okay." John took a deep breath. "It turns out I ask myself the same question sometimes. I don't know. I just never got into a relationship with a woman in that way." John thought about Ann Lingerfelt again.

"Me either," Matt said. "There is this girl, though, I've been seeing. We don't have much in common except maybe a feeling that we need each other. At least that's the way I see it. We're just such an odd couple, a PhD reject and a truck-stop waitress. I guess that's what I *really* wanted to talk about. I'm afraid to get too serious if there's no way it would work out. I mean, is there a way to know if this is right or not?"

John sighed. "I should tell you to pray about it. Other than that, I can't help you. You might as well ask me how to build a nuclear reactor. I'm as confused about intimate relationships as you are. I *can* say, though, from performing a lot of marriage ceremonies, that I've seen all kinds of couples. Some who appear to be right for each other end up not being able to make it work, and others who seemed like they didn't stand a chance are still going strong. So I don't think you can call it from the beginning."

"I mean, we're not even thinking about getting married. It's nowhere near that point yet. I just don't want to go down that road if it's not going to work."

"Wish I could help you there, but I can't."

Matt stood up. John rose and shook his hand.

"Okay, well, thanks for nothing," Matt said, laughing.

John smiled. "Glad to be of service!"

Matt left. John sat down and looked at his watch. It was four o'clock. If he left now he could make it to Shallotte by seven, ride around and find a cheap place to spend the night. Maybe the Twilight Motel was still open. Tomorrow he could take all day to look around town. He scribbled something on a Post-it note and put it in the church secretary's in-box.

• • •

John sped right by Shallotte. He was on Highway 17 and missed the turnoff. He had driven to Grissettown before he figured out he had passed it. There was a good reason, though, for his error. Highway 17 was now a four-lane highway, whereas it used to go through the middle of Shallotte. In fact, it had been Main Street. Nowadays, a person had to pay attention to see the sign indicating the exit from the four-lane to go through Shallotte. He made his way back to town and, much to his delight, the Twilight was actually still in business. A Walmart Supercenter was behind it where there had once been a tall pine forest. He had noticed a Hampton Inn on the four-lane bypassing Shallotte, but the Twilight suited the purpose of his trip.

After checking in, he got back in his car to drive around town and see if he recognized anything. The first thing he noticed across the street from the Twilight was a mini-mall of sorts with a Home Depot, a Belk department store, and a hodgepodge of other businesses. That was new. In the parking lot near the road was a McDonald's and a Burger King. He recalled when the first Hardee's opened in town. Just down the road, the old Gate gas station—cheapest gas in town—had been remodeled and was now a Kangaroo. He recalled that it had put Mr. Woody's Shell station out of business just a few years after it opened.

He drove on slowly. Ah, he recognized the building that had been Russell's Burger Barn. Best chili cheeseburgers anywhere back in the day. Looked like it was a used-car dealership now. Luke's Tire Service, a local landmark, appeared to still be in business. Going a little farther he recognized the old house that had been Doc Wardlaw's office. Across from that was the heating-oil distributor, apparently still run by the Hewitts. On the right was the old drugstore building; now it appeared to be some kind of insurance agency. Someone had painted the old bank building a light blue and it was some sort of nondenominational church. Wow, that was different. Brunson's Tire Store—gone. Ben Franklin five-and-dime—gone. Parker's Department Store—gone, replaced by a Family Dollar. Kimball's Hardware, practically an institution when John was growing up, was now an antiques store. Across the street, the Methodist church was still going strong. That was good.

John crossed the bridge over the Shallotte River, recalling the days he spent navigating its convoluted path through acres and acres of marsh grass toward the Intracoastal Waterway on a gray wooden johnboat powered by a twenty-five-horsepower Evinrude. John had learned to ski behind that boat. Needless to say, it had taken a long time for the small motor to pull him up out of the water. But he had done it. And so had his best friend, Pete. The boat belonged to Pete, who was killed in an automobile accident several years after graduating from high school. John remembered that funeral well.

Driving on, he saw that the strip mall where Bud's Barber Shop, the dentist's office, and Nick's Jewelry Store had been was now a different structure altogether with businesses he didn't recognize. Beyond that, the old Red and White grocery store was now a Food Lion and appeared to be a lot bigger. There was the little Presbyterian church on the corner where John and his parents had attended. The red brick that John remembered had been painted white. Back then his minister, Rev. Harris, had talked to him about going to Richmond for seminary after college. Said the church needed more young men entering the ministry. At the time, John had no interest in doing that. In fact, he had little interest in church at all. His main goal was to get out of Shallotte, become a doctor, and go live in a big city where he could remain socially anonymous. It was not to be, though. He smiled.

Well, that was about it. He saw other stores farther south along 17 but nothing he would recognize other than the armory, and that was still there. He turned the car around in a bank parking lot and headed back to the Twilight. In his room, he looked through the phone book for familiar names. He recognized many of the last names but not the first names they were paired with. And no listing for Lingerfelt. As he lay in bed that night, he wondered why he had come back. It had been an uncharacteristically spontaneous decision. And who would he talk to the next day? What would people think of him asking the whereabouts of former acquaintances? He was out on a limb here. Why?

• • •

John checked out of the Twilight Motel at 8 a.m. and drove to McDonald's to get a cup of coffee and a sausage biscuit. It was Thursday, so John thought there was a good chance he might recognize some locals. Not the usual weekend beach traffic. No luck; he didn't recognize a soul. He finished his breakfast and drove to Hewitt's Heating Oil. From the parking area he could see through the glass front of the small redbrick office building. He saw a man who appeared to be in his thirties standing behind the counter and an older woman sitting beside him. An electronic chime sounded as he opened the door. The man and woman had already been looking at him as he approached the building.

"Yes, sir, can we help you?" the man asked.

John hesitated. "Uh, maybe so."

The man and woman stared at him.

"I grew up in Shallotte and haven't been back in a long time and I'm trying to find someone."

"Who you looking for?" the man said.

"Well, I'm not really sure."

They looked at him suspiciously.

John said, "What I mean is I'm trying to find someone I might have known when I lived here, you know, to talk about old times and who is still alive and who's dead and where everyone ended up. Like I said, I've lost touch with anyone who might have been here then."

The woman said, "I was here. What's your name?"

"Haynesworth, John Haynesworth."

"I didn't know any Haynesworths. Did you have other family here?"

"Uh, no. My parents both passed on long ago, and I haven't really had any reason to come back."

The man started fiddling with some paperwork and turned away.

The woman said, "Can you think of any other names from back then?"

John shook his head. "No, I can't. . . . Well, there is one: Lingerfelt. Did you know any Lingerfelts?"

"There was an old lady in a wheelchair named Lingerfelt. She's dead, though. Is that who you're talking about?"

"Yes! Yes, that's the mother. What about her daughter, Ann?"

The man turned and looked at John suspiciously again.

The woman said, "Oh yes, I remember her. Used to see her pushing her mama around in that wheelchair. . . . I don't know where she is now, though. Come to think of it, I haven't seen her since her mama died. She might've left town."

"Oh . . . I see."

"I'll tell you who you need to talk to. You need to go see Toy."

"Who?"

"Toy. Runs Toy's Beauty Salon down there by the Food Lion. If anybody knows, it'll be Toy."

"How's that?"

"From fixing everybody's hair, for one thing. But she also fixes the hair of everybody who dies for Sadler's Funeral Home. She sees and knows everything that goes on in this town."

John smiled. "Thanks so much. Especially for talking to a stranger."

"No bother. Hope you find who you're looking for. That Lingerfelt woman . . . I'm sure I haven't seen her since her mama passed."

"Okay. Well, thanks anyway," John said and opened the door, "Have a good day."

The woman nodded.

John hopped into his car. The woman had said "that Lingerfelt woman." That meant she hadn't married. Maybe.

Toy's Beauty Salon was actually a double-wide trailer that had been converted to a salon complete with four chairs, three occupied, with sinks and mirrors behind them, where Toy or one of the other stylists cut women's hair. Two women sat in hair-dryer chairs at right angles to each other in one corner, and one wall had white shelves stocked with various hair-care products for women. The floor was covered with white-and-black checkered linoleum and the walls were painted peach. As he entered, all seven of the women in the salon stopped and stared at John as if he were a Jehovah's Witness.

John smiled and said, "Hi, is Toy here?"

An older lady with jet-black dyed hair wearing a white laboratory coat said in a nasal voice, "I'm Toy. What can I do for you?"

"Oh, hello. I'm John Haynesworth. A lady up the road at Hewitt's Heating Oil told me that you might know the whereabouts of someone I'm looking for."

"You must've been talking to Aileen. About my age? Sitting behind the counter?"

"Yes, that's right. She said you might know where Ann Lingerfelt is."

"Lingerfelt? You mean the old lady in the wheelchair?"

"I think that would be her mother. As I understand it, Ann took care of her mother."

"Oh, you mean the daughter. You know, she and her mama kept to themselves. Hardly anybody knew them. I don't know what's become of her. You're the first person to ask about them. Are you a relative?"

"No, I grew up here and went to high school with Ann."

Toy raised her eyebrows. "You're not one of them Facebook stalkers, are you?"

John blushed. "No, I actually don't do Facebook. I haven't been back here in so long I just wanted to talk to someone I knew when I was here."

One of the older ladies sitting in a styling chair leaned forward and said, "When did you graduate?"

"Uh, 1970."

"I know you."

John was startled.

She said, "You were a senior when I was a freshman. I remember your name. You were smart, right?"

"I don't know about that. I made good grades, though, if that's what you mean."

"Yeah, I remember you."

"I'm sorry; I don't know your name," John said.

"Norma, Norma Leonard."

"Well, it's nice to meet you, Ms. Leonard. You wouldn't

happen to know anything about Ann Lingerfelt, would you?"

"No. She and her mama didn't have much money. I think her mama got a disability check and Ann had a job, part-time maybe, at the sock factory before it closed. But when her mama died, she sold that little single-wide trailer they lived in. It's not even there anymore."

"I see. Do you recall who the Realtor might have been?"

"It probably would've been Louise Babson back then. Coastal Real Estate was the biggest real estate outfit around. But that was at least fifteen years ago."

"Is Ms. Babson still around?"

"Oh yes. She's in that fancy assisted-living complex near Holiday Acres."

"Holiday Acres?"

"Yes, just off the road to Holden Beach. Right there at Red Bug."

"What's Red Bug?"

Toy and another lady laughed. Toy said, "You never heard of Red Bug and you grew up here?"

"No, can't say I remember that."

Norma Leonard continued, "All you do is get on 130 toward the beach and it's about two miles past the Moose lodge."

"Okay, I think I do remember the Moose lodge," John said. "Is there a sign for the assisted-living center?"

The woman said, "Complex. Assisted-living *complex* is what they call it. The name is Tidewater Village Assisted-Living

Complex. We call it the TVA." She laughed and several of the women chuckled in support.

John said, "Well, I sure do appreciate your help. Maybe Ms. Babson will be able to tell me something about Ann Lingerfelt." John left with all the women still staring at him.

He got back in his car and sat for a moment. What was he doing? What would he do if he actually found Ann anyway? This little detective day trip was getting out of hand. It was nonsensical. He started the car and drove to Red Bug.

The Tidewater Village Assisted-Living Complex was indeed fancy. The front of it looked more like a hotel entrance than an assisted-living place. He parked his car and went into the lobby, where two white-haired elderly women sat side by side, manning an antique desk.

"May we help you?"

"Yes, I'm looking for Ms. Louise Babson."

"Louise? There's only one Louise around here and she'll talk your head off." Both women laughed.

The other woman ran her finger down a list of residents and said, "She's in C wing, room 304. I need to see your driver's license."

John pulled out his wallet and gave the lady his license.

She looked at it and said, "John Haynesworth. I don't know any Haynesworths. Are you from this area?" She didn't look up while waiting for John to answer. Instead she was copying his driver's license number into the visitor log.

"A long time ago. I'm just trying to track down an old acquaintance."

"Oh, really? And is that Louise?" the other lady asked. "She seems a little old for you." Both women cackled again.

"No, no, not her. Actually, I'm looking for a lady named Ann Lingerfelt. Someone told me Ms. Babson may know where she is."

The two elderly women looked at each other. Then one looked at John and said, "Did you say Ann Lingerfelt?"

"Yes, I did. That's who I'm looking for."

"Well, that's easy. She's a nurse's assistant on D wing, where we live. She's a sweet, sweet person." Both ladies looked at John. The one who had taken down his driver's license number handed the card back to him. "Did she know you were coming?"

John felt his heart beating. "No. She doesn't know. Are you kidding me? She's really here? I had no idea. I was just going to see Ms. Babson and—"

"So I guess you're not interested in seeing Louise anymore, then?"

"No, I won't need to do that now. Tell me, how can I get in touch with Ann?"

One of the ladies pointed and said, "Well, there she is right now coming across the parking lot on her way to work."

John spun around and saw a slender woman with gray hair coming directly toward him. She wore a white uniform— a blouse and slacks—carried a pocketbook over her shoulder, and walked with the gait of a much younger woman. She was not plain looking; she was pretty. He said to the two ladies at the desk, "Excuse me."

He stepped outside and met Ann walking toward the building entrance.

"Ann?"

The woman stopped and stared at John. She said slowly, "Yes?"

"Ann Lingerfelt?"

"Yes. Who are you?"

John smiled and said, "John Haynesworth. Do you remember me?"

Ann looked puzzled. "John Haynesworth? From high school?"

"Yeah, that's right. It's me. I've tracked you down!"

Ann just stared at John. "I can't believe it. I just can't believe it. Is it really you?"

"Yes. I can't believe it either!" He walked up to her and hugged her. She hugged him back.

"This is unbelievable," she said. "How . . . I mean, what are you doing back here, and why were you even looking for me?"

John laughed. "I don't know why. I just was. This is wonderful. There's so much to talk about." He stood back and looked at her. Ann shook her head in disbelief.

Then John remembered. "Oh, you have to go to work."

They turned and looked at the glass entrance doors, where both of the elderly ladies were standing, grinning at them.

John said, "Those two are a mess."

"Aren't they, though?"

"Look, what time do you get off? Can you go to dinner tonight?"

"Yes, sure. This is all so unbelievable. I never thought I'd see you again. And here you are! Yes, I can go to dinner. My shift here is over at 6 p.m."

"Okay, I'll be waiting for you and we can just go from here."

"I need to change out of this first!" Ann laughed.

"Oh, okay. Well, I'll follow you home and wait in the car for you."

"Okay, that's great."

Ann hugged John again. She shook her head as she walked toward the entrance, where the two elderly ladies were probably waiting to quiz her about John.

CHAPTER 26

Among all creatures, angels and men are most excellent. Concerning angels, Holy Scripture declares: "Who makest the winds thy messengers, fire and flame thy ministers" (Ps. 104:4). Also it says: "Are they not all ministering spirits sent forth to serve, for the sake of those who are to obtain salvation?" (Heb. 1:14). Concerning the devil, the Lord Jesus himself testifies: "He was a murderer from the beginning, and has nothing to do with the truth, because there is no truth in him. When he lies, he speaks according to his own nature, for he is a liar and the father of lies" (John 8:44).

THE BOOK OF CONFESSIONS, PRESBYTERIAN CHURCH (USA):
THE SECOND HELVETIC CONFESSION, 5.033

FRANKIE WAS EXHAUSTED. All of this traveling was starting to wear on her. She finished her cup of Sleepytime tea and put the cup on the floor beside her rocker. She was too tired to walk to the kitchen and put it in the sink. Instead, she slowly got up from the rocker and shuffled toward the bedroom. Walking through the den, she saw that George had fallen asleep in the La-Z-Boy recliner watching another History Channel special.

"George."

No response.

Frankie spoke louder. "George!"

George jerked his head up and looked around. "What? What is it?"

"I'm going to bed."

"Oh, okay. I'll be there in a moment."

"You'd better go on and get up now so you don't sleep all night in that chair. You remember what happened to your back the last time you did that."

"Yeah, alright, I'll be there in a minute."

Frankie continued down the hall to the bedroom and turned the light on. Maybe she could read a bit more of that book on Eleanor Roosevelt before she went to sleep. Frankie picked up the book and pulled the covers back. Crawling into bed, she heard George snore in the den. *Oh well, it'll be his own fault.*

Frankie turned on the bedside light. *Let's see . . . "Eleanor Roosevelt, a woman for all time." . . . Maybe so, but she was definitely not a woman for all men; there must have been some serious money behind that marriage.* However, Eleanor did forge ahead with her own life even when she knew her husband was cheating on her. There was something to be said for that. The world needed more strong women, for sure, but this book was just not drawing her in.

Frankie dropped the book over the side of the bed and pulled the covers up to her neck. Closing her eyes, she drifted off and . . . found herself running, a little girl running through the ruins of a village that had been bombed. A dark-gray sky was overhead. She was wearing her favorite Sunday dress. Frankie jumped into a hole behind some concrete rubble.

Her white dress had gray smudges on it. Mama was going to say something about that. Peering out of the hole, she saw World War II–looking soldiers running past her. Some were riding motorcycles with sidecars. There were mounds of dirt among the piles of concrete rubble that had footpaths worn into them. Everyone was running from something, something that was unstoppable, destroying everything in its path. Frankie heard it coming behind the soldiers. It sounded like metal grinding and clicking on metal, squeaking, scraping, and moving toward her. She looked around for a better place to hide. There—in that building over there with the walls that were pockmarked from machine-gun fire. The noise was getting louder: concrete crunching, metal squeaking, rumbling, and shaking the ground.

Her brother, Davie, appeared in the door of the building. "Frankie, come on; hurry up!"

She stood up to run to the building but her body just didn't have any energy. She was moving so slow. If only she could just lie down for a little while and take a rest.

"Frankie, run! It's right behind you!"

Frankie tried to answer but now she couldn't even talk. What was wrong? Some type of force was holding her back, making her tired. She got down on her hands and knees and tried to crawl to the building. Davie wasn't standing there anymore. Something behind her grabbed her braided ponytail and kept her from crawling. Frankie tried to pull her head from its grip but it was too strong. She felt herself being pulled backward and thought about how her dress was getting all dirty.

Suddenly, Davie appeared with a piece of iron pipe about four feet long and began to strike whatever was pulling her back. She watched as he swung with all his might, grunting with each strike. Whatever was holding her released its grip and she just sat still with her legs straight out in front of her.

"Frankie, get up! Run!"

Frankie started crawling again toward the building. Looking back over her shoulder, she saw Davie lying still on the ground with blood on his forehead. Then she felt something massive breathing hard just behind her. She turned around and—

"Why didn't you wake me up?"

"What?" Frankie propped up on her elbows, startled, as George walked over to the closet.

"I thought you would get me up before you went to bed."

"I did. Don't you remember? You wouldn't get up, so I just left you there."

George didn't say anything and kicked his bedroom slippers into the closet. Frankie fell back onto her pillow and stared at the ceiling.

"I had another bad one."

George walked over to the bed and stood beside it, looking down at Frankie. "Maybe it was that ravioli we had for dinner."

"Yeah, that's probably what did it."

George turned off the bedside light and crawled into bed beside Frankie. He rolled over and patted Frankie's gray head. "It's okay, baby. Let's get some rest."

Frankie closed her eyes.

CHAPTER 27

So the LORD must wait for you to come to him so he can show you his love and compassion. For the LORD is a faithful God. Blessed are those who wait for his help.

ISAIAH 30:18

BACK TO CHARLOTTE. Not to see the first guy again, who Dot thought was ugly, but to check out an associate minister who was looking for his own church. They had been on the road now for nearly an hour and everybody was wide awake, looking out the windows through the fog, at fields that had already been harvested.

It was too quiet. Nobody was talking, so Travis reached over and turned on the radio. A rap station just happened to be tuned in, but after a few beats Travis was able to quickly adjust the tuner to something that would be more appropriate.

Problem was he didn't know what kind of music everybody listened to. Country would be a good guess, but Joyce, Matt, and maybe Susie might not like that. Same for oldies. Definitely no rock. Now Travis was beginning to wonder what had moved him to turn on the radio in the first place.

Bill, sensing his quandary, spoke up. "Let's listen to some good old Sunday-morning gospel music, Travis."

"Yeah, that sounds good to me," Frankie chimed in.

"A lot of soul music and even some rap has its roots in gospel singing," Matt offered from the back of the van. Nobody responded. Matt pulled an iPod out of a small duffel bag he brought on this trip and put in the headphones.

"See if you can get that gospel station over in Dunn on AM," Bill said. "They play that old stuff."

Travis switched over to AM and immediately noticed the buzzing sound between stations as he turned the dial. He hadn't listened to AM since he didn't know when. It made him recall his younger days, when he and Jimmy went with Jimmy's dad—Travis's uncle—to the out-of-town high school football games. They would be driving home at night, and Jimmy rode up front while Travis was in the backseat of the old bluish-gray 1970 Pontiac Tempest his uncle had fixed up. Travis would lie down flat across the bench seat with his feet barely touching the other side of the car. His uncle would have one hand on the steering wheel and, leaning over with the other hand, would turn the AM dial so slow that it looked like he was adjusting the controls on some laboratory instrument. Stations would pop up and then disappear or give way to stations with a stronger signal. The buzzing sound was always there, though, until he could land right on a station with a strong signal. Travis would lie on his back and look up and out the side window at the stars moving through the pine treetops. Then he would close his eyes and go to sleep to the buzzing of the AM radio and the hum of the engine. Travis hadn't yet found a more comfortable way to go to sleep. He remembered being upset when he hit a growth spurt and couldn't stretch all the way out on the backseat. The memory was still clear as day to him.

"I think it's around 1510 somewhere," Bill said while looking at Travis's hand turning the knob.

Finally, he found a recognizable gospel music station and Bill, looking over at the radio, said, "That's it. Leave it there."

The radio announcer was saying, "Thank you for joining us this Sunday morning for the *Carolina Gospel Hour*. We have a great lineup this morning and we're going to start it out with the Singing Burkes and their runaway hit, 'Lord, Tell Momma.'"

"Ha!" Frankie blurted out. "'Lord, Tell Momma'? I've got to hear this one."

The song started out with a piano introduction and then a Tennessee-sounding tenor voice began singing, using an echo sound effect. It really was a good sound. Everybody got quiet and listened to the song. It was all about some guy thinking his momma was this wonderful Christian saint, like she could even walk on water when he was a kid, and how she always prayed for him. So now, apparently, this guy had gotten saved, and his momma was already in heaven, so he was asking the Lord to tell her that her prayers were finally answered.

Travis glanced around at the end of the song to get everybody's reaction. To his surprise, Frankie's eyes were moist, as were Dot's, Susie's, and Joyce's. Women would cry over anything. It was a pretty song, though.

There was a period of silence on the radio station following the song. Maybe the DJ had to use the bathroom or something. During the silence everyone turned around to look at Matt in the backseat. His head was leaning back, rocking from side to side, his eyes were closed . . . and he was singing, ever so quietly, in a high falsetto voice, something about a pretty, pretty, pretty, pretty girl. Hardly a Sunday-morning gospel song. But he sure got everyone's attention.

Finally, he opened his eyes and, blushing for the first time that Travis knew of, saw everyone looking at him. "Oh . . . sorry."

"What were you singing?" Dot inquired.

"Oh, just some Rolling Stones, that's all. You know, 'Beast of Burden.'"

"'Beast of Burden'? No, I don't know. Sounds like some kind of occult something."

Susie blurted out a one-syllable laugh.

"And you like that music?" Dot went on.

"Well, yeah. It's classic rock 'n' roll. I grew up with it."

"I guess that explains a few things," Dot replied, turning around in her seat, shaking her head with a frown.

The radio announcer started up again. "Friends, welcome! Praise God, hallelujah! We want to start off the hour by honoring those who have gone to be with the Lord. Hallelujah, praise God! Someday we will all cross that river, hallelujah! And there will be great rejoicing, praise God! And let's not forget to thank Powell Funeral Home, located here in town on Broad Street, which so generously sponsors the reading of the obituaries."

Then in another voice they heard, "At Powell Funeral Home, we stand above the rest, because we believe the most important service we provide is excellent body preparation. We know you expect it, and we deliver it. We make sure that the funeral experience is one that is reverent *and* memorable. When you need our services to take special care of a loved one, feel free to drop by and talk with us about our platinum plan. Financing is available on-site."

The first voice came back on. "That's right, folks—Powell Funeral Home has been serving our community for over twenty-two years. Your patronage will be greatly appreciated. Now for our daily obituaries.

"Mr. Fred Griffin went to be with the Lord on Monday evening after a heart attack at home. He was sixty-eight. His wife preceded him in death last year. Mr. Griffin is survived by a son, Tom, who lives in Aurora; a daughter, Ann, who lives in Dunn; and brothers Bill and Tom, both of whom live in Fuquay-Varina with their families. Arrangements have been made with Powell Funeral Home, and visitation will be tonight at eight o'clock at the Powell Funeral Home chapel. All family friends are invited to drop by and pay your respects. Memorials are asked to be given in lieu of flowers to the Bethel Methodist men's Sunday school class's Fred Griffin Memorial Fund for Burn Victims.

"Next, we have Mrs. Arlene Heath. Mrs. Heath passed away on Tuesday morning. She was eighty-six. She was preceded in death by her husband, Ray, three years ago this coming Monday. Funeral arrangements have been made with Parker Funeral Services.

"Next, we have Mr. Gordon Simmons. Mr. Simmons left us on Wednesday afternoon following some lung cancer complications. He was fifty-three. Mr. Simmons is survived by his wife, Earlene; two sons, John and James; a daughter, Connie; a sister, Doris; and two brothers, Mr. Bill Simmons of Tarboro and Mr. Danny Simmons of Pinetops. Funeral arrangements have been made with Powell Funeral Home, and visitation will be tomorrow night at seven o'clock. All family and friends are invited to drop by and pay respects. In lieu of flowers, the family asks that memorials be made to Carolina Hospice.

"The last one for today is Mrs. Viola Robinson. Mrs. Robinson passed away in her sleep on Wednesday evening and went to be with the Lord. She was seventy-seven. Mrs. Robinson was preceded in death by her husband, Bob, who died of a respiratory illness six years ago. Mrs. Robinson has no survivors. She was a twenty-seven-year pin recipient for perfect Sunday school attendance at Mt. Olive Baptist Church, where she played the organ and served as the church financial secretary for the past twenty-two years.

Mrs. Robinson was a noted collector of dessert recipes and was a significant contributor to the Mt. Olive Baptist Church dinner cookbook titled *Dinner-on-the-Ground Favorites*. A friend of Mrs. Robinson's has indicated that it was Mrs. Robinson's wish that, in the event of her death, donations be made to the church operating fund in lieu of flowers for her funeral. Powell Funeral Home was in charge of the funeral yesterday at Mt. Olive Baptist Church, and cars were lined up on the road all the way to Donny Smith's mailbox. It was one of the biggest funerals we've had this year.

"That's all for today. Please join us tomorrow at the same time for the reading of the obituaries. Now, let's go back to our music program, praise God! And listen to some good southern gospel tunes, hallelujah! Let's start it off with the Singing Cookes and 'Six Hours on the Cross.' Praise God!"

Dot broke the silence. "Good heavens, you reckon anybody's gonna be left by spring? Sounds like they're dying off pretty fast in that town."

"Makes you wonder, doesn't it?" Frankie added, smiling.

Bill reached over and turned the volume down slightly. "Hey, y'all want to stop at the Wadesboro Hardee's again?"

"Sure, I could use a cup of coffee," Susie said.

. . .

The associate minister they were going to hear was married with two kids. His current church was located right in town in an older neighborhood that was obviously going through a transition. This church was probably out in the country when it was built, but now it was surrounded by a neighborhood of seventies-looking houses—all that dark-wood stuff—and two apartment complexes. Across the street was an even older neighborhood with small brick ranch-style houses. A little farther down the road was an old Kmart that had been shut down and now had weeds growing up through cracks in the asphalt parking lot. Travis thought they needed to clean that up; it didn't look good.

They entered the church and, with confidence, sat in different spots. It was old hat now. The hymns were some good old ones, and for the anthem, a man and a woman in the choir sang a pretty duet of "Come, Thou Fount of Every Blessing." After the other regular stuff, the minister stood up and approached the pulpit. The bulletin said the associate minister was preaching today, so this must be the guy they'd come to hear.

"Our Scripture reading today comes from the book of Hosea, chapter 2, verses 13 through 16. Listen to the Word of the Lord. . . ."

Hosea? Travis recalled that was the guy who had to marry a prostitute. He wondered if the preacher was going to talk about that aspect of the story. Then Travis wondered how *he* would react to being married to a prostitute. It would definitely be awkward. What would you talk about over breakfast?

After reading the passage, the preacher began his sermon. "I love to read children's books, especially when my own children are sitting by my side, leaning on my shoulder, craning their necks to see the pictures that go with the words. One of my favorites is *The Runaway Bunny* by Margaret Wise Brown. I'm sure many of you parents recognize the book and the author. For those of you who haven't read the book, it is the story of a mother's unconditional love for her child. The baby bunny repeatedly threatens to run away to various places to get away from his mother, but she answers that she will always pursue him, no matter where or how far he strays.

"My kids do that to me sometimes. Unfortunately, my pursuit usually involves a flyswatter and any number of threats related to Christmas and birthday presents."

A lady up front blurted out, "Ha!"

"The childlike imagery in Margaret Wise Brown's book is quite beautiful. And while the analogy to our own parent-child relationships is pondered by my children during their silence at the end of the story, I am always confronted with the direct analogy to our relationship with God."

The preacher paused and took a drink of water from a glass on the pulpit.

"God pursues us just as he pursued Israel during Hosea's time, and many times under similar circumstances. In our Scripture reading this morning, we see that Israel willingly turned her back on God and actively sought other gods. After all he had done for the Israelites—rescuing them from slavery in Egypt, sustaining them in the wilderness, delivering them into the Promised Land—after all of this, Israel succumbed to the temptations provided by the surrounding culture, effectively turning their collective noses up at God. And yet

God chose to pursue Israel and bring her back into a right relationship with him.

"Are we shocked at Israel's betrayal? We shouldn't be; we would have done the same thing. To think that we wouldn't have is an admission of self-righteous arrogance. In fact, one of the things that is most shocking to me is when I realize that someone I know is really almost pure, someone without a grain of cynicism in their body, someone with truly pure thoughts. It makes me question my own faith, my own efforts at living a Christian life.

"Fortunately, the Bible is full of characters like most of us. Backsliders, doubters, hypocrites, ne'er-do-wells, adulterers, murderers, alcoholics. And then in our time there are the more common wanderers from God who worship their career, covet a neighbor's car, build a trophy house to show everyone they have made it.

"It goes all the way back to Adam and Eve eating the forbidden fruit and Jacob double-crossing his own brother with the help of his mother. Everybody with a younger sibling can empathize with Esau. Joseph started out as the favored son and bragged about ruling over his brothers someday.

"Moses was a murderer with a speech impediment. David was an adulterer and an accessory to murder. Jonah talked back to God and didn't want to go to Nineveh to speak on God's behalf. Peter denied knowing Jesus—three times. Paul was an executioner with an attitude before he had that bright-light incident on the road to Damascus.

"These are the men God chose to lead and preach to his

people. I often wonder how the world today would judge these men as leaders. Can you begin to imagine the Senate hearings?!"

Travis glanced at Bill and Frankie, sitting together and chuckling.

"Why does God so often pick a sinner to lead us, to warn us, to preach to us? There's a simple answer. Because God knows our hearts. He knows that we identify and relate to those who are most like us. It makes the messenger more believable."

Travis wondered if he was not so bad a sinner after all. Based on what the preacher was saying, he was in some pretty good company.

"But does God overlook our sin, knowing that later on we will get straightened out? No, he does not. Look again at the passage from Hosea. God is angry with Israel and, earlier in the chapter, accuses Israel of being like a wife who becomes a prostitute. Those are strong words. And yet he still pursues. He makes plans to woo Israel back to him, to 'speak tenderly' to Israel, to get Israel back into a full relationship with him."

Susie, sitting between Travis and Matt, leaned forward to cough and put her hand on Travis's knee for support as she did so. Travis's heart began to pound. He needed to think about something else—something horrible—to counteract his current thoughts. What about the bloating of a deer on the side of the road several days after being struck by a car? He made himself think about the decaying carcass. The buzzards picking at it. Okay, the other thoughts had passed.

The preacher was still talking. "There is so much to be learned from this passage in Hosea. What about our relationships with *our* children? God is patient with Israel; how do we measure up? Do we blow our top every time a glass gets broken or dirty clothes are left lying around? I don't know about other parents, but I know that I often do. Then while lying in bed at night after having sternly disciplined my children, I long to draw them close and tell them I love them no matter what. Sometimes the feeling is so strong that I get up in the middle of the night and go to their room to sit and watch them breathe while they sleep. Obviously, I'm still learning to be a good parent like God's example for us in Hosea.

"And what about the relationships between husbands and wives?" The minister stopped and smiled.

Travis shifted in his seat and cleared his throat.

"Does anybody want to talk about this? I see my wife over there shaking her head." Everyone laughed as the minister paused again and took a sip of water.

Travis felt his ears getting hot.

"It's too close, isn't it? How many grudges are you holding right now? When was the last time you wiped the slate clean, gave each other another chance? Forgiveness is a form of pursuit, is it not? In forgiveness, we say to the offender, 'That's okay; I'm still with you.' In forgiveness, we swallow our pride, take a deep breath, and say, 'That's alright; I'm ready to start again.' I'm not talking about abusive relationships; I'm talking about relationships like God had with Israel in Hosea's time. Anger? Yes, sometimes. But then forgiveness and speaking tenderly to bring back a full, loving relationship.

"We all wander in different ways. But God pursues us. We belong to him. He is not going to give up on us. We can cheat on him by worshiping idols like money, cars, houses, clothes, jewelry, social status, even leadership roles in the church. We can turn our back on God's grace and become prideful about our accomplishments. Sometimes we just kick him out of our lives. But God doesn't go far, does he? No, he doesn't. He patiently waits at the door, listening to the party inside, and when the fun is over and the house is trashed, he taps lightly, waiting for us to open the door. And if we don't open it, he knocks again. And again. And again. Speaking as one sinner to another, let me give you some advice. Open the door.

"In the name of the Father, the Son, and the Holy Spirit, amen."

CHAPTER 28

*When death comes, the church in its pastoral care immediately offers
the ministry of presence, of shared loss and pain, of faith and hope in
the power of the resurrection, and of ordinary acts of care and love.*

THE BOOK OF ORDER, PRESBYTERIAN CHURCH (USA): W-6.3006

JOYCE PULLED UP BEHIND BILL'S HOUSE and got out of her
car. The dog lying by the steps got up and made its way
toward Joyce, wagging its tail. She reached down and patted
its head and then climbed the steps to the screened-in back
porch. As she was beginning to knock she noticed that the
door to the house was open, and she could see Bill sitting at
his kitchen table . . . pointing a gun at his head?

She screamed. "Bill! Oh my gosh! Stop!"

The dog started barking.

Joyce pulled on the screen door but it was locked from the

inside. She banged frantically on the door frame. Bill stood up and walked toward her, pausing at the kitchen counter. He stepped out onto the porch and looked at her.

"Bill, open this door! What were you doing? Please let me in!"

Bill said nothing but walked deliberately to the door and unlocked it. His blue eyes were empty of all emotion, as was his face. He put one hand in his pants pocket and jingled his change and then sat down in a rocker just beside him. Joyce slowly stepped inside.

"Bill?"

Bill stared at the floor and didn't answer.

"Bill?"

Bill continued to stare at the floor.

Joyce was breathing hard and, at this point, not sure at all what should be done. She moved, very easy, over to the rocker next to where Bill was sitting and then sat down. Bill was not rocking at all but being perfectly still. Joyce didn't say anything and also sat still. The dog had come up the steps and had his nose pressed against the screen door. He was wagging his tail and trying to see what was going on. Joyce decided to just remain quiet for a while.

Neither Bill nor Joyce said a word for almost ten minutes. The dog sat down on the top step and looked out toward the yard. It was an unusually warm day for October and the dog was panting in the late-afternoon heat.

"I . . . ummm . . . don't see any point in this anymore. It wasn't supposed to . . ." Bill began.

"I know you miss her."

"Well, yes. . . . We were too close."

"There's nothing wrong with that." Joyce thought about how different her marriage had been from Bill and Mary Helen's. She and Bob had definitely not been "too close."

Five more minutes passed with no talking. The dog hopped back down the steps and resumed his post lying on the grass.

"I suppose it's a sin."

"What? To love someone more than anything else? I don't think so."

"No, I meant . . . what I was getting ready to do."

"I know what you meant. My response is still the same."

"I guess I don't know what to do now."

"You need to see a doctor. Today."

"No, I don't think so. I really just want to stay here. I suppose you're going to call the police."

"Why would I call the police?"

"Well, I don't know. I just thought—"

"Bill, you can't be left alone. You need to get some help in dealing with this."

"Yes. I know."

"So, can I take you to the hospital?"

"No, I don't need to go to any hospital."

"Yes, you do. People don't normally hold a gun to their head unless there is something wrong. You need help, Bill." Joyce leaned forward and took hold of Bill's hand. It was much larger than hers and was rough and dry.

"Just let me stay here."

"I can't leave you here like this. Let me stay with you awhile."

"I'll be fine."

"No, you won't. I'm staying."

Joyce let go of Bill's hand and stepped into the kitchen. She didn't see the gun. He'd probably stuck it somewhere when she screamed at him.

Joyce walked back to the porch.

"Bill?"

"Yes."

"May I take the gun with me?"

Bill didn't respond.

"Bill?"

"Okay . . . it's in the drawer below the coffeemaker."

Joyce turned and went back to the kitchen. She opened the drawer and picked up the gun. It felt heavy in her hand. She walked back out to the porch, where Bill was sitting, still staring at the floor.

"I'm putting this up."

Bill sighed but didn't say anything.

Joyce returned from her car and sat down in the rocker beside Bill. She took his hand again. She didn't say anything. She and Bill sat there together, looking out across the field behind his house.

Joyce looked at Bill. "You have a lot of life ahead of you. Everyone respects you so much."

Bill stared straight ahead.

"You're like a father to Travis. I've seen it in his eyes when he talks to you. And our church, our community, needs your leadership, your wisdom, your example. You have so much to offer. Can't you *see* that?"

Silence.

"I know how much you loved Mary Helen. But there are so many other people that love *you*, Bill. And your life isn't over. Do you think Mary Helen would want this for you? I don't think so."

Bill took in a deep breath and exhaled loudly.

"And you are a fine man. I wouldn't be surprised if a whole herd of widows came knocking on your door in this coming year. I know *I* would think about it."

He turned and looked at Joyce.

Joyce felt a slight blush come over her face. "Well, what I mean is that you're the kind of man that makes a good life companion. I know why Mary Helen was so taken with you."

Bill turned away again.

"Will you let me drive you to the hospital? They can give you something for your nerves. You need a good rest."

"I'm not going to go to a hospital. And, Joyce . . . don't tell anyone about this."

Joyce sighed heavily. "I'll tell you what. I'll make a deal with you."

"A deal?"

"Yes. I won't call the police or take you to a hospital if you let me stay here with you tonight and keep you company."

"What?"

"I can cook us a good supper and then sleep on the couch.

Then I'll get up tomorrow morning and fix breakfast, and if you're doing better, I'll go home."

"You can't do that."

"Why not?"

"It just wouldn't be right."

"Bill, it's not like I'm going to sleep with you. I'm just going to take care of you this evening. Somebody has to, and you won't go to the hospital, so I'm going to do it."

CHAPTER 29

Q. 89. What shall be done to the wicked at the day of judgment?
A. At the day of judgment, the wicked shall be set on Christ's left hand,
and upon clear evidence, and full conviction of their own consciences,
shall have the fearful but just sentence of condemnation pronounced
against them; and thereupon shall be cast out from the favorable
presence of God, and the glorious fellowship of Christ, his saints, and
all his holy angels, into hell, to be punished with unspeakable torments
both of body and soul, with the devil and his angels forever.

THE BOOK OF CONFESSIONS, PRESBYTERIAN CHURCH (USA):
THE LARGER CATECHISM, 7.199

FRANKIE ROLLED DOWN THE WINDOW as she pulled up to the cemetery. Stopping the car alongside a row of tombstones, she sat still and stared straight ahead. An afternoon breeze rustled the blades of corn in the adjacent field.

So much time had passed since she first heard that rustling sound, running after her older brother between rows of corn in the field behind their house. Their favorite game was playing tag in the cornfield. Her brother, being older and faster, would jump between rows and double back until Frankie often gave up, sitting down to cry in the gray dirt.

Davie would then come up behind her and pick her up, pat her head, and say he was sorry and to not worry, because he would never leave her there. He would hold her the same way after their father flew into a rage and whipped them with his belt or slapped them hard enough to knock them down, all because they stepped on a flower while weeding the flower bed or spilled a few drops of tea on the table while filling the glasses for dinner or stumbled bringing the eggs up to the house, causing one to fall out of the basket and break on the hard dirt yard.

And now, in a row of nondescript tombstones, her father's grave was one among many, giving no indication of the fear that, once upon a time, he could so easily summon in her—or of the fierce, intense anger that lived in his eyes. Now a plain marker with his name, date of birth, and date of death was all that remained of the evil force that had ruled their family.

Beside his tombstone was that of her mother, always quiet even in life. She was forced into submission by the power of her husband's hand, striking her face, leaving marks that brought humiliation—and withdrawal from all human interaction, even with her children. And next to her mother, a child's grave—her brother, Davie, twelve years old, killed by a single blow to his head from a glass milk bottle thrown across the dining room table by their father.

Her mother, drawing on her last ounce of courage, had picked up her son and carried him with his bloodied head into the kitchen past her husband, who continued eating his grits and two eggs, sunny-side up. She returned from the kitchen with a loaded shotgun. Walking up behind him, she pointed the double barrels at the base of his skull and pulled one trigger. Then, as he fell forward and his face broke the yolks of his breakfast eggs, she placed the barrels between his shoulder blades and pulled the second trigger.

Frankie, spattered with blood, ran screaming out of the house. She ran all the way down the long dirt road that led to the main road, not seeing Mr. Strickland, a neighbor, driving his wife to town. He blew his horn and slammed on his brakes, stopping only inches from Frankie's seven-year-old frame, shaking in the middle of the road. Mrs. Strickland, gasping with horror at Frankie's blood-spattered smock, ran to Frankie and picked her up and put her in the car while Mr. Strickland ran down the dirt road toward Frankie's house.

As he ran with his coattails flapping, Frankie heard another gunshot and looked toward her house, only to see her mother falling through the front screen door with the shotgun falling beside her.

• • •

Frankie got out of the car and carried two small potted mums over to her mother's and her brother's graves. She set one of the plants at the base of her mother's tombstone. Then she knelt, and while resting one hand flat on top of the ground in the middle of her brother's grave, she placed the other plant at the base of his tombstone and kissed the earth above his head. Frankie stood up and gazed at the earth covering her brother. Her mind was now empty of thought. She felt a breeze at her back, listened to the rustling of the corn. She stood there, still, for about five minutes. Then she turned and walked back toward the car.

Passing her father's grave, she didn't even glance toward the tombstone where, until just a few years ago, she spat after each visit before leaving the cemetery.

CHAPTER 30

How beautiful you are, my darling, how beautiful!
Your eyes are like doves.
You are so handsome, my love, pleasing beyond words!
The soft grass is our bed.

SONG OF SONGS 1:15-16

THE TRUCK STOP WAS NEARLY EMPTY except for two truckers in the corner booth and Matt and Julia sitting in a booth near the cash register.

Matt raised his eyebrows and asked, "You're kidding me, right? You've never seen the ocean?"

"Nope, never," Julia replied, looking away.

"How is that possible? I mean, we're only a couple of hours from the beach," Matt said.

Julia didn't reply. She folded her arms and looked down at the table. Matt finally realized the old hurt she was feeling.

Her entire life had been one of survival. Even if she could afford to go, there was no time for trips to the beach. And who would she go with, anyway?

"Hey, let's go camping this weekend at Cape Hatteras," he said.

"Really?" Julia said, looking up at Matt.

"Yeah, I'll get my old tent out of the attic and we'll go to the campground by the lighthouse."

"The lighthouse on the postcard over there?" Julia said, nodding in the direction of the door.

Matt turned to see a swivel rack of tourist postcards with scenes of North Carolina. He spotted the one Julia was referring to.

"Yep, that's the one."

"That would be fun," Julia said softly.

• • •

Matt picked Julia up from the truck stop after she finished her Friday-afternoon shift. He had his old white 1977 Toyota Corolla packed with camping gear in the backseat along with a duffel bag full of clothes. They drove to Julia's apartment, where she ran inside briefly and came out with her own bag of clothes. Then they hit the road.

Eastern North Carolina seemed to be about the size of Texas when trying to get somewhere. The only major roads cutting through it were I-95 and Highway 17, both running north-south, and I-40 going from Raleigh to Wilmington. Running east-west, Highway 64 out of Rocky Mount and

Highway 264 out of Greenville both went to Manteo and the Outer Banks, but neither was exactly a cruising highway. Matt opted for Highway 264 through the backwater town of Washington and around the shore of Lake Mattamuskeet and then up to Manteo.

Julia was sitting up straight and not missing anything as they drove along in the dusk. This was all new territory for her.

"What's it like?" she asked.

"What's what like?"

"The ocean, what's it like?" she repeated.

Matt thought for a second. "It kinda depends on the weather."

"I figured that, but you know, like, it's the edge of our continent, right?"

"Yeah, it's the end of dry land."

Matt wondered what preconceived vision Julia had of the ocean. All she had to go on were the postcards at the truck stop and the Weather Channel during hurricane season. On the other hand, most people who visited the coast probably didn't look too far past the breakers. Matt viewed it as a Portuguese sailor might, hypnotized by the horizon, knowing the possibilities beyond it. And then there was the sea itself: scary big, almost endless, with who knows what kind of life-forms existing a mile beneath the surface. His scientific eye pondered the fluid dynamics along the shoreline with waves forming and breaking, currents running in several directions, and the rush and fall of the foamy salt water on the beach. At night the beach was alive with ghost crabs scurrying about, the smell of damp salt air, and the twinkling lights of beach cottages.

It was nearly dark by the time they reached Buxton, just north of the lighthouse. It was too late to get in the campground so they pulled into an old one-story redbrick strip motel with a red neon Vacancy sign on in the office window. Matt went into the office to check in while Julia waited in the car.

"Can I get a room for the night?" he asked the clerk, a tired- and angry-looking brown-headed woman with a permanent. She looked to be in her late thirties and was significantly over-weight, wearing a loose-fitting white top and some light-blue expandable-waist polyester pants.

The clerk looked out the office window at Julia. "Is that your wife?"

"No, just a friend," Matt replied.

"Girlfriend?" she continued.

Matt suddenly remembered it was against the law for an unmarried couple to share a motel room in North Carolina, although he thought that law had recently been declared unconstitutional. He didn't think the point was worth argu-ing. "No, just a friend. Can we have a room with two beds?"

The clerk studied his face momentarily and then said, "Okay, if it's just a friend. I'll need a credit card and an ID."

After checking in, Matt went back out to the car. "Pretend we're just friends. She'll be spying on us."

"Why?" asked Julia.

Matt looked at the office window, where the woman was staring at them. He waved and pulled the car away.

"Because it's against the law for us to share a motel room if we're not married."

"That's dumb. So how did you get a room, then?"

"I told her we were just friends. Only friends."

Julia laughed.

Matt parked the car at the far end of the building. They carried their bags into the room and locked the door behind them. The room had a faint odor like a badly managed nursing home. The two queen beds were covered with dark-green bedspreads that matched the old carpet. A small television and a laminated list of channels sat atop a cheap chest of drawers in front of the aisle between the beds. Matt watched Julia walk through the room to the bathroom. A sink and vanity mirror were at the end of the room. A small door opened to a toilet and fiberglass insert tub and shower with a yellow stain around the bottom of the tub.

Julia turned and frowned.

"I don't want to do anything in this room but sleep," she said. "And I think I'll leave my clothes on when we get in bed. This is awful."

Matt's face flushed. "We can go back to Manteo if you want and stay at the Hampton Inn," he offered.

"No, it's okay. I just don't want to remember this room in connection with us," Julia explained.

"Oh, okay," Matt said, barely hiding his disappointment.

Matt put the duffel bags on the bed by the door. He stood still, looking around the room where they would spend the night together. "You want to go for a walk on the beach?"

"At night?" Julia replied, surprised at the suggestion.

"Yeah, that's the best time," Matt said, trying to sound upbeat.

"Well, okay, let's go."

They turned the light off in the room and opened the door slowly. Matt peeked his head out the door to see if the clerk was watching them. The office light was on but she must have been doing something in the back, because he couldn't see her. They quietly closed the door behind them and headed for the boardwalk to the beach from the motel parking lot.

A salt-air breeze was blowing through the sea oats as they crossed the small dunes separating the motel from the ocean. When they reached the beach it was completely dark, but the tide was high and the foam from the breakers could be seen approaching the shore. They could see a few lights looking north toward Nags Head but nothing was visible looking south until—*whoosh*. A flash of light passed high above them from the lighthouse.

"Whoa, that was cool," Julia said.

"That's your lighthouse," Matt replied. "I think it's one flash every seven and a half seconds."

Just then another beam of light passed overhead. Julia took hold of Matt's hand, and they began to walk toward the lighthouse in the thick sand near the dunes.

"It's so beautiful, even in the dark," Julia said.

"Do you see the ghost crabs?" Matt asked.

"Where?"

"Over there."

"Oh, look at them. They're so fast!" Julia exclaimed.

"Try to catch one," Matt said.

"Won't they pinch me?" Julia asked.

"No, because you can't catch them."

Julia ran at the crabs and they scattered. She stopped and laughed. "You're right; they're too fast," she said, out of breath.

Matt caught up with her and took her hand again.

She leaned against him as they walked.

After several minutes of just walking, she asked, "What happened to you, Matt?"

"What do you mean?"

"Why did you come back home to live with your dad?"

Matt didn't reply and they strode on for a while.

Finally, he spoke. "I don't really know what happened. I think part of it was I wasn't really living. Just playing a game that someone said was the right game to play, if that makes any sense."

"Keep talking," Julia said.

"Well, I've always done what I thought I was supposed to do, what everyone thought I would do, though it probably sounds hokey: make some type of contribution to science."

Matt paused, waiting for Julia's reaction, but she didn't say anything.

He continued, "Somewhere along the line I began to look outside my narrow world and realized that being a research scientist wasn't my purpose, or at least wasn't what I wanted to spend my life doing. It just didn't seem right. There had to be something else. Have you ever felt like you were in the wrong place?"

"No, not really. I've never thought about being any other place but where I am right now."

Matt thought about that as they continued to walk. He was too full of himself. Of course she hadn't felt like that. She hadn't had the freedom to know anything else. Her life was one paycheck at a time. And yet there was something about her that was so true and so real that it made the smartest and most successful people he knew, even the most religious people, seem silly in comparison. What was it? He also realized that his pontificating was almost childish compared to Julia's daily efforts to just survive. He felt slightly embarrassed.

"I'm sorry for all this 'meaning of life' stuff. I just haven't had my head on straight for some time now," he said.

"That's okay. I like talking with you about it. You've done so much more than me—I'm just a waitress," she said, laughing.

They continued to walk toward the lighthouse with only the sound of the surf beside them.

"Do you think we have a soul?" Julia asked.

"Yeah, I think so," Matt replied.

"One that lives after we die?"

"Yeah, otherwise life seems so pointless. There has to be something else."

"I think so, too," Julia replied, "but I don't think life is pointless otherwise. Life is what it is, you know? I think that's the point."

Matt laughed. "Now *I* don't understand."

Julia put her head on his shoulder as they walked. "Well, I've never really had anything to look forward to, so I just try to enjoy where I am. I don't have anything else. Right now I have you."

They walked on.

"Do you think God knows who I am?" Julia asked.

Matt said, "He has to know who you are, Julia."

"Why do you say that?"

Matt paused. "Because you're what God is all about."

They kept on in silence until they reached the lighthouse point.

"Want to head back now?" Matt asked.

Julia didn't say anything but turned around and took Matt's other hand.

They walked to the motel without saying anything. At the boardwalk, Matt turned and kissed Julia. They stood there awhile, embracing.

"I like the ocean," Julia said.

They slowly made their way back to the room, making sure they weren't holding hands in case the night clerk was watching them. After opening the door for Julia, Matt closed it behind him and turned on the light switch by the door. While Matt closed the front curtain, Julia sat down on the edge of the bed and sighed.

"That was so cool," she said, smiling at Matt.

Matt sat down beside her. He brushed her hair out of her face and leaned over to kiss her. Julia let him. Then Matt was not sure what to do next. She had said she didn't want to do anything but sleep in this room, but now the way she was looking at him, and she was so beautiful, and they were all alone, and . . .

"Matt, are you confused about me, too?" Julia asked.

"What do you mean?"

"Well, we're here alone and we're sitting on this bed," Julia said, still smiling.

"But you said you just wanted to sleep," Matt replied, knowing as soon as he said it what an idiot he was for not making a move.

"You really are a space cadet," Julia said, laughing. Then she stood up and went to the bathroom, closing the door behind her.

Matt sat on the bed with his hands on his knees. What was he supposed to do? Did she or didn't she want to do something? Women were so hard to read. What was she doing in the bathroom anyway? He sighed and started untying his shoelaces. Maybe a baseball game was on tonight. Wow, he had really blown it.

Just then, the door to the bathroom opened and he looked up. Maybe they weren't going to sleep right away. Maybe.

• • •

The next morning they woke up early and walked down the beach again. Julia picked up shell after shell and studied them, asking Matt questions about each one. She stood on the edge of the surf with her hands on her hips and watched the water rush past her ankles and then pull the sand around them back into the sea. Matt sat down on the sand and watched her. Finally, she came running up to him and sat down beside him. They both looked out toward the horizon.

"Have you ever been out there?" she said.

"No."

"You don't want to go?" she asked.

"I don't know. You get out of sight of land and then you're surrounded by water. It would be a little unnerving, I think."

"But eventually you would end up somewhere, right?"

"Maybe, if you know what you're doing," Matt said, laughing.

Julia jumped up and held out her hand to help Matt up. "Let's go exploring," she said.

"Okay, sounds good to me," Matt replied as he took her hand and stood up. "North to Nags Head or south to Ocracoke?"

"Ocracoke!" Julia replied.

• • •

They checked out of the motel and drove to the ferry landing in Hatteras. Matt noted that riding an Outer Banks ferry supplied plenty of romance for women that men otherwise wouldn't know how to provide. Matt laughed as Julia threw pieces of Lance cheese crackers up in the air for the seagulls to catch on the fly. Then they went to the front of the ferry and watched as they approached Ocracoke Island. Julia was absolutely mesmerized by the ferry ride. Even Matt recognized that.

After spending the day kicking about Ocracoke village, they returned to the ferry to go back to Hatteras Island and the campground by the lighthouse. Matt bought more crackers for Julia to throw to the gulls, and at the bow of the ferry, he stood behind her, holding her tight to his body as they looked forward. Something was different now. She had a different posture that somehow fit his body more naturally.

They checked into the campground at 4 p.m. Matt unpacked his old tent and began laying it out on the ground.

"Do you have any Off?" Julia asked.

"Ah, no, I forgot it," Matt replied, looking up at her swatting in the air.

"These bugs are pretty bad. Will it be like this all night?" she asked.

Matt watched her slap her leg, her arm, and then her other leg. Then he had an idea that excited him as if he had just solved a math problem for a prize. He was getting better at this after all.

"You know what? They are going to be real bad. I was wrong. Let's go back to that motel, okay?" he said, almost in the form of a proposal.

Julia stopped swatting bugs and laughed. "Okay, let's go."

CHAPTER 31

One Sabbath day as Jesus was teaching in a synagogue, he saw a woman who had been crippled by an evil spirit. She had been bent double for eighteen years and was unable to stand up straight. When Jesus saw her, he called her over and said, "Dear woman, you are healed of your sickness!" Then he touched her, and instantly she could stand straight. How she praised God!

LUKE 13:10-13

BACK ON THE ROAD. Today they were going to hear a guy with six kids. Travis couldn't figure out how a Presbyterian could allow something like that to happen. The church was over in a hilly part of the state, near Seagrove, on the edge of the Uwharrie Mountains, a small mountain range right in the middle of the state. It was an old country church that sat up on top of a big knoll. This was real pretty country through here, lots of rolling hills and pastures and little creeks.

Travis had already seen two good signs on the way to Seagrove from Sanford. One was *Be fishers of men. You catch 'em; he'll clean 'em* and the other one said, *Try to be the person your dog thinks you are.*

On that last one, after some discussion, the committee decided that some kids must have switched the *D* and *G* in *God* to make it *dog*. On the other hand, Travis figured the dog message made good sense too, unless you happened to think about somebody like Bruce Simmons. He beat his dogs all the time, so it was hard to be sure that they thought highly of him.

By now Travis had filled up a whole page in his little blue notebook with these church-sign messages. Most all of them were some kind of pun that made everybody smile. But there were other signs that people put up in their own yards that had no puns at all. These homemade billboards had messages like *Get right with God before it's too late* and *Jesus saves!* and *The wages of sin is death.* These people were serious. It made Travis wonder what kind of conversations they had at dinner. He guessed it was kind of quiet.

They pulled up to the church and went inside without drawing a lot of attention. They mixed it up some so that Bill sat with Joyce, Travis sat with Susie—*Yahoo!*—Dot sat with Frankie, and Matt sat alone. He said he didn't mind. Not wanting to suffer through another Tibet-inspired humiliation, no one objected.

The interior of this church was decorated like John Calvin would have prescribed; that is, it was pretty plain. No pew cushions here. And these were country people like the ones in Travis's church; lots of Sears suits and brown necks and balding white heads. He felt right at home. The choir came in from the left wearing royal-blue robes with gold stoles, and Travis could tell they were country people also. Maybe a little too country.

He scanned the bulletin to check out the hymn lineup. Looked okay, except these hymns were all in the Baptist hymnal too. Everybody knew them from their childhood, not from their present church.

The preacher came in from the right wearing a black robe with a white stole and looking altogether normal. Travis glanced over at Dot to see what her take was, and she appeared to have given him the approval that the preacher did not yet know was required. He was tall, maybe six foot two, with wide shoulders that made him look like he might have played football in college. He was prematurely gray and kind of jerky in the way he moved around the pulpit.

He had the kind of voice that sounded more like he was talking *with* you than *at* you, like a conversation, almost. That could be good and bad; some people needed to be talked to, while others would run straight to the Episcopalians if you talked too sternly to them. He didn't have an associate minister to help him. It was clear in looking around at the congregation that they admired him and trusted his leadership.

This was the kind of scenario that made Travis feel guilty about stealing a preacher. What would happen to those people left behind? How would they feel about losing their pastor? Of course, the committee had already been through that whole scene, but it still made everybody feel uncomfortable and slightly dishonest.

Travis wondered why it couldn't be done another way. Why couldn't the minister tell the congregation that he felt called to move on and that he was submitting his personal information form to the presbytery for consideration at another church? Then search committees could come hear him preach in his own pulpit without having to sneak around. If everybody was up-front about it, then maybe people would get more used to it as a regular part of the church's mission in the world and feel like they were part of the calling too, in supporting the guy. Travis wondered who started the whole sneaking-around thing—probably somebody who had a streak of insecurity about them and didn't trust anybody. Somebody like Dot.

In the third row from the front sat a woman, attractive but not a lot of makeup, wearing a navy-blue straw hat with a matching ribbon around it. You didn't see a lot of hats anymore in church other than a few at Easter, mostly worn by women nobody had ever seen before. Beside her were six small heads that just cleared the back of the pew. Two of the heads were a little bigger and sat taller than the other four that . . . all looked the same size! Travis wondered if they were . . .

Oh my goodness! They were quadruplets! Had to be. That would explain the six kids. The preacher had two kids and was going for one more, probably, and it turned out to be quadruplets. So he really *was* a pure Presbyterian. They couldn't help it they had quadruplets; they were just going for three altogether. *Man,* Travis thought, *I bet they go through some milk at that house.*

The bulletin said the title of this guy's sermon was "Healing Power!" *Hmmm.* Sounded a little Pentecostal, but they would just have to wait and see. The opening anthem was pretty good even though you could catch a little bit of twang coming through. After the choir finished and sat down, the preacher got up to recite a prayer of confession with the congregation.

"Heavenly Father, we come and come again to seek your help in times of trouble. During these times that we feel closest to you, we pray often, but in prosperous times, we fail to give you praise. Help us to keep our thoughts focused on you and your will for our lives. Help us to be selfless, to serve others, just as your Son did during his life when he was fully human and fully divine. We have been blessed by you, Lord, but many times the blessings right in front of us go unnoticed. Forgive us, heavenly Father."

After the assurance of pardon and the children's sermon, it was showtime. Well, that was probably a little irreverent, but it did pretty much sum up the situation.

"I hope the title of my sermon hasn't frightened anyone into thinking we were going to try an Ernest Angley–type service today."

Travis heard chuckles from the congregation. He recalled one time when he was real little, before Robby was born, some people from a church near their house came by and talked his mama into going to a healing service they were having during a tent revival. Travis and Lou Ann tagged along, after taking a quick bath and putting on some clean clothes. He remembered two of the ushers helping his mama walk to the front of the tent, where a preacher in a white suit was doing a lot of yelling about something and pounding his fist on a Bible. The preacher had walked over to Mama and put his hands on her shoulders and looked toward heaven while saying a prayer with his eyes open. Travis and Lou Ann watched closely to see what would happen.

As the revival preacher prayed, Travis recalled him saying something about his mama's faith helping to heal her. Looking back on it, that must have been the guy's way of getting out of it if it didn't work. As it turned out, nothing happened except for Mama shuffling back down the aisle by herself as everyone looked at her and her lame side like she was a sideshow at the county fair. She had motioned to Travis and Lou Ann to follow her, and two ladies in the back had jumped up and given them a ride home.

The Seagrove pastor had started his sermon. "We know that the real way people are healed from various illnesses is through modern medical science. Just look at the advances in technology over the past fifty years. Diseases like polio, for instance, that ravaged previous generations have been all but wiped out. And now we can keep people alive for as long as we want by doing their breathing for them, pumping nutrients and medicines into their body for them, and in short, by allowing technology to control their bodily functions when they can't. That's the incredible ability of modern medical science."

Travis noted that paralysis caused by stroke hadn't been fixed by modern medical science—at least not yet.

The preacher paused and shuffled his notes around. Then he took a sip of water from a glass that had been placed behind the pulpit. He cleared his throat and went on.

"Recently, at the request of the family, I visited a young woman from one of my former churches who had struggled with mental illness most of her life. She had tried to do herself in by swallowing the entire contents of a Tylenol bottle as well as the contents of an aspirin bottle. She was in intensive care, unconscious, with a tube going into her mouth and down her windpipe to do her breathing for her. The tube was kept in place by adhesive tape wrapped very tightly around the tube and then around her entire head.

"I counted at least four IVs, one in each wrist and one in each lower arm. Then there was another tube for the fluids leaving her body and a heart monitor attached to her index finger. The monitoring screens above her bed showed the rhythmic beat of her heart, her blood pressure, and her breathing rate. I spoke with the attending doctor, and he said that in addition to the toxicity in her blood that was threatening her liver—and her life—she also had a very bad case of pneumonia.

"The fluids that were being pumped through her body to help flush the liver caused her hands and feet to swell, and her neck was so swollen that, lying flat on her back, she had no visible chin. But later, when I was alone with her and sitting beside her bed, I looked through a small opening in the bedside railing that revealed only her eyes and forehead . . . and saw the beauty that she possessed. Looking at her whole body and head, the beauty was hidden. Yet through this small opening, I saw it.

"Standing up, I looked at her comatose body, dead but for the ventilator pumping air into her lungs. The doctor also feared that she had bleeding on her brain because the aspirin had thinned her blood to a dangerous level. It was hard to imagine that she would be better off if she survived. The doctor was doing everything available to him to save her life, and he said that she still had only a fifty percent chance of making it. Fifty percent. That's either a yes or a no. Black or white. Life or death. And it was beyond man's control. Nothing else could be done, he said. I prayed for her. But I recall thinking it was hopeless."

He paused, glanced down, and then looked out at the congregation again.

"Apparently, God also saw the beauty. The woman made a complete physiological recovery. Had my prayer made a difference? Maybe so, maybe not. Or was it just a matter of biology? Did her body have the power within it to heal itself? No, it did not. One pull of a very ordinary plug would have ended her life."

The preacher paused again.

"It was God. It wasn't a televangelist striking her on the forehead or laying hands on her. It wasn't the advanced medical technology that saved her. She was past all of that. Her body had reached a fork in the road. One way was life. One way was death. God took her hand and led her down the road back to life.

"The hapless cynic would say it was only a matter of statistics. But that doesn't cut it with me, because I was a math major in college. The results of events are what statistics describe. But the control of the event is something different altogether. It was the process, not the result, that was important. And the process? For this woman, the process was God's healing touch to save . . . the beauty.

"Our God is a mighty God. We sometimes forget that. When talking about sickness and disease, we are embarrassed to say that God might play a role in fighting disease or healing the critically injured. Am I saying that we need not rely on modern medicine to heal our ills? Not at all. And I want, as much as anyone else, to receive the best medical care available when I have to be put in a hospital.

"What I'm saying is that when we have done all we can do and there is nothing else—when we become powerless—we need to remember that our God can do infinitely more than we could ever ask or even imagine. Because he can."

The preacher took another sip of water.

"But what did God really see? Did he see the physical beauty that I saw through the rail of a hospital bed? I don't think so. I think God saw something else. The something God saw is what is inside each of us. It is the love of a woman lying in a delivery room, giving birth to her child. It is the joy of the husband watching the birth, then looking at his wife holding their baby—a joy that makes him speechless. It is the sorrow of a child losing her sister to leukemia and never forgetting it. It is the perseverance of a cleaning lady working forty-five years cleaning other people's bathrooms, all the while raising her own family. It is the excitement of a graduate student lying awake at night with a new idea, impatient for the morning to come. It is the courage of a father laid off from his job, interviewing for jobs beneath his skill level in a humble attempt to make ends meet. It is the hope of a Vietnamese mother, following her husband to America with their children.

"These are the things I think God notices—intangible things that make a human life valuable beyond measure. These are the things God saw when he looked down at this young woman, nearly lifeless and having little or no chance of survival. I believe her life was spared because God still needs her for his purposes on earth. And so he touched her with his healing power. After the power of medical technology had given up on her, it was her only option for survival. God's healing power.

"In the name of the Father, and the Son, and the Holy Spirit, amen."

CHAPTER 32

Above all, you must live as citizens of heaven, conducting yourselves
in a manner worthy of the Good News about Christ. Then, whether
I come and see you again or only hear about you, I will know that you
are standing together with one spirit and one purpose, fighting together
for the faith, which is the Good News. Don't be intimidated in any
way by your enemies. This will be a sign to them that they are going to
be destroyed, but that you are going to be saved, even by God himself.

PHILIPPIANS 1:27-28

"Mee-Maw, it's me!"

"I'm cooking. Come on in here."

Dot walked into the kitchen. Ernestine was standing in
front of the stove, wearing a white apron and dropping bat-
tered squash into a frying pan of hot grease. A paper-towel-
lined plate of fried spot sat on the small table in the kitchen,
and a pot of collards seasoned with fatback was cooking on
another burner. The smell of the fried fish commingled with
the pungent aroma of collards made Dot feel safe and comfortable. This was a standard meal at Ernestine's house.

"You got any corn bread going?"

"What do you think?"

"Well, I timed it just right today. I haven't had good collards since I don't know when."

"Have a seat at the table and give your feet a rest."

"You're the one that needs to rest. Why are you cooking so much food? Is somebody coming over?"

"Yeah, they done here and already started running their mouth. Sit down over there and talk to me."

"Well, alright. Where's Sonny?"

"He's gone to the store for some more milk. I ran out this morning."

"Oh. Well, Mee-Maw, I look like the fool now."

"What are you talking about, child?"

"I thought I had caught Fred with another woman the other day, and it turns out I've been wrong about that all along. He was just helping out Susie's boy, the troubled one I told you about. The boy was playing the stock market, and Fred was helping him so he could buy his mama a new car." Dot paused. "See, I told you I was a fool."

Ernestine didn't say anything.

"He laughed at me when I confronted him about it. What made it so bad was that I got Frankie and Susie to help me confront him and now they're feeling like fools too. Frankie hasn't called me to talk about anything since. She used to call me at least once during the week to get caught up on the gossip, but lately I haven't heard a word out of her."

Ernestine still didn't say anything.

Dot looked at Ernestine, waiting for her to respond with some type of comment, but Ernestine was still silent as she moved the fried squash around in the skillet with a spatula.

"Anyway, I just wanted to let you know about Fred so you could stop feeling sorry for me."

Standing in front of the stove and flipping the squash over, Ernestine said, "So he told you he wasn't sneaking around with another woman?"

"Yeah, and he really rubbed it in, saying, 'You're never gonna hear the end of this' and—"

Ernestine interrupted. "He *is* cheating on you, sugar."

Dot looked at her, confused. "What did you say?"

"I said he *is* cheating on you. Sonny saw them."

"What do you mean?"

Ernestine turned to face Dot, holding the spatula down by her side. "Sonny was over in Kinston the other day to see a man about a truck he had for sale, and he saw Fred and some girl coming out the Red Roof Inn parking lot. I'm sorry, sugar, but I couldn't keep it from you."

Dot's face flushed red and she couldn't speak. Finally, after a long pause, she said softly, "What were they doing over there?"

"Look here, sweet girl, you need to get rid of that one. He's no good. I thought he was . . . but I was wrong."

Dot put her head down on the table and began to sob.

Ernestine walked over and patted her head and then rubbed her back between the shoulder blades. "I'm sorry, sweet girl. You'll be fine, though. You just wait and see. You'll be fine."

Dot looked up from the table with red and puffy eyes. "Mee-Maw, now I *am* ruined."

"No, you're not, sugar."

"Mee-Maw, I don't want to go through with this. Maybe Fred will stop doing what he's doing if I ask him about it."

"You already did, and he lied. He's no good. But go on and do what you want to do. I'm just telling you what I think."

Dot sniffed and wiped her nose with her index finger. She looked out the window at the woods behind Ernestine's house. She had looked out that window from this chair many times when she was a little girl. At those same trees. And now this, forty years later. She was older, the trees were bigger, and things were more . . . complicated. Why couldn't she start again? Go back to those days. Playing in the yard. Picking gardenias and taking them home to her mother. Doing cartwheels on the grass. Climbing the mimosa tree and thinking it was really big.

"Okay, Mee-Maw, I'll have to think about it some. And pray about it. Will you pray for me, Mee-Maw?"

"I already do, sugar. Every day. Every single day."

CHAPTER 33

Then God blessed Noah and his sons and told them, "Be fruitful and multiply. Fill the earth."

GENESIS 9:1

TRAVIS WAS KILLING TIME at the local Walmart looking at some new flat-screen televisions when the manager of the store came on over the PA and asked everybody to exit through the front door in an orderly manner, as there was an emergency-type issue that was being dealt with. Well, Walmart being what it was—a gathering place for all sorts of people, most of them trying to demonstrate some type of fad but not quite getting it right—pandemonium ensued.

Travis strolled up to the front of the store and was doing exactly what the manager told everybody to do when he got run over, literally, by a 260-pound woman wearing a tube top and gym shorts, holding a thirty-six-roll package of toilet paper under one arm and pulling behind her—or more like dragging—a mop-headed toddler with a dirty bottle. He guessed she didn't see him. Anyway, he got hit from behind by this locomotive carrying toilet paper and it knocked him forward so hard that he tripped and fell on the floor. Travis didn't think she even felt it, because she just kept heading for the front door. As he was getting up, he looked over his shoulder in time to see another such creature headed his way, so he sprinted through the front door like everybody else.

Out in the parking lot, people were standing around looking anxious, many of them speculating on what had happened, when all of a sudden the volunteer fire department started racing into the parking lot from the highway. A sheriff's deputy's car came screeching into the lot as well, sirens blaring and lights flashing. One of the volunteer firemen jumped off the truck with his axe and ran toward the front door. The problem he encountered was about two hundred people moving toward him in the opposite direction. Frustrated, he began to yell, "Get out of my way. I've got to get inside to where the bomb is!"

This of course set off a second stampede toward the outer reaches of the parking lot, with many people later turning around and running back against the crowd to get in their cars and move them away from the building. It didn't take long for gridlock to set in, complete with horns blowing and some yelling accompanied by middle-finger gestures.

A fight broke out between the driver of a two-tone 1975 Monte Carlo, the big long kind, and the driver of a bluish-purple Dodge Neon. Travis would normally have bet on a Monte Carlo driver, especially one with an older model, but the guy who crawled out of the Neon must have had his real car impounded, because he was a huge unit. Massive with a flattop. Must have been some kind of military dude. The Monte Carlo guy was a rail-thin redneck with a bushy moustache and a Petty Enterprises ball cap. Of course, he was evening things up by carrying a tire iron along for his weapon. He took one roundhouse swing at the Neon's head but the Neon was ready for it. He ducked and came up swinging, catching the Monte Carlo with a left hook that knocked his ball cap right off and sent him staggering backward.

Travis thought it was over for him, but the little wiry guy regained his composure and went right back at the Neon driver. This time he threw the tire iron at the Neon's head when he was about five feet from him; it would have killed him if it had found its mark. Instead, Neon ducked and the tire iron traveled on through the air, unimpeded until it met the head of the Walmart employee who worked in the electronics section, where Travis had been.

After he hit the ground, the fight broke up and everybody rushed over to the electronics-section guy to see if he was dead or alive. Once it was determined he was alive, the Neon guy looked at the Monte Carlo guy and smirked. Monte Carlo picked up his tire iron and smirked back. Then they both walked back to their cars and sat there, still and silent.

The volunteer fire department guys came walking out the front doors of the Walmart, looking disappointed that they didn't get to deal with a real bomb. Travis was sure some of those guys were nuts in a bad way. As soon as the crowd realized the bomb threat was a fake, everyone began moving as a herd back toward the store to finish up their shopping. Travis couldn't stand it anymore. He crawled into his car and left the scene.

Pulling up in his driveway, he noticed that there were several new fire-ant hills spread around the yard. Fire ants just didn't go away. Those things were going to take over the world one day if somebody didn't do something. Nothing he'd tried to date had really worked.

He'd tried it all. He'd poured boiling water onto the hills, trying to scald the ants to death. He'd poured diesel fuel all over a hill and lit it with a match, watching their little bodies sizzle and shrivel up as they burned. He'd poured grits all around their hill. This latter action was based on the theory that when an ant ate the grits, the grits would absorb moisture and expand inside the ant's body, ultimately causing its insides to irreversibly swell, killing the creature. That did not work either. He'd tried every poison Home Depot carried; he'd even mixed some of them together, but nothing worked.

It was like a modern-day plague had hit eastern North Carolina, but why? All Travis knew was that you couldn't get rid of the dumb things no matter what you tried.

He went into the garage and looked around at the various

bags of fertilizer and other lawn chemicals he had. Over in the corner was a jug of Prestone antifreeze. Maybe that would work on the ants. It sure did a number on dogs and cats. He walked out to the front yard and poured it on several of the hills. He was bending over one of the hills, looking for some type of reaction, when somebody blew a car horn with a long, slow blast right in front of the house. Travis snapped upward to see who it was.

It was Jenny. She pulled into the driveway and got out of the car. "What on earth are you doing pouring antifreeze all over our yard?"

"What does it look like I'm doing? I'm trying to kill these fire ants. They're ruining our front yard."

"With antifreeze?"

"It makes dogs and cats sick. Some of them even die. Maybe it will work on ants too."

"Travis Booth, you are a one-man show for the ages."

"What does that mean?"

Jenny walked over to where Travis was standing, holding the jug by his side.

"It means," Jenny said while putting her hands on Travis's waist, "that I love you very, very much." She kissed him on the cheek. "Guess what?"

"What?"

"I'm late."

"You're what?"

"I'm late. I might be . . . you know . . ."

"But how? We've been doing everything we're supposed

to be doing to keep from getting that way. How could it happen?"

Jenny pulled back from Travis and frowned. "So you're not excited?"

"Well, yes, but . . ."

"But what? You don't want to have a baby, do you?"

"Well, yes, but . . ."

"You better get one thing straight, Travis Booth. We're going to have this baby and you're going to be happy about it."

Jenny turned and walked toward the house.

"Wait, Jen. I didn't mean I wasn't happy. All I was saying was—"

"Just shut up." Jenny turned to face Travis. "All you want is to maintain this little life you got going and never do anything else but stay in this stupid little town. All I ever wanted was to—"

"What does this town have to do with—?"

Jenny sobbed loudly and turned to walk into the house.

• • •

The fire ants seemed to like the antifreeze. No effect at all. It looked like they were slurping it up, hanging around the edges of it. Maybe a better approach would be to draw them out of the ground with some sugar-coated bread or something like that. Then, when they were all over the bread, light them up with a propane torch and leave their dead bodies lying around the top of the hill, discouraging the surviving pests from settling in this yard. It might work.

CHAPTER 34

O God, you know how foolish I am; my sins cannot be hidden from
you. Don't let those who trust in you be ashamed because of me,
O Sovereign LORD of Heaven's Armies. Don't let me cause them to
be humiliated, O God of Israel.

PSALM 69:5-6

SITTING ON THE BENCH he had made between two cypress
knees by the swamp river, Matt turned as he heard a car pull
up to the house. He stood and watched Julia tug at her jeans
as she knocked on the back screen door. His dad let her in.
Matt sat back down on the bench and waited.

In a few minutes he saw Julia leaving the house and walking toward the swamp, toward him.

"Matt!" Julia called.

"Down here!"

Julia continued walking down the dirt road, letting her
arms swing by her sides. "Matt!"

"Over here!"

She made her way toward the path through the trees. As she stepped into the sparse shade, Matt motioned to her to come and sit beside him.

"You better not slip off that seat," she called. "That'd be a hard injury to explain at the emergency room. Ha."

"Why are you so peppy? Is it meat loaf day at the truck stop?"

Julia smiled as she approached him. She leaned over and kissed the top of his head. "Hey, I need to tell you something."

"Shoot."

She looked subdued. "Uh, it's not a good thing. I'm pregnant."

Matt bolted upright, causing Julia to step backward, looking like she was ready for a fight. "How could that . . . ? I mean, we didn't . . ."

"That's right. It's not yours."

Matt stood still with his mouth slightly open, staring at Julia's contorted face, her eyes brimming with moisture.

"Oh. So who is the father?"

"Matt . . . I'm sorry. . . . It was a mistake. . . . The guy's truck broke down and he needed a place to spend the night, and . . . I started drinking with him, and . . . It was a mistake."

"When did this . . . ? Was it recent? Are you getting married now?"

Julia laughed while she cried. "No, the guy is long gone. I don't know where he is. He'll never come back. I know that kind."

"So what . . . are you going to do?"

"I'm going to keep it."

"But how can you do that? You don't have the money for . . ."

Now Julia was sobbing so hard her thin frame was convulsing.

Matt suddenly saw her. All the smart talk, all the flirting, all the hardness was gone. There was nothing now but Julia. In a town that had already decided she was insignificant, part of the background the important people never saw. A servant.

But what a person she was, beautiful in mind and body. It didn't matter that they had come from completely different backgrounds—that she was a pragmatic waitress and he was a spacey PhD. The fact that he had even considered that an issue was almost silly, an indication of his own fragile ego. And he didn't care what anyone else thought about them; he only cared about her right now. What the truckers at the truck stop would say about her and what the church people would say about an unmarried pregnant waitress didn't matter at that moment. Their present context was the shady stillness of the swamp, the black water, the gnarled cypress knees, and each other. The only thing that mattered was the present. And Julia.

Matt took a deep breath and pulled her to him. She kept shaking in his arms.

"Matt, I'm so sorry . . . so sorry."

Matt was silent. They stood there awhile until Julia stopped shaking.

She pushed away from him. "Good-bye. Thanks for everything. I can't believe I screwed it up like this. Bye."

She turned and started to make her way back to the house. Matt watched her as she moved out into the sunlight. "Julia!"

She turned around but didn't respond.

"Julia, I have an idea!"

She looked startled when he came bounding out of the woods toward her. He stopped in front of her, breathing hard, and grabbed her shoulders. "I have an idea. . . . Why don't we . . . get married?"

"What?"

"Get married. You know. I'll be the husband and you'll be the wife. Like that."

She jerked away from him. "No, Matt. I know what you're doing. Don't screw your life up. Let me go now."

She started walking again. Matt ran and got in front of her. He grabbed her again by the shoulders and she stopped. "Julia, I'm not screwing anything up. I love you. I want to marry you!"

She took a deep breath and looked at him through dulled eyes. She didn't say anything.

"Julia, listen. This is what I want! We can get married this month and nobody will think anything of it when the baby comes, and if they do . . . so what?"

"It's not your baby."

"It can be. We can raise this baby together."

Julia looked down at the ground. She started sobbing again, quieter this time.

Matt put his arms around her and whispered, "I love you, Julia. Please marry me."

She sniffled and looked up into his eyes.

"I don't deserve you. I'm trash, and everybody knows it. I don't know what I was thinking. . . . Just let me go." She pulled away.

Matt watched her as she bypassed the house and went around the side to her car. She got in and backed out of the driveway, leaving him standing in the bright sun.

• • •

Matt walked into the church office and stopped in front of the secretary's desk. John's door was closed.

"Hi. May I help you?"

"Uh, yes. Is John in?"

"Did you want to see him?"

"Yes. I didn't call, but I thought I might drop by for a quick chat."

"I see. Well, let me check to see if he's busy."

She got up and went into John's office. Matt looked around the sparsely outfitted room and wondered what she did all day. The door opened and John came out, followed by the secretary.

"Well, hello!" John said.

"I hope this isn't an interruption. I just wanted to talk with you about something."

"Of course. Come on in." John walked back to his desk as Matt closed the door behind himself.

John sat down and said, "So how is the scientist doing?"

Matt shook his head. "You might not have noticed, but there's not a lot of science going on around here."

John chuckled. "What's up?"

Matt took a deep breath. "Remember our earlier conversation about the waitress I'm dating?"

"Hmmm, PhD and truck-stop waitress. That's kind of hard to forget." He smiled.

"Well . . . she's pregnant."

John frowned.

Matt sighed. "No, it wasn't me. We had a chance on a trip to the Outer Banks, but we didn't go through with it. We just . . . didn't."

"So someone obviously did go through with it."

Matt sighed again. "She said it was a mistake. They were drinking. His truck broke down and he needed a place to stay."

"Sometimes things happen that you can't control. Is she in love with this other guy?"

"No. He was a trucker, passing through town. A one-night stand for him. Didn't say good-bye to her or anything."

"I see. Still, it doesn't sound like the kind of girl for you, Matt."

"It seems like that on the surface. But you would think differently if you really knew her. My dad would agree with me. I just don't know what to do."

"And what does she say about all this?"

"She wants to keep the baby."

"Well, that's a good start. What about her family? Will they help her?"

"She doesn't have any family. She left home when she was eighteen and hasn't been back."

"So . . . she wants you to marry her?"

"No."

"Okay, Matt, what is it you want from me?"

"Some advice."

"Solicited advice, the best kind."

"I want to marry her and help raise that baby."

"Matt, are you sure you've thought this through? This is not something you can do halfway. And this is a small town. Not that it should matter, but people talk."

"Remember how we talked about God's will for our lives?"

"Yes, I do."

"And how it was hard to know what it was?"

"Oh yes."

"I know this is it."

John looked at Matt for several seconds. "Do you think she wants to marry you?"

"She would have, if this hadn't happened. But now she says she doesn't want to mess up my life the way she messed up her own."

John paused again. "Well, you know, Matt, there's nothing wrong with what you want to do. In fact, it is quite noble. But do you really know what you're committing to? I mean—"

"You're right; I probably don't appreciate how hard it will

be, at this point. But for me, it's more than just the right thing to do . . . I'm in love with her."

"So did you tell her this?"

"Yes. That's when she left, crying."

"She left, crying?"

"Yeah."

"After you told her you loved her?"

"Yeah."

"Well, you should get out of here and go get her."

"What?"

"Go get her. I think she loves you too."

"But she—"

"She wants to marry you too. Go get her."

CHAPTER 35

Q. 159. How is the Word of God to be preached by those that are called thereunto?
A. They that are called to labor in the ministry of the Word are to preach sound doctrine, diligently, in season, and out of season; plainly, not in the enticing word of man's wisdom, but in demonstration of the Spirit, and of power; faithfully, making known the whole counsel of God; wisely, applying themselves to the necessities and capacities of the hearers; zealously, with fervent love to God, and the souls of his people; sincerely, aiming at his glory, and their conversion, edification, and salvation.

THE BOOK OF CONFESSIONS, PRESBYTERIAN CHURCH (USA):
THE LARGER CATECHISM, 7.269

JOHN LEANED BACK IN HIS CHAIR and put his feet up on the corner of the borrowed desk in his room at the Blue Vista Motor Lodge. The bare-bones efficiency apartment wasn't very homey, but he still preferred to work there occasionally for a change of scenery. Today he had thought the lack of available distractions might help him concentrate. Since reconnecting with Ann Lingerfelt, he had hardly been able to focus on his work. Or anything, really. He was in uncharted territory. An odd feeling of nervousness had taken over his body. Very unsettling. The day he had driven to Shallotte to find her had become a pivotal experience.

That evening at dinner, their conversation had been awkward. At one point he had looked up from his plate to see her looking at him with sad amusement. She had quickly glanced away. So much time had passed, and they were both beyond the age that would allow them to start a life together. Weren't they?

Shaking his head, he tried to get back to the business at hand—writing a sermon. What could he say that would test the congregation's faith, something to make them uncomfortable? Something to make them question, and then affirm, their beliefs?

Hmmm, maybe something on homosexuality would stir them up, especially since he was a bachelor. It would be a deviation from the lectionary, but that was okay every now and then. So what angle to take? Maybe it would be good to bring in a recent conflict in a church, like that church in Washington, DC, that split over the issue. That would keep them awake alright. And a little tongue-in-cheek to rouse their suspicion. Then hit them hard with the Scriptures at the end. Yes, a little drama.

The gay debate had consumed the Episcopal church last year, and now it was the Presbyterians' turn to become a single-issue denomination for a while. It was a sin, no doubt. The Scriptures said as much in several places. But was it worthy of so much discussion? Clearly, the church had more important things to do in carrying out God's will than to focus exclusively on one sin.

Pride was a sin, too, as were telling a lie, committing adultery, and stealing a person's retirement funds through some fancy financial shenanigans. And then there were the more inward sins such as lust, greed, and arrogance. Didn't they deserve just as much attention? Would a church ever split over the sin of arrogance? No. How about greed? Wasn't being fully engaged in capitalism a form of greed? Was that really bad? Was it justifiable?

The sins most easily forgiven and forgotten were those having nothing to do with sex. If sex was involved in some form or fashion, forgiveness suddenly became more difficult and the memory of the offense never ceased. Was the sexual relationship people had with one another more important than being prideful?

And what if a homosexual came to church after asking for God's forgiveness? Would the church ever forget the person's past? It was easy to forgive, say, someone who used to be arrogant and a swindler but then turned his life around and became a regular churchgoer. But what if a gay person stood up one Sunday and made a public profession of faith and then said that he was no longer going to engage in homosexual relationships? That was what the church was asking for, wasn't it? Could they ever forget? Let the former homosexual teach Sunday school? Could they live up to their own standard?

And then, what if . . . what if they were wrong? What if homosexuality was a genetic condition? Would God forgive them for singling out homosexuals as the enemy to be fought?

Now there was an angle. How should the church respond to this issue? What if the church was wrong?

John stared at the ceiling in the corner by the window. Someone had pinned a strip of flypaper there before he moved in and he had left it hanging. Now he saw that a single fly had been captured by its own desire for food. He got up and walked over to get a better look. The fly was still alive. Perhaps it had just landed several minutes ago. As the fly struggled to lift one leg, and then another, John considered helping it escape. The flypaper was really sticky and the fly's effort to escape was clearly in vain. John reached up and tried to give the fly a nudge. When he did, his finger stuck to the flypaper and in quickly trying to get his finger unstuck, he accidentally squashed the nearby fly.

John walked over to the sink to wash his hands, pondering the fly and the flypaper. And wondering what to do about Ann Lingerfelt.

CHAPTER 36

Q. 192. What do we pray for in the third petition?

A. In the third petition (which is, "Thy will be done on earth as it is in heaven"), acknowledging that by nature we and all men are not only utterly unable and unwilling to know and do the will of God, but prone to rebel against his Word, to repine and murmur against his providence, and wholly inclined to do the will of the flesh, and of the devil: we pray that God would by his Spirit take away from ourselves and others all blindness, weakness, indisposedness, and perverseness of heart, and by his grace make us able and willing to know, do, and submit to his will in all things, with the like humility, cheerfulness, faithfulness, diligence, zeal, sincerity, and constancy, as the angels do in heaven.

THE BOOK OF CONFESSIONS, PRESBYTERIAN CHURCH (USA):
THE LARGER CATECHISM, 7.302

THEY FINALLY NARROWED IT DOWN to the Havelock guy and the Seagrove guy. Today they were headed back to Havelock for a second look, and if they still weren't sure after hearing the sermon, they planned to visit Seagrove again. Travis was glad for a second chance to hear the pastor at Havelock, since he'd fallen asleep during his sermon the first time around. He didn't want to have to admit that—or to make up something when the others asked him what he thought.

The most direct way for them to get to Havelock was to

go through Greenville over to Highway 17, head south to New Bern, then pick up 70 and take it into Havelock. They would be approaching Havelock from the north side of the Croatan National Forest, so, thank goodness, they wouldn't have to deal with that again. It wasn't that far a drive, so they didn't have to get up real early and they all had their coffee before they hit the road.

Travis didn't know if it was because they were taking it easy or what, but everybody was kind of quiet all the way to New Bern. Matt was in la-la land, as usual, but today he was in some kind of deep-thinking mode. There was no telling with him. Susie and Dot hardly said a word. Dot didn't even seem snappy; she was almost humble. Travis didn't know what was up with that.

Bill didn't joke around any and kept his eyes on the road without looking around like he normally did. He would have missed at least two good church signs if Travis hadn't pointed them out to him. One said, *If you're not right with God, you're left.* The other one said, *Plan ahead—it wasn't raining when Noah built the ark.*

And Joyce, she wasn't her usual polite self and even seemed a little agitated. The only one who appeared to be the same as always was Frankie. She was the only one talking, and she was the one who told Bill to stop at the Hess station just before they got to New Bern. "Turn in here, Bill," she said from the back of the van. "I've got to go."

"I don't think this station has an indoor bathroom. You want to wait until we get to New Bern?" Bill replied.

"No, stop now or you'll be wishing you did pretty soon."

"Alright, alright."

Bill turned into the Hess station parking area. Frankie was already up by the side door, waiting for the van to stop so she could get out. When Bill finally stopped, she jerked open the door, made a grunt as she stepped down to the pavement, and then hustled inside. In less than five seconds, she came out of the store holding a key that was attached to a long piece of Plexiglas. She scurried around to the other side of the station where the outside bathrooms were located.

"Anybody want anything?" Bill asked over his shoulder.

"I could use a pack of Dentyne if somebody will go get it for me," Dot offered from the middle of the van.

"I'm fine," Susie said.

Matt said to Susie, "How about a cup of coffee? My treat."

Susie paused, then said, "Well, okay. But I'll go with you to get it."

"Okay, let's go," Matt said and stepped out of the van, followed by Susie.

Travis watched Susie walk into the station. She seemed so out of place here; an attractive, well-dressed woman, all ready for church, walking into a dirty-looking gas station. And why was Matt offering to buy her coffee? Did they have something going now? But what harm would there be in that, and why should Travis care anyway? Maybe Matt was just being nice. That had to be it, because Travis just couldn't visualize Susie with Matt, ever.

As Susie was coming out of the store, Frankie came around the corner shaking her head.

"What's wrong with her?" Dot asked no one in particular.

Susie got in the van first, followed by Matt. As Frankie got in, she said, "Well, I never!"

"What?" Dot asked.

"That was about the nastiest bathroom I've ever been in. I couldn't sit down on the seat because it looked like something might jump up on me."

"So what did you do?"

"I took some tissue and went outside behind that dumpster storage area."

"You did what?"

"It was the only choice I had. I had to go, and I didn't want to catch something from that bathroom, so I just went behind that storage area."

Bill laughed. It was the first time on this trip that he had even smiled. "Good heavens, Frankie, why couldn't you wait until we got to New Bern?"

"Just drive on and forget about it. Men don't have any idea what it's like when a woman has to use the bathroom on a road trip," Frankie replied.

"Amen!" Susie piped up.

"Alright, alright. I'm sorry I said anything. I should have known my place," Bill said, looking over and smiling at Travis.

"Bill Duncan, I don't know how Mary Helen put up with you all those years," Frankie replied.

Travis looked around at everybody, and everybody was

smiling . . . except Joyce. She was just looking out the side window. That was odd. She was always smiling. Oh well, must be one of those woman days. Jenny had been upset recently too, but for another reason. Turns out it was a false alarm and she wasn't pregnant after all. Fortunately, Travis had enough good sense to keep his mouth shut. Jenny had been silent too. Not talking at all.

Crossing over the bridge at New Bern, Travis could look right over into the little riverside town. It was a nice place with old-looking orange brick. You could park your boat right there on the waterfront. Travis didn't know what these people did for a living. Probably retirees, mostly, and not from around here.

He had come to New Bern one time with his daddy to look at a workboat that some old guy had for sale. He didn't know why his daddy wanted a boat—the closest big water to their house was at least an hour away. Anyway, the boat was pretty beat up and his dad talked with the old man for about thirty minutes before he told Travis to crawl back into the truck. They didn't get the boat. Apparently, the old man wouldn't come down on his price, and Travis's dad always had to get a good deal on any major purchase. So they went home.

The four-lane between New Bern and Havelock was bounded on one side by the tall pines of the Croatan National Forest and on the other side by the Neuse River. Travis kept his eyes peeled for a dirt road coming out of the national forest to see if Tabby Lake Road made it all the way through the forest like the map said.

"There it is!" he announced to the group. No one else seemed quite as interested as Travis was in finding it.

"It doesn't look good from this side either," Bill said as they passed by, looking at the sandy entrance with deep ruts evident from earlier adventurers.

"I get tired just thinking about it," Dot said with a heavy sigh.

"Well, at least the map was right. It does make it all the way through," Matt said from the back of the van. "I wouldn't mind trying it again."

"Well, you can have at it—but not on this trip," Dot ordered.

Matt closed his eyes and rested his head on the back of the seat.

They arrived at the church just in time to see the choir marching to the sanctuary from the educational building, and it made Travis wonder, once again, how hard it must be to hear somebody preaching a sermon with his back turned toward you. It couldn't be the same effect that the congregation experienced when a preacher was making a serious point and all you could see was the bald spot on the back of his head. No facial expressions, just a bald spot with a few strands of hair trying to cover it up. He guessed over a period of time you could observe the progress the hairline made as it moved south and note the exact date when the preacher gave up on the comb-over. Little observations like that made life interesting. He bet somebody in a choir somewhere had done it.

Anyway, they parked on the back side of the parking lot so

as not to draw unnecessary attention, and then they crawled out, one by one. Somebody needed to write a manual on covert tactics for search committees. It got a little tricky when you went to a small church. You either played it to the hilt and lied about who you were and what you were doing there, or you just fessed up right away, smiled, and left.

Travis remembered how one smaller church around Andrews, South Carolina, almost nailed them. What happened was somebody went up to Frankie and Bill to shake their hands after the service and said, "Hi! My name is Don Avery."

Frankie shook his hand and said, "Hi. I'm Frankie, and this is my husband, Bill."

The church member asked, "Are you folks just visiting with us today?"

Bill answered, "Yes, we are. We enjoyed the service."

"Where are you folks from?"

Frankie spoke up and said, "We're new to the area and we're just checking out the various churches that we might attend."

"Is that right? Well, there's only a few churches to check out around here and this is the *only* Presbyterian church. Where did you move to?"

At that point, Frankie glanced at Bill to signal that she needed some help getting out of this one.

Bill smiled. "Oh, in that little neighborhood out on 41 coming into town."

But it didn't work. The church member said unexpectedly, "Hey, that's where I live. What street do you live on?"

Bill looked to Frankie. She took a breath, then said, "It's that first one on the right after you turn into the neighborhood."

"Why, that's the street I live on. Which house did you move into?"

Frankie looked at Bill, smiling, but with raised eyebrows. Bill deliberately lifted his arm to check his wristwatch. "I'm sorry, sir. Honey, we need to get going if we're going to make it to that new restaurant in Georgetown."

Frankie looked relieved. "Oh, that's right. I almost forgot. It was so nice to meet you and I hope we run into you in the neighborhood."

"Well, sure. And please call me Don. I hope y'all come back for another visit. We got a real good preacher here and I think he'll be with us a good long while."

So Frankie and Bill vowed to never go near Andrews, South Carolina, again for fear of being spotted by Don and being caught in a lie.

The Havelock church was one of those slick redbrick one-story buildings with an A-frame sanctuary, built in the late sixties or early seventies. A-frames had gone out a long time ago. Travis recalled its being a hot day the first time they'd visited—the time they'd gotten lost in the national forest. Today it was a little cool and the sky was bright blue. The air seemed fresh and dry, not heavy and humid.

There was a big crowd today; maybe they were going to jump the committee as soon as they walked in. They didn't. Everybody just smiled and welcomed them to the church, which made Travis feel guiltier than any direct accusation of preacher-stealing would have. They had split up in their normal pairings, and after Travis sat down he skimmed the bulletin to see what hymns they would be singing.

Okay, let's see . . . "Be Still, My Soul" was the first one. The one right before the sermon was "There Is a Place of Quiet Rest" and the finale was "He Leadeth Me"! *Alright then.*

And the sermon title? "Waiting for God~~ot~~." What? Travis couldn't believe somebody misspelled *God.* And just crossing through the mistake and leaving it in the bulletin? Sloppy.

The service moved along pretty quickly and before Travis was actually thinking about it, it was time for the minister to get up and do his thing.

"Our Old Testament Scripture today is a familiar one, Psalm 23. I'm reading from the New Living Translation.

"'The Lord is my shepherd; I have all that I need. He lets me rest in green meadows; he leads me beside peaceful streams. He renews my strength. He guides me along right paths, bringing honor to his name.

"'Even when I walk through the darkest valley, I will not be afraid, for you are close beside me. Your rod and your staff protect and comfort me.

"'You prepare a feast for me in the presence of my enemies. You honor me by anointing my head with oil. My cup overflows with blessings. Surely your goodness and unfailing love will pursue me all the days of my life, and I will live in the house of the Lord forever.'

"And our New Testament reading is taken from the book of Hebrews, chapter 11, beginning with the first verse.

"'Faith is the confidence that what we hope for will actually happen; it gives us assurance about things we cannot see. Through their faith, the people in days of old earned a good reputation. By faith we understand that the entire universe was formed at God's command, that what we now see did not come from anything that can be seen.'"

The minister shuffled his notes and looked out at the congregation.

"Samuel Beckett is a controversial literary figure who wrote the play *Waiting for Godot*. For those of you familiar with English literature, you may fondly recall—or maybe not so fondly—trudging your way through this seemingly meaningless plot and then wondering how some academics could have devoted their entire careers to the interpretation of this one piece of literature. I know I wondered about that.

"In this story, two men are waiting for someone named Godot. They have never seen Godot, and they can't remember why they are waiting for him. And he never comes. They pass the time in a purposeless manner, reacting to circumstances affecting them.

"Beckett never offered any interpretation of his piece, and the play has been the subject of much analysis. Many believe it to be a humorous and yet tragic portrayal of mankind's existence—that life has no purpose and mankind only reacts to events or invents distractions to pass the time. Others feel that it is a modern-day allegory for their perception of Christianity—waiting for a Savior who doesn't respond and never comes.

"Waiting is an uncomfortable feeling for most people, isn't

it? Especially in these times when we rely on fast food, fast Internet access, interstate highways, overnight mail delivery, and the list goes on and on. It wasn't so long ago that there was no Internet, no overnight mail delivery, and no big highways. I remember when the first fast-food restaurant came to my hometown of Wilmington. It was a Hardee's. People flocked to it, primarily out of curiosity, to sample what was advertised as a great-tasting hamburger in no time flat. I remember when my parents took our family there for lunch one Saturday. I was in complete awe of the production-line activity behind the counter. Amazing. It was a huge success.

"Can you imagine businesses operating nowadays without some type of overnight mail delivery? Or a computer? Does anybody remember how we got along without these things?"

The minister paused and shuffled his notes some more.

"Most people can't remember. These time-saving devices and systems are as much a part of our life as soap or tooth-paste. We expect—no, we *demand*—that these things be available to us. And so, waiting is uncomfortable.

"But waiting has always been uncomfortable, for it implies that we are not significant enough to demand immediate attention. It belittles our self-esteem. I remember when I was about ten years old, my mom would normally pick me up after school, but occasionally my dad would pick me up. I sat on the front steps of the school at the end of each day until they came. My mom was always there on time. I had no doubt that she would be. My dad . . . well, sometimes he would get stuck in a meeting, or some type of emergency would happen at work, or sometimes he would just plain forget to pick me up. So I sat. And sat. And sat.

"I came to know every indentation in the concrete steps, every spot of chipped paint, the number of tongue-and-groove boards in the ceiling of the overhanging porch, every freckle on both of my arms, the prevailing wind direction, how to twiddle my thumbs in both directions, and thousands of figures formed by the passing clouds. And I learned to hide my embarrassment at being forgotten as the last of the other students were picked up and as the last of the teachers left. Even when it was just me and the principal, I learned to pretend that everything was cool, that I was completely okay with having to wait.

"And then, when my dad finally arrived and apologized to the principal, I ran and jumped in the car like nothing was wrong—until we pulled away. Then it never failed; a flood of emotion would pour out into the car. I told my dad I hated him, that he hated me, that I didn't ever want to go back to school, that I wished I were dead. And my dad would say he was sorry, give some reason for being late, and try to hug me. If I really put up the stone wall, he would just prop his elbow on the open window and hold his tilted head in the palm of his left hand and stare straight ahead, driving home in silence.

"The twenty-third Psalm is perhaps the best-known Scripture in the Bible. Many of us had to memorize it as children. Many of us chose to memorize it as adults. It's our security blanket. No matter what, no matter where, no matter who, we know that God is our protector and companion.

"But do we really know? Or do we just hope? Is one less than the other? If we say we know but events don't happen or if they turn out the other way, does that mean our faith is weak? If we say we hope but events don't happen or if they turn out the other way, does that mean God has no control in the world?

"When God doesn't answer some obvious need that we have been praying about every night for the last two weeks, we sometimes ask a different type of question. Like 'Why isn't God answering my prayer?' or 'Why is he allowing this to happen right now?' Some people go even further and start negotiating with God. 'Okay, God, if you're not going to do that for me, then I'm not going to church for a couple of months' or 'If you hurry up, God, I promise I'll really tithe next year.' Then a desperate few will even wager their salvation on God's response.

"But God makes you wait.

"And wait.

"And wait.

"And the bill collectors call. And the tumor returns. And you really do lose your job. And your daughter continues to rebel. And your grandmother dies. And where . . . is . . . God?

"Well, he's right there with you. Always has been. Look at the twenty-third Psalm again: 'Even when I walk through the darkest valley, I will not be afraid, for you are close beside me.' 'He leads me beside peaceful streams.' 'He guides me along right paths.'

"He is with us. He's not sending us off on our own or waiting at the end of the trail. He is with us.

"Our problem is that we want to know—actually, we want to *control*—how things turn out. We don't like to admit how little control we have over our circumstances. Especially here in America with our Puritan work ethic, our free-enterprise system, our superior military might, and our wealth relative to the rest of the world. But if we're honest with ourselves, we would admit that things don't always turn out like we planned, do they?

"We struggle to understand what God's will is for our lives. Most of the time we come up with a solution of our own making and try to make things work. Then we struggle and toil and work so hard that we convince ourselves that what we are doing must be the right solution because it requires so much effort. Then when things don't work out, we ask God why he allowed our failure. Why didn't he give us the right result? Why did he make us go through all that pain and then not come through for us? Why is it that his answers are not always the answers we prayed for?

"The end. The solution. We are usually praying for something at the end. Something to end the struggle. Something tangible. Something we can see and touch. A solution that will reward our hard work."

The minister paused.

"It's not about the solution, folks. . . . It's about the journey. It's about what happens to us on the way. How we grow. How we respond. How we wait.

"Let's look at that wonderful verse from the book of Hebrews, 'Faith is the confidence that what we hope for will actually happen; it gives us assurance about things we cannot see.'

"We read that verse and think we already know what the things are that we hope for. We say to others, 'See there, if you only believe hard enough, you will get what you want!' But that's not what it says. 'Assurance about things we cannot see' doesn't say 'assurance of things we want,' does it? No, it does not. If it did, then where would God fit in? We would become the masters of our own destiny.

"'Assurance about things we cannot see,' to me, says, 'Assurance about knowing that God will prevail.'

"Some of you might question that and say, 'Why do anything, then, if God does everything?' Because our job—and hear me on this—our job is to live our lives in service to God. That's hard work, folks. Try it sometime. You can do great things by doing God's work. And at the end of the day, trust that God will take care of you, that he is the master of your destiny. Then, no matter what comes along to confront us, we can be assured that God is present, standing by our side, seeing us through it, and leading us in his will.

"Beckett got it only partly right. We do wait . . . but God does come. In fact, he is already here.

"In the name of the Father, the Son, and the Holy Spirit, amen."

Travis looked around at the other committee members to get everybody's reaction. Hard to tell. Looked like they were going to Seagrove again.

CHAPTER 37

Anyone who injures another person must be dealt with according to the injury inflicted—a fracture for a fracture, an eye for an eye, a tooth for a tooth. Whatever anyone does to injure another person must be paid back in kind.

LEVITICUS 24:19-20

DOT LEANED BACK in the La-Z-Boy chair in the den, pulling on the lever to raise the leg rest. After she got settled, she folded her arms across her chest and jutted out her lower lip.

This was a real pickle. Fred was cheating on her with Stephanie, his bookkeeper. She just couldn't imagine how Fred had wooed a younger, attractive woman. He must have spent a lot of money on her; that would be the only way he could have pulled it off. He had turned out to be exactly like her daddy had warned—worthless.

Should she confront him about it? Or maybe confront

the girl? It probably wouldn't make any difference. What could she hope to accomplish? If she confronted him and he repented, she certainly would never be able to trust him again. If she left him, all their friends would know why, and she figured they wouldn't necessarily blame Fred. It just wasn't fair that he should get off scot-free and hardly anyone would know or care what he had done. There had to be a way, a way to make him pay.

Hmmm. Make him pay. Hardly anyone would know. Maybe that was the answer. A slow smile spread across Dot's face.

• • •

At the post office, Dot waited in line for about ten minutes until it was her turn. She approached the counter.

"How do I get a mailing list for everybody in this town?" she asked the dumpy middle-aged male postal clerk.

"Well, I can't provide that to you, but if you go over to Randy's FastPrint, he'll sell you a list like that for about twenty-five dollars," the clerk replied. "In fact, he'll do a mail merge for you as well. Of course, there's an additional fee for that."

"Thank you," Dot said emphatically. Then she turned and walked out of the post office.

Randy's FastPrint was on the end of the new stucco strip mall that had just gone up on 301.

At one end of the tall white counter that separated the customers from the employees was a greasy-looking young man wearing a Randy's FastPrint T-shirt and working on something. His black-dyed hair was hanging down over one eye.

"May I help you?" he asked, looking up from his work.

"Maybe so," Dot replied. "How do I get a mailing list for everyone in town?"

"We can sell you one for thirty-five dollars."

"Thirty-five dollars? The man at the post office said it was twenty-five," Dot protested.

"That was last year. Prices have gone up," the young man replied matter-of-factly.

"Well, I guess it is what it is. Tell me, how would I go about sending something to everyone on the list?" Dot inquired.

"Like a Christmas letter, you mean?"

"Well, not exactly. But a letter, anyway."

"It's not too hard. You just write whatever it is you want to send in Microsoft Word format, and we can mail merge it for you. You'll have to pay for the postage, of course."

"I see," said Dot. "Let me put it together and I'll come back later."

Dot drove to Frankie's house and knocked.

Frankie answered the door. "Well, hey there. What are you doing out and about today?"

"I need a hand with something."

"Sure, what is it?"

"I need your help to write something on the computer," Dot explained. "A letter."

"Come on in. George has gone to the grocery store, so we can get on his computer in the kitchen."

"Okay," Dot answered, walking into the house.

Frankie sat down beside Dot at the computer and they began to work. After several minutes Frankie said, "Dot, are you sure you want to do this? I mean, what you're wanting to do, there's no turning back."

"Yes, I am 100 percent sure."

Frankie said, "Okay, but this could get ugly. People will talk and Fred will definitely leave you. For good."

"I know, but I won't be able to hold my head up in this town if I let him get away with it."

"Suit yourself. I'm just saying there's no going back."

• • •

As Dot left Frankie's house, Frankie stood on her front stoop and called, "I'm here if you need me."

"Don't worry; I'll be fine," Dot yelled back from the driveway.

Dot walked into Randy's FastPrint for the second time that day. The greaser was still working at the end of the counter.

"Okay, so what do you have?" he asked when Dot entered the store.

Dot handed him the letter and the CD on which Frankie had saved the letter electronically.

The young man said, "So this is going out to everyone in town? You know that will be a lot of postage."

"Yes, you're right. What's the cheapest way to do it?" she asked.

"I would just print it in a small font on a postcard. That

way, everybody will see it without having to open an envelope. You want to make sure they read it, right?" he asked.

"I wouldn't be sending it if I didn't want them to read it, now would I?"

The young man blushed. "Well, sure. I just meant a post-card would be the easiest way to get your message out."

"Okay, so how much will it cost to send these out on a postcard?" Dot asked.

"Let's see, if you send it bulk rate, I think it will be around ten cents a card. The list has about five hundred addresses on it, so that would be what, say, about fifty dollars?"

"It's worth it. Let's do it."

"Well, there will be the printing charge as well."

"And what will that be?"

"For this, I would say about fifteen dollars."

"Okay, do it. How long will it take?"

"We can do it right now if you want."

"The sooner, the better."

When the young man finished printing the postcards with Dot's message on them, she removed the card on the top of the stack, sliding it out from beneath the rubber band holding the stack together.

She turned it over and read to herself,

To Everyone in Our Town,
  My husband, Fred Spivey, has decided to break his marriage vows by cheating on me. He has been seeing Stephanie Wood, a much younger woman than

I, who is also his bookkeeper. Last week they spent at
least one day together at the Red Roof Inn in Kinston.
A trusted friend witnessed their coming and going.
I have been a good and faithful wife and don't
deserve this kind of treatment. I am truly heartbroken.
This is very hard for me to tell everyone about, but
I just wanted to let everyone know what I'm going
through.
If you think it will help, please pray that I will make
it through this tough time.

Love to all,
Dot Spivey

It barely fit on the card but it would do the trick. This
would run Fred and his girl out of town for sure. Dot would
come out smelling like a rose, with everyone sympathetic to
her situation. Ah, revenge was sweet. She paid the greasy kid
and left the store.

• • •

Two days later it happened. The calls started coming in.
"*Dot, I am so sorry. Please let me know if I can do anything.*"
"*Dot, I've been there, done that. Send that dog packing.*"
"*Dot, I will pray for you and hope that your husband gets*
what he deserves."
"*Dot, leave his sorry carcass behind. He's not worthy to be the*
doormat on your back steps."
And so it went, on and on. She had to delete the messages

on the answering machine at least three times that morning, there were so many of them. Dot sat in the kitchen and waited for the Fred fallout.

At 11:30 a.m., Fred's car came to a screeching halt in the driveway. He slammed the door and stomped to the front stoop.

Opening the front door, he yelled, "You're the one that drove me to it!" He walked into the kitchen. "I was going to stop seeing her, but you had to go do this! I'm leaving! Thanks for ruining my life!"

Dot didn't say a word. It was only what he deserved. Wasn't it?

Fred walked down the hall and into their bedroom. Dot heard drawers opening and shutting. In less than two minutes, he was ready to leave.

Opening the front door, he yelled, "Good-bye and good riddance!"

Then he slammed the door and left.

Dot sat still at the kitchen table. It had worked perfectly.

Payback.

Revenge.

He was gone, punished, and the girl would likely leave town as well.

Everyone knew it was his fault.

Dot put her head down on the table and began to cry.

CHAPTER 38

Q. 90. What shall be done to the righteous at the day of judgment?
A. At the day of judgment, the righteous, being caught up to Christ
in the clouds, shall be set on his right hand, and, there openly
acknowledged and acquitted, shall join with him in the judging of
reprobate angels and men; and shall be received into heaven, where
they shall be fully and forever freed from all sin and misery; filled with
inconceivable joy; made perfectly holy and happy both in body and
soul, in the company of innumerable saints and angels, but especially in
the immediate vision and fruition of God the Father, of our Lord Jesus
Christ, and of the Holy Spirit, to all eternity. And this is the perfect
and full communion, which the members of the invisible Church shall
enjoy with Christ in glory, at the resurrection and day of judgment.

THE BOOK OF CONFESSIONS, PRESBYTERIAN CHURCH (USA):
THE LARGER CATECHISM, 7.200

FRANKIE TIGHTENED THE BELT on her bathrobe and walked over to turn on the radio, an old, big, black plastic model with a handle across the top and a silver-colored grille, which sat in one of the cubbyholes in her bookcase. George had won it playing bingo at the Halloween carnival over at the high school about eight or nine years ago. Even though the antenna was broken at about the halfway point, it could still pick up several stations like that gospel station in Dunn, a Spanish-speaking station in Greenville for all the Hispanics who had moved into the area, another gospel station coming out of Kinston, a rock station over in Fayetteville, and the country station in Wilson. Frankie had it tuned to the Dunn gospel station. She sat down in her rocker and opened her women's devotional Bible.

She heard the radio announcer inviting listeners "to the grand opening of the new Dollar General store in Erwin beside the Food Lion. We'll be handing out flyers there today that tell all about the Southern Gospel Quartet Sing-Off on Saturday, December 17, at Erwin Bible College in the multi-purpose room. The cost is four dollars at the door, or you can pick up your tickets here at the station and get a one-dollar discount. Y'all really need to come out for this event, because I can promise you that you will receive a blessing from it, and God will be glorified on that day."

Frankie closed her Bible, leaned back in the rocker, and closed her eyes. She started a slight rocking motion by pushing off the floor with the balls of her feet. The radio announcer droned on. "And now we pause for the reading of the obituaries, praise God! Hallelujah! There will come a time, blessed Jesus, when we all meet on that wonderful shore, praise God! And one by one we'll cross over to the Promised Land, hallelujah! Praise the Lord! Today, fellow Christians, we honor those who have gone on before us, praise God! Hallelujah! Our first beloved today who has gone on to meet her maker is Frances 'Frankie' Leonard Fulford, wife of George Fulford for fifty-three years. Parker Funeral Home is handling the arrangements."

"What?" Frankie sat up and looked at the radio.

"Yes, she was a fine Christian woman and what you might call a servant leader."

"What is going on?" Frankie said out loud. She stood up.

The radio announcer continued, "Mrs. Fulford will be greatly missed by all who knew her, because she made such a dramatic impact on their lives, living the gospel so that all might see and believe, praise God!"

Frankie whispered, "Something is wrong here. I need to go fix it. Everybody thinks I'm dead."

Frankie left the house, and she was suddenly downtown, walking along the road in front of the Methodist church. An old blue Chevrolet station wagon passed her, and a child, a young, dark-haired boy wearing a red shirt, waved at her from the backseat. She kept going.

She looked in the direction of the Presbyterian church but it wasn't there. Instead there was some kind of motel, painted yellow, occupying the lot where the church should have been.

Frankie asked, "Where is our church? What is that?"

She turned and went down a side street with no sidewalk. No one was at home in any of the houses along this street. Frankie passed all of the houses and came to a cornfield on the left side of the road. She jumped across the small roadside ditch and walked into the field, putting her hands in front of her to keep the sharp leaves from striking her face.

The wind picked up. The rustling corn blades sounded like fine sandpaper on a smooth kitchen countertop. Frankie began running down the row. The blades of corn were sting-ing and cutting her arms.

She stopped and crossed over to another row. The corn was taller here. Looking ahead and then behind her, she saw nothing but tall, green cornstalks loaded with new corn.

She ran deeper into the field. Now the blades were strik-ing her face, and she squinted to keep them from hitting her eyes. Then she heard footsteps. Frankie stopped and squatted down to see better. There weren't any blades near the ground, so she could see through the rows.

"Frankie! Wait up! I need to talk to you!" a boy's voice shouted. He was running and getting close but he was not in her row.

"Davie?" Frankie whispered.

"Frankie! Stop running! Where are you?"

"I'm over here!" Frankie shouted.

"Where?"

"Here!"

Davie parted the corn and stepped over to Frankie's row. He was out of breath and bent over to rest with his hands on his knees. He was still twelve. "Whew! I thought I'd never catch up to you, girl. You can really run now."

"Davie, what are you doing here? I thought—"

"Yeah, well, listen. I've been wanting to talk to you for a long time, but I wasn't allowed to until now."

"What do you mean, you weren't allowed to?"

"Oh, it's nothing. I can tell you about it some other time. I need to talk to you about something else now."

"What is it?"

"Well, I just wanted to let you know that I'm okay. Everything's alright—you can stop worrying about me."

"Davie, I don't understand. Why are you here? You died, remember? Daddy killed you with that milk bottle."

"Yes, you got all of that right. I am dead, kind of—but not really, because I'm here talking to you, aren't I?"

"I don't get it, Davie. What's going on?"

"Just don't worry about it. I can't stay long. I've got to get back so that me and Mama can sing in the choir together."

"Mama?"

"I'm sorry. I know this is really strange for you. Yes, me and Mama are doing fine. She said to tell you hello and that she wants to see you sometime too, but I don't think they'll let us do this again."

"Who's *they*, Davie?"

"The—look, I can't tell you everything, okay? I just wanted you to know that I'm doing real good now, and you don't need to worry so much about me. I'm fine."

"But you're dead. I saw it."

"I know you did, and that's what I wanted to talk to you about. It's okay now. I'm in a better place. I'm safe, Mama's safe, and everything is fine."

"So how long can you stay?"

"Just a couple more minutes. This sort of thing is kind of unusual. I've been working on them for a long time to get to do this."

"Davie, don't leave me. You can stay at my house. I've got a real nice place and you can meet . . ." Frankie looked down at her clothes and held out her small arms, twisting and inspecting them. "Wait—I'm a girl again. . . . What happened?"

"That's part of the deal. You have to be the same age as when I last saw you for me to be able to talk to you. . . . Look, just relax now. Me and Mama are waiting for you. There's a place for you there. Hey, I got to go. I love you, Sis."

Davie stood up straight and started to walk backward, then ducked and crossed over to the next row. He was gone and Frankie stood alone, surrounded by green blades of corn.

"No, come back, Davie! Don't go!" Frankie shouted in the direction that Davie had gone. She ran down the row, back toward the road. Bursting out from the sharp green blades, she jumped the ditch and saw that she was standing in front of her and George's house.

How did that get here?

She wiped the sweat from her forehead, noticing that her hands were now brown and leathery with familiar liver spots on the back. They were an old woman's hands.

"Wake up, darling! You're having another bad one!"

"What?" Frankie said with her eyes half-open.

George was gently shaking her shoulders. "Come on. Get up. You had another bad one."

Frankie sat up straight in the rocker and looked around past George. "Davie?"

"Who are you calling, honey?"

"Davie, my brother. He was here. Not here, but out in the field with me. I talked with him."

"Come on, sweetie. Let me help you." George reached down and helped Frankie stand up. He grabbed the arm closest to him with his left hand and put his other arm around her to lead her to the bedroom.

"I talked to him, George. I talked to him. I really did."

George rubbed her back as they walked. When they reached the bedroom, he pulled the covers back for her as she stood still beside him. "Come on; crawl in."

Frankie got into bed and lay down on her back, staring at the ceiling. "George?"

"Yes, hon?"

Frankie turned her head to look at him. "I really did talk to him. I talked to Davie."

"That's great, sweetie. Let's get some sleep."

Frankie looked up at the ceiling and smiled. He was okay. . . . Davie was okay.

Frankie's body felt unusually light and her breathing seemed effortless. She rolled onto her side and, closing her eyes, fell into a deep, comforting sleep.

CHAPTER 39

Bend down, O LORD, and hear my prayer; answer me, for I need your help. Protect me, for I am devoted to you. Save me, for I serve you and trust you. You are my God. Be merciful to me, O Lord, for I am calling on you constantly. Give me happiness, O Lord, for I give myself to you.

PSALM 86:1-4

A MONTH HAD PASSED since Julia had driven away. Matt had gone to her apartment in town, but she wasn't there. Panicking, he had driven around for several hours looking for her, going to the truck stop to see if she had stopped there, even going out on the interstate and stopping at several exits in either direction. He had returned home and sat at the kitchen table with his dad, no words spoken, just silence. The next day he had gone back to the truck stop to ask if anyone knew where her folks lived. Julia had mentioned once that they lived in South Carolina near Lake Marion, but she had not been back there since leaving home at the age of eighteen. Her father had told her to get out for no other reason than she was old enough to be on her own. Her mother had raised no objection.

After leaving home, she had taken a waitress job at one of the fish camps on the lower lake, Lake Moultrie, renting one of the ramshackle rooms behind the restaurant that the owner rented to bass fishermen. After three months the owner's wife became suspicious of her husband's intentions for Julia and had him fire her. One of the other waitresses gave her a ride to a friend's apartment in Santee, a small town built around an I-95 exit, where she walked from tackle shop to gas station to fast-food joint to convenience store until she landed a waitress job at a seafood restaurant. After several months, the friend lost her job and headed for Charleston, leaving Julia to pay all of the rent, which she couldn't afford. That's when a lady trucker she served at the restaurant agreed to give Julia a ride to Dunn, North Carolina. Julia lied, saying she had relatives there. She only knew it was near I-95 and in North Carolina after hearing some other truckers that day talking about stopping there. Fortunately, the lady trucker sensed Julia was completely on her own and had called her bluff. Julia had broken down, and while she was sobbing uncontrollably the lady trucker called a friend at a truck stop a little farther north up I-95, who agreed to give Julia a place to stay and a waitress job at the truck-stop restaurant. That's where Julia landed and had remained for nine years, until now.

Matt had searched the Internet for any listing of Julia's last name, Truesdale, in any of the towns around the lakes. He had actually called several people with that name, but none claimed to know anything about who Julia was or who her parents were or where she might be.

• • •

It was warm, especially for December. Matt's dad had gone into town to talk to the Massey Ferguson dealer about having them rebuild the hydraulic pump for his tractor. Matt didn't want to go with him. The black cloud was back. He was floating again, not sure about anything, not wanting to do anything. Fortunately, it was winter break from school.

He decided to walk down to the swamp. He sat on the bench he had tacked across two cypress knees and stared at the black water, trying to remember something Julia had said about her past, anything to give him some clue where she might be. Methane bubbles broke the surface of the water and floated with the current briefly before popping. She had said something else about Lake Marion once, something about the swamp. Something about rafts. What was it? He just couldn't recall what she said. But it did have something to do with her past. He remembered that.

The door slammed on his dad's truck up at the house and Matt went to see what his dad was up to. When he reached the house his dad was sitting at the kitchen table, drinking a glass of milk.

Matt opened the back door and walked to the table. "Dad, I want you to help me find her."

Matt's dad didn't say anything.

"I think she went home," Matt said.

"And where would that be?" Matt's dad asked without looking up.

"I don't know. I think it's around Lake Marion. She never said exactly where she was from, but I remember her once saying something about growing up around Lake Marion."

"It's a big lake," Matt's dad replied dryly. "What's your plan?"

"No real plan. I don't know what else to do other than to drive down there and ask around about her."

"Son, I don't think that will turn out well. You're probably not going to find out anything you haven't already uncovered, and it will just get you all torn up inside. Why don't you just try to get on with your life? If it's meant to be, she'll come back. She probably knows you're looking for her."

Matt felt his ears get hot. "So is that how you dealt with Mom's death? Just getting on with your life like nothing happened?"

Matt's dad stood up, looked down at the floor, and walked out the door. He walked across the yard to the tractor shed. Matt sat down at the table. He stared at nothing in particular, just stared. Nothing seemed to work out, ever. Why was that? The black cloud began to close in on him. He felt its pressure. He put his head down on the table and closed his eyes.

Five minutes later the back door flew open and his dad's big frame filled up the doorway.

"Alright, let's go find her. Get packed."

Matt stood up and looked at his dad. His dad smiled. Matt walked quickly to his room and shoved some clothes into a duffel bag.

• • •

Two days had passed with no luck. They had asked every store and restaurant owner in Santee if they had seen or heard anything about Julia Truesdale. No one knew her. Same response when they traveled down to Eutawville. Same thing up above Santee at Elloree. Then they crossed the lake on I-95 and began working their way up the other side. They stopped at Jake's Landing and Tackle Shop near Rimini. The old man behind the counter was smoking, but you could tell by the way he held the cigarette in his mouth that he had no teeth or at least had not put his dentures in that day. He was wiry, brown, and leathery with wrinkled-up skin on his face and arms. He was stocking cigarettes on a shelf behind the counter and didn't acknowledge Matt and his dad when they entered the store.

"Hi," Matt offered.

The old man didn't say anything but did look at them as if to say, "What now?"

"We're looking for a friend of the family who's a Truesdale. Any Truesdales in these parts?" Matt asked.

"No."

"How about a girl named Julia? Heard of anyone by that name traveling through here?" Matt continued.

"No."

"Okay. Thank you," Matt's dad replied and turned to

leave the store. Matt followed but then turned and asked, "Are there any rafts on the lake around here?"

"What?" the old man asked, squinting his eyes at Matt.

"Rafts. I don't know, like some kind of raft somebody might live on or something."

The old man stared at Matt for a moment before asking, "Who are you with, the power company?" Before Matt could answer, the man continued, "Because if you are, you can just get on out of here. Ain't got no use for you."

"No, we're not with the power company. We're just passing through. We're from North Carolina and we're looking for a friend of the family."

The old man didn't reply but seemed partly satisfied with Matt's answer. He resumed stocking the cartons of cigarettes.

"Does the power company not like rafts on the lake?" Matt asked.

The man turned around with a look of disgust. "No, the power company'd just as soon get rid of all those rafts."

"People live on the rafts?"

The old man again studied Matt for a while and said, "Are you sure you're not from the power company?"

"No, we're not from the power company. I'm a teacher. My dad's a farmer. We're looking for a friend."

"And your friend's on a raft?"

"I don't know where she is. We're looking for her. Where are these rafts?"

"Sorry, can't help you there," the old man replied and returned again to stocking cigarette cartons.

Matt's dad had come back in and was listening to the conversation. Finally, he spoke up. "Would twenty dollars help you remember where these rafts are located?"

The man didn't say anything and continued to stack cartons.

"Okay, what about fifty?" Matt's dad continued.

Still no response.

"A hundred dollars is my last offer," Matt's dad said, raising his voice.

The old man turned around. "Put it on the counter and I'll talk."

. . .

Matt and his dad rented a johnboat from the old man and headed out into the lake. The man also tried to sell them a gun. Said they'd need it. Matt and his dad turned down the offer. "Suit yourself," the old man had replied.

While making all the arrangements for renting the johnboat, the old man had rambled on a bit about the rafts and the power company. Apparently, there was a part of the lake near the headwaters where only a shallow draft boat could reach. Locals called it Touchberry Swamp. It was hard enough navigating through the upper part of the lake anyway because the area had never been completely cleared before the power company built the dam and formed the lake. They ran out of money during the Depression. Cypress trees, knees, and stumps were thick in some areas, and in the area where the rafts were supposedly located there was no distinguishable open water at all. It was basically a flooded forest but it was full of bream beds. Fishermen had originally built the rafts with a room and maybe a cot to have their own fishing cottages. The entire raft was typically no more than eight to ten feet across and twenty feet long and was tied to surrounding cypress trees.

Fishermen used to cook their catches on Coleman stoves, drink whiskey, and generally have a good time with their pals. Mostly, they just spent the weekend there or maybe an entire week if they were on vacation. Nowadays, fishermen no longer used the rafts, as far as the old man knew. Instead they were occupied year-round by people with no other place to go. Poor, generally illiterate white folk. They had formed an isolated community, sustaining themselves on fish and corn bread cooked on woodstoves and grills, rarely coming out for supplies.

The power company had tried unsuccessfully to remove the rafts because the people who lived on them were squatters on public property and they also used the water around them as their septic tank. Furthermore, the squatters had become adversarial in a cantankerous sort of way. There were only a few navigable routes through the trees to get to the raft area. The local word was to get out of there by any possible route if you heard a chain saw. The raft people would cut down a tree to block your way out.

After relaying this last bit of information, the old man pointed out that they were leaving their pickup truck at his store and it would be his if they didn't return the boat.

Matt and his dad had purchased a laminated map with soundings from the old man and were headed to an area where he had claimed they would run into the raft people. It was already afternoon and they didn't want to waste time on the lake. The weather could turn nasty, and where they were going was not a good area to be in after dark.

They followed the channel going west in the big water until the flooded forest came into view; then they turned at a channel marker noted by the old man and headed south, directly toward the flooded forest. They slowed the boat to a crawl.

Matt sat at the bow peering down into the brackish water for signs of stumps or any other thing that might damage the motor. His dad had one hand on the outboard motor's tiller and the other hand on the top of the outboard, ready to raise it out of the water if Matt warned of something they were passing over.

They stopped and scanned the area. There was no discernible channel through the flooded forest from their position. They decided to move along the perimeter of the forest to see if there was any way in. After several hundred yards they came to what was obviously the entrance to a small channel meandering through the trees. They entered the forest, slowing to idling speed, peering through the trees for any signs of rafts.

Finally, they spotted one. It appeared to have been constructed from fifty-five-gallon drums tied together, with rough planking on top. An unpainted plywood shack with a tin roof had been built on the planks, and the whole thing was tied between two big cypress trees. They approached it slowly. No sign of anyone living there. They came up to it and Matt hopped onto the raft. His dad grabbed one of the planks and held the johnboat alongside.

"This is pretty nice," Matt said, looking around.

"Look inside the place," his dad suggested.

Matt opened the makeshift plywood door. There was no lock. Inside were two cots, a barbeque grill, a five-gallon bucket with a toilet seat mounted on top of it, and some old *Field & Stream* magazines in one corner. This one was apparently still used by fishermen.

"Not much in here," Matt said, walking out of the shack. "Just a couple of cots and a grill." He got back into the johnboat. "Looks like a regular fishing shack from what I can tell."

His dad shoved off and they continued to follow the winding channel through the trees. They went on like this for what seemed to be an entire hour, looking through the trees for any signs of raft houses, until they reached a point where the channel split into two. They stopped the boat at the fork.

"What do you think?" Matt's dad asked.

"Don't know. Cut the motor and let's see if we can hear anything."

Matt's dad pulled the kill-switch cord and the outboard stopped running. They sat still, listening for sounds of anything that might give them an indication of the correct channel to take. A woodpecker broke the silence and began to make a lot of racket somewhere off to the left.

Matt wondered how Julia could voluntarily choose to live separated from the rest of the world in a dark place like this. And how would she survive living on a raft in the swamp? It didn't seem possible.

On the other hand, if this was truly her home, it was the only family she had. Perhaps she thought they would welcome her back after being gone for so long. But hadn't her father told her to leave? Would they take her in now with a baby on the way? The more he thought about it the more unlikely it seemed that she would have returned here. She was probably waiting tables at another truck stop somewhere along I-95.

Ting . . . ting . . . ting.

"What was that?" Matt asked.

"Sounds like somebody hammering on a railroad spike."

Ting . . . ting . . . ting . . . ting.

"Coming from that direction," Matt's dad said, pointing toward the right-fork channel. He turned and pulled the cord to start the outboard. They began idling along the right-hand fork, trying to follow the hammer sound.

As they got closer to the sound, it stopped.

"They stopped hammering," Matt whispered.

His dad didn't respond but kept looking out through the flooded forest for any type of manmade structure. They continued to idle along.

"Look over there," Matt's dad whispered, nodding in the direction he was looking.

Matt turned and looked through the trees to his right at

what appeared to be several shacks tied together. No sign of people, though. "What do we do now?" he whispered.

"I don't know. You're the one who wanted to come look out here."

Matt cupped his hands and shouted toward the raft shacks, "Helloooo?"

No response.

He tried again. "Helloooo?" He strained to get a better look as his dad kept idling the boat along in the direction of the rafts.

KAPPOWW!

A shotgun fired behind them, scaring Matt and his dad so that they nearly fell out of the johnboat turning around to see who was shooting at them. A string bean–looking fellow with long blond hair was about fifty feet behind them in a dugout canoe. He was reloading his shotgun.

"Don't shoot, for crying out loud!" Matt's dad yelled. "We're not here to harm anyone, and we're not from the power company!"

Matt was down on all fours in the middle of the boat. The man finished reloading his gun and drew a bead on the johnboat. Matt's dad had pulled the kill-switch cord during all of the commotion so the outboard stopped running.

"Who are ya and what're ya doing out here?" the man shouted.

"We're looking for a friend!" Matt answered, rising up.

The man put the gun across his lap and picked up his paddle. He moved the dugout canoe through the water, barely making a sound. He stopped about twenty feet from the johnboat. "They ain't nobody out here but us, so you'd best be gettin' on back to the big water."

"Are you a Truesdale?" Matt's dad asked.

The man picked up his gun again and pointed it at them. "No, they ain't no Truesdales out here. Now get on outta here."

"We're looking for Julia Truesdale," Matt said. "She's my girlfriend."

The man looked at Matt and said slowly, "I told you to get on outta here."

Matt's dad said, "Okay, okay. Let us get the boat turned around and we'll be gone."

Matt stood up, turned toward the raft shacks through the trees, and yelled, "Julia! It's Matt!"

KAPPOWW!

Matt jumped and fell backward into the boat. His dad moved quickly to see if he had been shot. When he realized the man was just scaring them again he turned and said, "Stop shooting that gun! We're leaving, alright?"

The man in the canoe didn't reply. Instead he pulled another shell from his pocket and began to reload the gun while staring at them.

"Matt, sit down and shut up so we can get out of here."

Matt sat up and rubbed the back of his head where it had hit the metal boat seat when he fell. Matt's dad picked up a paddle and began to maneuver the boat around to return the way they had come.

"Matt?!" a woman's voice shouted from the raft shacks.

Matt looked at his dad and then at the man in the canoe. "Julia! It's me, Matt!"

The man in the canoe pointed his gun at Matt.

Matt's dad held up his hand and said, "I hope you can reload faster than that, because if you pull that trigger I'll pull your sorry behind out of that boat and bury it on the bottom of this swamp."

The man pointed the gun at Matt's dad.

"Ray! Ray! Don't shoot. I know them!" Julia shouted from a raft shack. "Ray! Bring them over here. I know them!"

The man slowly lowered his gun and picked up his paddle. He muttered as his dugout canoe glided past the johnboat.

Matt's dad was still wound up and ready to fight.

"Calm down, Dad. It's okay. We found her," Matt said softly.

His dad reached down and pulled the cord to start the motor. They idled along behind the canoe toward the raft shacks.

Julia was standing in a small ray of sunlight on the front of the center raft. She was smiling, hands on her hips, and shaking her head from side to side. Ray paddled his canoe around to the back side of the raft. Matt's dad pulled the johnboat alongside the raft where Julia was standing.

Matt jumped out of the boat. He embraced Julia, lifting her off her feet. "Marry me," he whispered in her ear. "Marry me."

Julia began to laugh and pulled back from him. "Watch out," she said, pointing to her belly. Matt quickly let her go.

TIM OWENS

"You guys are crazy. How did you find me in the middle of this swamp?"

Matt's dad said, "It wasn't easy, that's for sure. Your canoe friend there didn't help either." He was still ready to fight.

"Ray, come here. I want you to meet my friends from North Carolina," Julia said, looking toward the back of the raft. Then turning back to Matt and his dad, she said, "Ray's my brother. He came back here to take care of our mama after my daddy died a few years back."

"Is your mama here?" Matt asked, looking around at the three rafts tied together.

"No, she died last year. Ray said she had a bad cough and died one night in her sleep. There's an island near here in the middle of the swamp where some friends buried Daddy. Ray buried Mama beside him."

Ray stepped out of the shack and propped the door open with his shotgun.

"Ray, this is Matt Fischer and his daddy. Remember, I told you about them. They were real good to me when I worked at the truck stop," Julia explained, looking at her brother.

"So he's the one?" Ray said, looking hard at Matt.

Julia paused and then said, "Yes, he's the one."

Ray turned and went back into the shack, picking up his gun and closing the door behind himself.

Matt looked at Julia. "What did he mean about me being the one? Did you tell him I'm the father?"

Julia turned away and said, "No, that's not what he meant."

"Look, Julia, I want you to come back," Matt said.

Julia looked up at him. "What he meant was that you were the one . . ." She paused and then continued, "The one meant for me."

"Does that mean you'll marry me?"

She smiled. "Wait just a minute. I'll be right back."

Matt looked at his dad. "What now?"

His dad shrugged.

Julia came back out of the shack with a scrap of paper in her hand. She handed it to Matt. He unfolded it and smiled.

CHAPTER 40

Our faith and its assurance do not proceed from flesh and blood, that is to say, from natural powers within us, but are the inspiration of the Holy Ghost; whom we confess to be God, equal with the Father and with his Son, who sanctifies us, and brings us into all truth by his own working, without whom we should remain forever enemies to God and ignorant of his Son, Christ Jesus. For by nature we are so dead, blind, and perverse, that neither can we feel when we are pricked, see the light when it shines, nor assent to the will of God when it is revealed, unless the Spirit of the Lord Jesus quicken that which is dead, remove the darkness from our minds, and bow our stubborn hearts to the obedience of his blessed will.

THE BOOK OF CONFESSIONS, PRESBYTERIAN CHURCH (USA):
THE SCOTS CONFESSION, 3.12

IT WAS SUNDAY MORNING and time to go to the church. John opened the door to his efficiency and stepped outside. Wow! What a beautiful day. Blue sky and seventy degrees. There were only a handful of days like this during winter, but those few days made the coastal plain seem like heaven. For John, the blue sky and warm air in the middle of winter was nearly as renewing as the first few days of spring, when some primal physiological machinery in the body triggered the production of a different sort of hormone. Then the normal, predictable thought life took a wild vacation and everyone headed outdoors on the weekend to be counted as part of nature, marking their spot and proclaiming that they were part of all this. But that would be later; this was only a hint.

The fine weather, however, did little to dampen the ruckus among the town's church folk. One of the elders had stopped by earlier in the week to tell John about the trouble at the First Baptist Church, where on the previous Sunday the preacher, a thirtysomething, muscular fundamentalist, announced that he had been fornicating with the organist, a twentysomething, sickly-looking, blond-headed fellow who had joined the preacher at the pulpit when the announcement was made.

Apparently, one of the deacons, a local farmer, had rushed the pulpit and punched the preacher squarely on his nose, causing blood to spatter all over the new pale-blue carpet. The preacher's wife, along with their two children, ages two and four, were sitting up front, and when the husband made his announcement, she had started crying uncontrollably.

In the middle of the chaos, the preacher and the organist managed to escape through the choir room and then into a utility closet at the rear of the church, where they were able to climb through a small window and drop to the asphalt parking lot. They had driven off in a lime-green Volkswagen Beetle belonging to the organist. The congregation had poured out of the front doors of the church and had hurled white landscaping gravel at the car as it sped out of the parking lot.

Later that week, on Thursday, the leader of the Wednesday

Sunrise Prayer Breakfast Women's Group at the Baptist church had come to John's office to say her group was leaving their church to attend the Presbyterian church where, they felt, such spontaneous public humiliation was less likely to occur. But she first needed to understand some things about Presbyterians. Among other things, she had wanted him to explain why full immersion was not necessary for baptism. He had answered her questions politely.

John had spent the better part of the week fleshing out the thought-provoking sermon on homosexuality that he'd started before Christmas. He had not anticipated the impact of the goings-on at the Baptist church the previous Sunday. Entering the sanctuary from the choir-loft door, he looked out at the congregation and was startled to see the sanctuary completely full, so much so that metal folding chairs had been placed alongside the end of each pew to provide additional seating. His mind began racing, trying to determine if he had forgotten that today was some special event. Finally he noticed the leader of the Wednesday Sunrise Prayer Breakfast Group from the Baptist church sitting in the second row, almost directly in front of the pulpit. That might explain it.

After the announcements, the call to worship, the prayer of confession, and the anthem by the equally startled choir, it was time to begin the sermon. John, sitting nervously by the pulpit and still a little taken aback by the large crowd, stood up and faced the congregation. He noticed several members of the session staring hard at him. Glancing around the congregation nervously, he recognized several search committee members, who were sitting with their families. They still had not found a new minister, but he recalled they were not traveling this weekend because the van was in the shop.

And in the back pew . . . Ann Lingerfelt? Yes, it was! Smiling at him.

Suddenly a warm calmness flowed through his body. He could feel it—he felt young again, as though he were twenty-two years old, ready to conquer the world. And his mind was perfectly clear, not cluttered with distractions or frustrated at some forgotten piece of information. Looking out upon the congregation, he felt a certain peace and compassion, and then inspiration. He walked deliberately to the podium and, glancing down at his carefully prepared notes, smiled, folded them in half, and moved them aside. He picked up his Bible and began thumbing through the pages as several of the session members exchanged concerned glances. Then, without any notes, he began.

"Today . . . today is a special day. A gift from God. Does anyone believe that?" He paused. "We say to ourselves that we do. But *do* we . . . really?" He smiled. "Our lesson from the Old Testament is from Psalm 130. Let us listen—really listen—to the Word of God." He carefully and slowly put on his reading glasses.

"'From the depths of despair, O Lord, I call for your help. Hear my cry, O Lord. Pay attention to my prayer. Lord, if you kept a record of our sins, who, O Lord, could ever survive? But you offer forgiveness, that we might learn to fear you.

"'I am counting on the Lord; yes, I am counting on him. I have put my hope in his word. I long for the Lord more than sentries long for the dawn, yes, more than sentries long for the dawn.

"'O Israel, hope in the Lord; for with the Lord there is unfailing love. His redemption overflows. He himself will redeem Israel from every kind of sin.'"

John paused and began thumbing through his Bible again. "And from the New Testament, the apostle Paul writes in his letter to the Philippians, 'I don't mean to say that I have already achieved these things or that I have already reached perfection. But I press on to possess that perfection for which Christ Jesus first possessed me. No, dear brothers and sisters, I have not achieved it, but I focus on this one thing: Forgetting the past and looking forward to what lies ahead, I press on to reach the end of the race and receive the heavenly prize for which God, through Christ Jesus, is calling us.

"'Let all who are spiritually mature agree on these things. If you disagree on some point, I believe God will make it plain to you. But we must hold on to the progress we have already made.'"

John removed his reading glasses and placed them on the podium.

"Once, a very long time ago, when I was a boy, eight years old, I had a tree house. My father had built it for me as a birthday present. It seemed like a rustic clapboard mansion to me when, in fact, it was only four feet wide and eight feet long, the size of a standard sheet of plywood. Inside the tree house, I had placed many of my prized possessions: my baseball glove—though I was never any good at baseball—a deck of playing cards; a buffalo nickel and an 1894 silver dollar; an old, crinkled-up, black-and-white picture of my parents at Niagara Falls; a copy of *Boys' Life* magazine; and a pair of US Army–issued field binoculars that my father had somehow acquired.

"I remember thinking one day that it would be very handy to have my footlocker in my tree house so that I could bring even more . . . stuff . . . up there. I didn't really need more stuff up there, but I had it in my mind that it was quite necessary. Well, needless to say, getting the footlocker up the ladder and into the tree house was a mighty struggle. After getting the footlocker off the ground, holding it with one hand with the other hand grabbing the rungs of the ladder, I quickly realized that I would not make it with all of the stuff already loaded in the footlocker. So I unpacked some of it and tried again, and again I failed to reach the summit. After completely emptying the footlocker, I managed to get it up the ladder and into the tree house. Exhausted, I looked back down the ladder at the stuff on the ground and began to think all of that stuff wasn't really necessary to enjoy my tree house . . . so . . . I left it on the ground and later put it back in my bedroom."

John tapped the pulpit with his index finger. "You might ask, what does an old man's recollection of his boyhood feats have to do with anything, much less the Scripture read earlier?"

He paused and looked down. Then he looked up again,

making eye contact with as many people in the congregation as he could, including Ann Lingerfelt. "My friends, it has *everything* to do with our Scripture reading today. In fact, it has everything to do with the gospel, the loving forgiveness given to us by God through his Son, Jesus Christ.

"You see, we all have stuff, baggage, that we carry with us everywhere we go. I'm not talking about baggage like a physical or mental disability, but things from our past that ride on our shoulders, always there on our conscience, mocking our attempts at a better job, a better marriage . . . a better life.

"Why didn't my career ever take off like I planned in college? Why isn't my marriage the Camelot I dreamed about? Why are my children so rebellious? Why have I turned out to be an angry and frustrated parent, constantly yelling at my children, even more than my parents yelled at me? Why did I do such and such—you fill in the blank—to that person? I never thought I would do something like that to anyone. Why, why, why? Why, God, did my life turn out like this?

"All of us, from the very poor to the very rich, from the illiterate migrant worker to the English professor, from the introvert to the life of the party, from you to me, we all have disappointments. All of us. Why? Well, for one, because we live in an imperfect world and are faced daily with imperfect decisions that must be made.

"But I suspect—no, I *know*—there is another reason. We just can't let go of the baggage. We can't leave the footlocker on the ground. Why does it have to go in the tree house? We don't need it there. It takes a lot of energy to overcome its weight pulling down on you as you climb the ladder. It makes you stop your progress up the ladder to rest. And it continues to weigh you down, even when you reach the top. It would be so much easier to just leave it on the ground. But we don't. We are determined to carry it with us. And in the end, all that stuff in the footlocker we thought was important doesn't really matter.

"And so, weighed down by our baggage, we find that things don't turn out as we planned. We get interrupted in our progress. We can't do anything without being conscious of the load we are carrying. Our compromises become lingering disappointments.

"The apostle Paul knew about disappointments. Following his dramatic conversion on the road to Damascus, his life didn't turn out to be an easy street, full of glory, love, and joyful celebration. No. For one, he didn't plan on spending time in prison. Who would? And the church in Athens that never really got going? He didn't plan for it to happen that way. And the church in Corinth—always arguing, always quarreling over trivial matters, much like a modern-day school board or county council? He didn't intend for that congregation to relate to one another like that, and he acknowledged as much in one of the letters he wrote them.

"And what about you? Do you even remember the dreams you had when you were twelve years old? What you wanted your life to be like when you became an adult and began to make your own way in the world?

"You wanted to have a happy marriage, didn't you? You

didn't wish for the silence that exists during dinner at your house. None of you did.

"You wanted to be a well-known, successful farmer, didn't you? A hardworking man of distinction. You didn't plan on the drought for the last two years, the never-ending struggle with the bank, reliance on government subsidies, the children who had no interest in farming and wanted more than anything else to leave the farming life, only to head to the city to get in a line of traffic every day for several hours to drive to an office and push paper around. And that, somehow, was more fulfilling to them than watching a crop grow? How could it have turned out this way?

"So now you think there is no hope for your children to have a meaningful life, no way for you and your spouse to look at one another the way you once did long ago, no way for the dirt surrounding you to provide a life of integrity, producing something that people really need. No hope . . . for happiness.

"But I'm not a Jeremiah. I'm also preaching to myself. Interim assignments like I have here usually involve semi-retired ministers who have spent many years at one or two churches. I never did that. I've never had my own church.

"You see, it's easy to bounce around from church to church, never really setting down roots, running from failed attempts at leadership, running from God's will. And why? It seems like such a trivial matter. It's hard to believe that every major decision in my life has been impacted by one incident in my past.

"When I was fourteen, in the eighth grade, I loved sports. I loved baseball, I loved basketball, and I loved football—the only school sports in those days. Although I was a little scrawny, I dreamed every night of playing one of these sports on the high school team. I practiced throwing and kicking the football in the fall, shooting and dribbling the basketball in the winter, and throwing and hitting the baseball in the spring.

"It was a little hard to do all this because I didn't have many friends, at least not enough to get the experience of a real practice game. Nonetheless, I went on to ninth grade and tried out for the football team. A chubby kid beat me in the forty-yard dash. I couldn't budge the blocking dummy, even without the coach riding it. And I had a muscle spasm during the second practice. Needless to say, I didn't make the team.

"But I still had basketball and baseball. I tried out for the basketball team. The same chubby kid beat me in the one-on-one tryouts, not because he had better skill in dribbling and shooting, but because I couldn't drive around his big gut for a layup without getting thrown off balance and landing on my rear end. Both of us were cut that day.

"No big deal. Baseball season was just around the corner. I oiled my glove, started swinging my bat with a sack of rocks tied to the end, and drew a big red circle on the side of our chicken house to practice my pitching. I should have gotten the hint from the chickens. They were not at all impressed, or pleased, with my flinging of the little white orb in their general direction.

"After being cut from the baseball team, it suddenly hit me like a ton of bricks—I was a failure. I didn't measure up. My dad took me fishing and talked to me about how sports weren't really that important, but I didn't believe anything he said. I knew I was second-rate, and that feeling came to reside in my memory long after the memory of the failed sports tryouts had faded. It just stayed there, waiting for me to think about trying to do something a little above my ability or station in life. Then it would rear up, mocking me, telling me to forget about my dreams, that I needed to be content with what I had already accomplished and shouldn't try doing something that would stretch me a little. I would probably fail at the attempt, and why risk all the bad feelings and regrets that accompany failure? This silly logic is what I live with, even to this day.

"And what does God say to us about all this? This is what he says: 'Two thousand years ago, I sent my Son to live among you, to experience the joy of family relationships, to understand human grief, to know the oppression of religious law as interpreted by man in your daily life, to feel all that you feel. Then, after teaching you how to love one another, showing you what is really important to me, giving you an opportunity to hope for something better than life on earth can offer—after all that, my Son died for all of your short-comings, all of your sins, in order that you could be set free from your past.

"'Forgiven. The past, forgotten . . . my own Son . . . and yet you continue to drag it around with you, holding you back from being all that you could be, forgetting that you are forgiven, still hoping for a better past. Not believing that your sins could be, and have been, forgiven. Going to church, going to Sunday school, blessing each meal, even praying on your knees every morning. And still, after all of this, your past holds you back.

"'Hear me! The past is past! What you do today or tomorrow does not have to depend on what you did yesterday. This is the hope that my Son, in his death, has given to you as a gift, a token of my love for you. If you believe it, you will live and grow. If you don't believe it, you are already dying.

"'Believe! Tomorrow is a new day. Leave your past where it belongs . . . on the ground.'"

John paused and scanned the congregation. Every single face was looking at him, eagerly waiting for his next word. "That is the gospel, my friends, the saving grace of Jesus Christ, the forgiveness of our sins, the freedom from our past. That is why the prostitute on Bourbon Street can become the missionary in Tegucigalpa. That is why the convicted murderer can become the homeless-shelter manager. That is why the lying, thieving ghetto child can become a minister of the Word and Sacrament. That is why *you* can become what you dreamed for your life at the age of twelve, glorifying God in all that you do.

"In the name of the Father, the Son, and the Holy Spirit, amen."

He closed his Bible and scanned the congregation again. They were all looking at him, eyes wide open, and not a single whisper could be heard. He smiled. They smiled back. He just stood there for a moment. It had been too many years since he had felt this way, since he had been moved by the Spirit during a sermon. He was born again, again.

"Let us now return a portion of what God has so graciously provided to us. Let us present our tithes and offerings."

The organist began to play the offertory and the ushers came down the aisle. Following the presentation of offerings, the congregation recited the Apostles' Creed. The final hymn was "Holy, Holy, Holy." During the last verse, the sopranos in the choir sang a descant, sounding like angels singing in heaven and bringing tears to John's eyes. He bowed his head. *Thank you, Most Holy One, my Savior and my Redeemer. Amen.*

• • •

Travis caught Bill's eye. He was smiling. Then he saw Frankie. She was smiling. So were Matt and Susie and Joyce. And . . . Dot! They were all smiling.

They had traveled far and wide over parts of three states for more than a year, looking for someone who was already in their pulpit.

EPILOGUE

Q. 55. How doth Christ make intercession?

A. Christ maketh intercession, by his appearing in our nature continually before the Father in heaven, in the merit of his obedience and sacrifice on earth; declaring his will to have it applied to all believers; answering all accusations against them; and procuring for them quiet of conscience, notwithstanding daily failings, access with boldness to the throne of grace, and acceptance of their persons and services.

THE BOOK OF CONFESSIONS, PRESBYTERIAN CHURCH (USA):
THE LARGER CATECHISM, 7.165

SIX MONTHS LATER

It had taken a little doing, but the presbytery had voted to allow John Haynesworth, the interim minister, to become their new preacher after the search committee made their recommendation and almost everybody from the church went to the presbytery meeting to show their support.

The Sunday-afternoon reception for the new preacher in their fellowship hall was one of the biggest that Travis had ever attended. Bill came in holding hands with Joyce and looked, for the first time in a long while, like his old self.

Normally Dot would have been cranking up the rumor mill about that, because it had not quite been a year since Mary Helen died. But Dot hadn't been herself for the past few months. She was there just acting polite, and Travis didn't hear her speak even once. That was good, because Matt brought his new wife, who was obviously in a family way, and Susie's son was sporting a tattoo on his neck. The rock of the committee, Frankie, was there with her husband, George, and looked ten years younger than she had when they went on their first trip. And everyone noticed that Pastor John had invited a "lady friend," an attractive woman about his age who was very gracious and polite.

As the party was winding down, Travis volunteered to take all of the trash to the dump the next day. Monday morning was busy at the grocery store, but late in the afternoon Travis found some time to get away and make the trip to the dump. He turned down Blueberry Farm Road and looked over his shoulder to make sure the bags of trash were okay in the bed of his pickup. Facing forward again, he flipped down the visor to shield his eyes from the late-afternoon sun and then noticed someone coming toward him along the side of the road. It looked to be an older person, a black woman, moving slowly and carrying a big pocketbook. As he came alongside her, Travis saw it was Mrs. Bryant, the lady he had delivered food to with Jenny for Easter last year. She didn't look up.

What was she doing walking out here by herself? She must be at least three miles from her trailer and another mile and a half from town. Travis watched her in his rearview mirror as he continued on with his trash.

At the dump he crawled into the bed of his pickup and threw the bags of trash into the closest dumpster. Someone had set an old black-and-white TV on the ground next to one of the dumpsters and had attached a handwritten sign that said *Free to Good Home*. Travis looked at the television and briefly considered taking it home and getting it fixed so he and Jenny could have a TV in their bedroom. *Hmmm. Might be hard to get parts. Jenny probably wouldn't want it anyway.* He left it alone.

He started up his truck and turned to go back to town. As he got closer to town he saw Mrs. Bryant again. He slowed down, leaned over, and rolled down the passenger-side window.

"Mrs. Bryant, you need a ride?"

Mrs. Bryant looked into the open window at Travis, like she was trying to recognize who he was.

"I'm Jenny's husband. We brought you some food last Easter."

"Oh yes, I remember you."

"Can I give you a ride into town?"

"Bless you, son. That would be mighty sweet of you."

Travis leaned over and opened the door. Mrs. Bryant approached the truck and paused to look up at the seat. Travis saw what she was thinking and said, "I'm sorry, Mrs. Bryant. Let me come around there and give you a hand."

Travis hopped out and walked around the truck to help Mrs. Bryant in. He extended his hand to her but she grabbed his forearm instead. She placed one foot on the floorboard and pulled down on Travis's arm to lift her body into the truck. Travis grabbed her other arm from behind and helped her get inside. Then he closed the door and walked back to his side of the truck.

As he got in, Mrs. Bryant asked, "Did you know my husband?"

"Uh, no, ma'am." Travis recalled her asking the same question when he first met her.

"His name was Milton. He was a fine man." Mrs. Bryant looked straight ahead and sighed. "I miss him."

Travis started toward town again. "How long were y'all married?"

"Fifty-two years before he passed."

"If you don't mind me asking, how did he die?"

"The good Lord took him in his sleep. I woke up one morning and turned on the light to get my clothes on and saw he was still in the bed. He usually got up around four thirty, but I couldn't get up before five. Still can't. Anyhow, he was still in the bed and so I reached over to shake his arm to wake him, but he didn't move a muscle. I thought he was just worn out from helping me put up all that corn the day before so I said, 'Milton! Get up! It's already after five!' But he didn't answer. I shook his arm again and he didn't budge. I put my hand on his chest to try to feel his breathing but it was like touching a sack of flour. Nothing. Then I knew he was gone."

"What did you do next?"

"Oh, nothing much. I sat with him all day and talked to

him about all the arrangements that needed to be made and how I was going to miss him."

"You didn't call anybody?"

"No, I didn't see any need to right away. My niece, Jessie May, stopped by the next morning on her way to work and she found out about it. She called in sick to work and helped me get everything together."

"I'm sorry to hear he died. I bet it was hard to find him dead like that." Travis drove on without saying anything for a while. Then he asked, "So where in town are you headed?"

"I was going to the store for some milk and fatback."

"Walking? Your niece couldn't give you a ride or get it for you?"

Mrs. Bryant looked out the side window. "No, she passed last year. The cancer got her and took her quick. She was a good girl. I don't know why the Lord took her like that."

"I'm sorry to hear that. You've sure had a lot of sadness to deal with in recent years."

"That's alright; I've had a good life. God blessed me in all my years. I love the Lord. He's been good to me."

"Don't you have some other family that could help you with rides and stuff? You don't need to be walking like that."

"No, son, they're all gone. I've lived too long. They're *all* dead. I don't know why God leaves me here like this, but I trust it's for some good reason. I've asked Jesus about it, but he won't tell me either. But about the rides—God always sends somebody to come along and pick me up. Today it was you." She turned to Travis and smiled.

He smiled back. "Did you say your special prayers today?"

Mrs. Bryant squinted and said, "Why yes, I did. How did you know about that?"

"You told me about them when we took you that food."

"Oh yes, that's right. Now I remember. You didn't believe me. I remember."

Travis blushed. "Yes, I did. It's just that I don't pray like that."

"I see. Well, how *do* you pray then?"

"Well, like most everybody else. I pray sometimes at night and at every meal and then in church along with everybody."

Mrs. Bryant nodded her head and looked out the side window again. "Do you and your wife have any children?"

"No, not yet. We plan to, though."

"Oh, I'm glad to hear that. Children are the greatest blessing of all. Jesus loves the little children, all the children of the world. . . ."

"We've had a couple of false alarms, so I haven't really got excited about it yet."

Mrs. Bryant turned to Travis. "Well, how does your Jenny feel about it?"

"She obviously wants one real bad. Actually . . . she's mad at me for not being excited about it yet. I was hoping I could finish up at the community college first."

Mrs. Bryant didn't say anything.

"Did y'all have any children? I mean, I guess not, if you don't have any family left now."

"No, I lost two babies and then I didn't want to try anymore.

Something changes inside of you after that. I wish we would have been blessed with little ones. That would have been good for Milton. I guess it turned out for the best. I ended up taking care of everybody else's little ones, so I got blessed like that. But Milton never got that blessing."

Mrs. Bryant was quiet as they rode through town toward the Food Lion. Travis looked at every car he passed to see who was inside and if they noticed that Mrs. Bryant was riding with him. Pulling into the Food Lion parking lot he asked, "So you were going to walk all that way for a gallon of milk and some fatback and then carry it back?"

Mrs. Bryant smiled. "Yes. Thank you, son, for the ride." She opened the door and turned to step down onto the asphalt.

"Mrs. Bryant?"

"Yes?"

"Look, I've got some time. I'll give you a ride home when you're done."

"I don't want to put you out, now. You've got your own family to tend to."

"Oh, that's alright. Jenny will be glad I could help you."

"Well, okay then. If you're going to do that, then I'll get a few more things."

"Take your time. I've got to check on some things in the store anyway."

. . .

After Mrs. Bryant finished with her food-stamp transaction at the register, Travis picked up her bags. "I can get this," he said, and then turning to the checkout girl, "Tell somebody to straighten up aisle three. Somebody dropped a jar of Pace salsa on the floor."

The girl nodded. Travis turned and escorted Mrs. Bryant out to his truck.

"This is mighty nice of you, son."

Travis didn't say anything. He opened the door for Mrs. Bryant and helped her up into the truck. Then he put the two bags of groceries in the back and crawled in his side. "I called Jenny and she said to tell you hello."

"That's nice. I remember she was a sweet girl. You can tell that her mama and daddy raised her up right."

Travis pulled out of the parking lot and headed toward the other end of town and Blueberry Farm Road. They drove through town without talking, just looking at the storefronts and people passing by. As they reached the other side of town, Mrs. Bryant asked, "Do you love her?"

"Excuse me?"

"Do you love her? Your Jenny?"

Travis felt the blood rush to his ears. This old lady had some kind of nerve asking a question like that. Especially after all he was doing for her. "Well, yes, I love her. I don't think I would have married her otherwise. Why are you asking me that?"

"I didn't mean to rile you, son. I was just wondering, because it took my Milton a little while after we were married before he really loved me. I loved him from the get-go, and he said he loved me. But he really started loving me later on."

Travis wondered if she thought he was some dumb boy who was born yesterday. Why did everybody treat him like that? He didn't respond for about a minute. Finally, the feeling of indignation passed. "How many years were y'all married when you thought he started to really love you?"

"Four years and three months. That's when I lost my first baby. We went through that together and then he started to really love me."

"Oh. . . . Well, I do love Jenny, but we haven't had anything like that happen to us."

"That's good, son. I wouldn't wish that on anybody. But Milton was different after that baby died."

"You mean the baby was . . . I thought you had a miscarriage."

"No, we had that baby for three days and then he died."

"How?"

"The doctor said he was born too early and his lungs weren't right."

"I'm sorry."

"It's alright. I'm sorry I asked you that question. That wasn't very polite of me. I just wonder about things a lot in my old age. You know, how other people think about things and like that."

"That's alright."

"Most people give up on their marriage before they even get a chance to love each other. I'm talking about regular folks, not those that hit each other and all that. If the regular folks would just hold on a little longer, God would put the love in there. It doesn't always come about in an easy way, but if you be patient with one another, it will come. How long have you and your Jenny been married?"

"Five years next month."

"That's good." Mrs. Bryant paused. "And seeing as how you already love her, then it will get even stronger in a few more years. Y'all are going to be fine. I just know it."

Travis thought to himself, *No, you don't. You think I'm young and dumb just like everybody else does.*

"I'll start praying for y'all to be blessed with children. You just let me know when you have enough and I'll stop praying," Mrs. Bryant said with a raspy laugh.

Travis smiled. Okay, she had a good sense of humor. Maybe she didn't think too badly of him. "Alright, I'll let you know."

Travis turned down Ned Simmons Drive and headed toward Mrs. Bryant's trailer. He pulled up to her front porch and got out to help her into the house. She held his arm until she got up on the porch. Travis went back to the truck to get the groceries while she fiddled with her key in the door lock.

They went inside, and he put the bags on the table and then turned to go.

"Wait," Mrs. Bryant said, holding her hand out to Travis.

He walked over and took her hand.

"You were a blessing to me today. I thank you and I'm going to talk to Jesus about you. I want to show you something."

She tugged Travis over to an old, cheap piece of furniture that looked like it was part of a desk from Walmart or somewhere like that. Mrs. Bryant opened a drawer and pulled out a worn brown leather photo album. She opened it up and started thumbing through the pages. "Here he is."

Travis looked at the faded black-and-white photograph with a crease mark on one corner that Mrs. Bryant was pointing at with her finger. It was a picture of a young black woman sitting in a chair and wearing a housecoat—Mrs. Bryant, he guessed—holding a baby wrapped in a small blanket.

"That's Milton Jr. when he was two days old. . . . He died the next day. I miscarried the next baby, so I didn't get to hold it, but I got to hold Milton Jr. for three days. Three days . . . then he died right in my arms." Mrs. Bryant's voice began to crack. "That poor little boy. He never had a chance. . . . But God let me hold him for three days. I had that blessing for three days."

She looked up at Travis with moisture brimming in her eyes. "I want you to remember my baby when Jenny has your baby. Hold that baby as much as you can. Love on it as much as you can. A baby is God's greatest gift. Don't ever forget that, son." Mrs. Bryant wiped her nose with her finger, sniffed, and then closed the photo album and put it back in the drawer. She turned to Travis. "I'll let you go on now. Thank you for all you did for me today, and tell your Jenny that I said hi back."

"Yes, ma'am."

Travis walked out onto the porch and down the steps. At the bottom of the steps he turned to see if Mrs. Bryant was standing at the door. She wasn't.

He got in his truck, backed out of Mrs. Bryant's boggy

driveway, and headed back up Ned Simmons Drive to the highway. He didn't turn on the radio but just drove along quietly.

He turned down Cedar Street and took it out of town to where it connected with 301. He passed the spot where he had grown up in a ramshackle, unpainted clapboard house on cinder-block piers. It wasn't there anymore. Instead, someone had built a Family Dollar store on that property. Ironic. When he had lived there it had been a "family-without-a-dollar" house.

He began to think about how he got from that house to where he was now. Had it not been for his aunt Kay taking on three more kids when his mama died . . . She had loved Travis, Lou Ann, and Robby even more than their mama had, or at least she had shown more love than his mama had shown them. Lou Ann and Robby had made good, too: Lou Ann, now a bank teller and married to a high school teacher, and Robby, a lineman for the electric co-op, which was pretty hard work for a guy with only three fingers on one hand. But Robby enjoyed the challenge and even laughed about it.

And then Travis getting the job as a stocker at the grocery store, when jobs in a small town were hard to come by, and working his way up to assistant manager. Some of the older folks in town remembered where Travis had come from. They were always telling him how proud they were of him as they pushed their carts past him in the grocery store. It used to embarrass him, and he really hadn't wanted people to remember that about him, but now he just smiled and said thanks. All things considered, his life had been a miracle parceled out over time.

Turning south onto 301, he noticed how the black-eyed Susans had come out along the ditch banks. Volunteers. About a mile later, he saw an old Walker hound trotting along the side of the road. The hound paused and looked up as Travis passed, hoping to recognize its owner, and then continued its trot.

Farther down the road he passed a sharecropper's house, abandoned now but for a large oak shading the front yard, hinting that a family had once filled the old house with life. What happened to that family? To those children? He thought about his old house again and his mama moving around in it, dragging her leg. And Robby, his baggage. That's what the preacher was talking about, that day they realized he was the man they were looking for.

The road passed through a cypress swamp with knees poking through swirls of pollen floating on the still, black water. A snapping turtle was making its way across the road in front of him. Travis swerved to miss it.

He continued to drive along, not really going anywhere but just driving. Mrs. Bryant's baby—why had it been taken from her? Then having to spend her life taking care of *other* people's babies? Lost her husband. Walked to town for groceries. And now she talked to Jesus for a solid hour and a half every day. She had an itty-bitty bit of faith and had shared the secret with Travis. He hadn't recognized it.

On both sides of the road now, corn was waist high,

waiting on the next rain. He passed a farmer on a large tractor going in the opposite direction. The farmer waved and
Travis waved back. Everybody waved. The ones who didn't
weren't from around here. Passed a field of watermelon vines.
No melons yet. Several bee boxes were sitting across the ditch
between two other fields. Travis looked closely and was
able to focus on several bees flying around the boxes. Working bees. Ahead, a thundercloud was building in the early-
summer heat, momentarily hiding the sun, getting ready to
provide a late-afternoon shower.

He was part of all this—not separate from it, but part of
it. Just as Mrs. Bryant was part of it. And the boy he caught
shoplifting at the grocery store. And Bill. And even Dot.
They were all part of this. Bound together, not separate.

He drove on for another ten or so miles. Then he decided
to turn around and head home.

• • •

Pulling up in his driveway, he saw Jenny weeding her zinnias
on the side of the house next to the carport. He stopped
and sat in his idling truck, looking at her bending down in
her pink rubber garden boots, khaki shorts, and untucked,
red-checkered sleeveless shirt, wearing a large, wide-brimmed
straw hat. Beautiful. He was blessed.

She didn't look up. He parked his truck and walked over
to her.

"Jen?"

She stood up straight, red-faced and glistening with sweat,

holding a trowel by her side, and looked at him with a puzzled expression. "So how's Mrs. Bryant?"

Travis looked down and kicked at the ground as he spoke. "Uh, she's fine."

"So why are you acting so funny? Did something happen?"

"Jen . . . I'm ready."

"Ready for what?"

"To start."

"To start what?"

"You know, to start. The baby thing."

Jenny didn't respond.

Travis looked up at her.

She tossed her hat on the ground and dropped her trowel. Then she put her dirty, soiled hands on his cheeks and laughed.

Q. 129. What is the meaning of the little word "Amen"?

A. Amen means: this shall truly and certainly be. For my prayer is much more certainly heard by God than I am persuaded in my heart that I desire such things from him.

THE BOOK OF CONFESSIONS, PRESBYTERIAN CHURCH (USA): THE HEIDELBERG CATECHISM, 4.129

DISCUSSION QUESTIONS

1. Have you ever served on a pastoral search committee or a similar team where you were partnered with people very different from yourself and whom you may not have known very well? What are some of the challenges in working with such a group? What are the benefits? What kinds of surprises might you experience?

2. Which member of the search committee did you most identify with at the beginning of the story? Did that change for you at any point in the book? Did you recognize other people you have known in the different characters?

3. What was your first impression of Mrs. Bryant? Eventually Travis realizes that she is a woman of great faith, and that perhaps her faith has been increased by the adversity she has faced. What experiences have you had that increased your faith?

4. Frankie has nightmares due to atrocities committed in her family when she was a young child, but no one on the committee knows this and she doesn't share it. Do you know anyone who has shared a story with you and very few others? Why is it hard to share such painful and intimate memories? Do you think it is important to talk about them? Why or why not?

5. Frankie is later comforted by her deceased brother in a dream. Do you think God sometimes uses dreams to comfort us or help us with a problem? Have you had a similar experience where something was resolved in a dream?

6. Dot instills fear in Travis due to her confrontational personality and insensitive comments. Yet she is a different person with Ernestine, the lady who helped rear her. What characteristic in Dot causes these two reactions? Are there situations or relationships in which you feel like two different people? Is that good or bad (or neither)?

7. Bill believes he is in control of his life and Mary Helen's, too. With Mary Helen's death, he learns he is not, and he doesn't know how to respond to that revelation. What events in your life have proven to be beyond your control? This may be painful or personal, but can you share how you responded to them? How did God help you respond to those events?

8. Do you know any young person like Shawn who has demonstrated a desire to look after a single parent? What strengths might a young person develop in such a situation? What extra challenges might they face?

9. Is there a particular minister's sermon in the book that spoke to you more than the others did? How so?

10. How does his father's alcoholism affect Travis? What specific examples in the book make this evident? Why do you think the choices of parents can have such an impact on their children?

11. Matt suffers from depression and takes medication for it. Do you think it's appropriate to seek medical help for mental-health conditions? Why or why not?

12. How does Julia help Matt? Why do you think Matt wants to marry Julia and help her raise a baby that isn't his? Have you ever had the opportunity to do something really difficult for someone you love? How did you make the decision? If Matt had come to you for advice, what would you have told him?

13. Discuss the racial issues that come up in the book. (For example, Travis's initial reaction to Mrs. Bryant; the man staring at Travis at the gas station; Dot's relationship with Ernestine contrasted with the way she downplays it to her friends.) Look up and discuss one or more of the following biblical examples of racial

differences highlighted between individuals: the parable
of the Good Samaritan (Luke 10:25-37); Jesus and
the Samaritan woman (John 4:5-42); Philip and the
Ethiopian eunuch (Acts 8:26-39).

14. What do you think happens beyond the end of the
book? Does John marry Ann Lingerfelt? How many
children do Travis and Jenny have? Does Julia continue
to work at the truck stop after her baby is born? Do
Bill and Joyce get married, and if so, do they remain in
their town or move elsewhere? What else happens?

AN INTERVIEW
WITH THE AUTHOR

This is your first published novel. Is it the first one you've written? Can you tell us a little about your journey to publication?

Yes, this is the first book I've written. I did most of the writing about five years ago when my kids were relatively young, so I had to write late at night after the bedtime drama had dwindled down. It took about a year to get it done. Then I collected exactly thirty-nine rejection letters and put the book aside. Forty seemed like a threshold I didn't want to cross.

Then about two years ago, I got the book out again, dusted it off, moved some chapters around, added more life to some of the characters, and sent out five more query letters. In about two weeks, I received a call at work from a well-known agent, Ethan Ellenberg, who said he wanted to see the whole manuscript. He liked it! Then he made some calls and suggested that I enter it into the Operation First Novel contest put on by the Jerry B. Jenkins Christian Writers Guild. So that's what I did, and that's how I ended up here answering this question.

I must add something about Kathy Olson, my editor, and the other folks at Tyndale. I've had as much fun editing as I did writing—actually, *more* fun because of the encouraging feedback and interaction and coaxing of details from my head to the keyboard. It's been a great learning experience.

Can you tell us about your other creative endeavors as an inventor? I understand you hold a couple of patents.

Well, it's important to not know what you don't know. That way, you try to do things that others wouldn't, because you don't know how difficult it's going to be. So it helps to be stupid like that.

For example, I have several patents on a hollow metal-core golf ball that a company has licensed and is trying to bring to market. It goes straight. Most folks in the golf-ball industry were able to immediately point out why it wouldn't work. But it does.

And then I wanted to build a big wooden boat for my family to use, because we live near the water. I found some plans online and moved some junk around in my garage to make room for the project. One of my son's friends came by one day and saw it and said it wouldn't float. He was twelve. Of course he had moved on by the time I (successfully) finished the project—it was a simple one that only took me six years to complete. But that's the kind of harassment you have to be willing to put up with.

For my day job, I'm an environmental engineer, and in that

line of work I've patented a pollution-control device for coal plants as part of my PhD work. But that's not very exciting.

Let's see, what else? Oh yeah, after Hurricane Mitch hit Central America in 1998, I designed, along with the owner of the engineering firm where I was working, a drinking-water treatment system that would fit on the back of a pickup truck and treat about ten thousand gallons of water per day. I spent over a year going back and forth to Honduras to install these units in remote villages, and that led to a project in Mozambique to install units there following the floods in 2000. Lots of travel, plus one poisonous spider that almost did me in.

How did the idea for this story come to you?

I served on a search committee about twenty years ago to find a minister for the church my wife, Ruth, and I attended. The whole concept sets up nicely for a book. You have a group of people on a journey, in close quarters, with a common purpose. Things are bound to happen, and they did. And I just made up the rest of it, except for the parts that are true.

How much of Travis did you draw from yourself? Are there parts of you in some of the other characters as well?

It's probably easier to answer that by looking at it another way: I'm about two parts Travis, two parts Matt, half a part Bill, and maybe a little Dot. And I know the other people.

The church signs Travis writes down during their travels are priceless. Where did the inspiration for these signs come from? How do you feel about the role of laughter in the church?

It helps to live in South Carolina. Humorous church signs are an art form here. It mostly started when the trailer-mounted letter signs with flashing arrows were invented, which I believe was in the late 1970s, but I'm not exactly sure. Just now I Googled "church signs" and one of the first ones that came up was *There are some questions that Google can't answer.* I suppose there are more than a few people who think laughter should not be a part of our faith. That's fine; I just don't want to be in their Sunday school class. Which is exactly the point of the church signs—they're using a little humor to get you inside.

What do you hope readers will take away from this novel?

The characters find themselves in a lot of silly and awkward circumstances as they travel and in the churches they visit. But what they experience in their personal lives is the real story here. Reconciliation, redemption, forgiveness, spiritual growth, and grace—especially grace. "For my prayer is much more certainly heard by God than I am persuaded in my heart that I desire such things from him" (*The Book of Confessions, Presbyterian Church (USA):* The Heidelberg Catechism, 4.129).

ABOUT THE AUTHOR

TIM OWENS grew up in eastern North Carolina and now lives in Summerville, South Carolina, with his wife, Ruth, and their four children. He is an environmental engineer, and in addition to writing, he enjoys working on his old Ford tractor at his farm near Ehrhardt, South Carolina. Once the backsliding son of a Southern Baptist preacher, Tim was led gently by his wife into the Presbyterian church, where he is now an elder. This is his first novel. Visit his website at www.timowensauthor.com.